VICIOUS

FACES OF EVIL

DEBRA WEBB

PINK
HOUSE
PRESS

PINK HOUSE PRESS
WebbWorks
Huntsville, Alabama

First Edition November 2013

ISBN 10: 0989904415
ISBN 13: 9780989904414

ACKNOWLEDGEMENTS

I must acknowledge my amazing editor. She keeps me straight and gives generously of her time. She is truly priceless. Thank you, Marijane, for all you do.

Thanks to Linda in Reno, Nevada, for her pointers and for loving the series even when I give Jess a classy suit and high heels to go with her badge and gun—which she keeps in her bag rather than in a holster.

This book is dedicated to a very nice man whose loving brother volunteered him to play a wicked part in this novel. Enjoy, Rick. You're a killer character.

"The age of our fathers, which was worse than that of our ancestors, produced us, who are about to raise a progeny more vicious than ourselves."

~Horace

CHAPTER ONE

"Do you know who I am?"

His guest moved her head side to side in swift, frantic little shakes. Her dark eyes were round with fear and every desperate breath echoed that same fear in the quiet room.

Satisfaction made him smile. She was unaware of his name or his reputation, yet she instinctively understood that her life as she knew it was at an end.

Rory Stinnett was going to die.

How fortunate she was to be the first chosen to join him in this final round of the game. Before the last ounce of life drained from her, she would know the name Eric Spears intimately. And he would know every sweet, luscious part of her, inside and out.

This one was truly beautiful. Long, silky hair as black as the deepest part of the night. He traced the length of her throat with his eyes. She shivered as if he'd stroked his fingers there. Her extraordinarily sculpted body lay naked before him. The restraints at her wrists, waist, and ankles, chaffed her smooth, tanned skin.

1

His gaze lingered on her breasts, nipples erect from the low temperature in the room or from the terror coursing through her veins, either way they begged for attention. Anticipation stirred inside him. Not yet, it wasn't time to play. Her role in the game was immensely important, far more so than she could possibly comprehend.

"You will know me in time." His promise prompted another delicious shiver of her exquisite body.

"But not until the perfect moment," he explained. "Not until the others are here."

Not until *she* was here.

His body tightened with excitement as the image of the guest of honor for the upcoming coup de grâce filled his mind.

Once Jess was here, the final game would begin.

He could hardly wait.

CHAPTER TWO

Deputy Chief Jess Harris waited in the austere private room for the patient to decide she was ready to continue. The uncomfortable plastic chair squeaked each time Jess shifted. She crossed her legs to stop her knee from bouncing with impatience and frustration. Didn't help. Her worst nightmare was coming true and she couldn't just sit here and pretend she wasn't worried.

Eric Spears, the sociopathic serial killer who haunted her every waking hour, had taken his first victim. Equal measures of fury and fear erupted inside her all over again. She struggled to hold back the emotions welling up in her throat. Breaking down at this point wouldn't help anyone, least of all the woman he'd chosen to use in his sadistic scheme.

As soon as Jess received word from the Bureau that two of the three missing women had been found, she and Chief of Police Dan Burnett were on their way. With no nonstop flights out of Birmingham,

3

Alabama, they'd had to endure a plane change in Atlanta. Every wasted minute had cranked Jess's tension a little higher. By the time they arrived in Knoxville the Bureau and local law enforcement had already finished their interviews, and Jess had felt ready to snap with mounting tension.

Unless the two survivors of this perverted reality game could provide some additional insight into where Spears had held them, or why he hadn't freed the third victim, or what he intended next, they had nothing. Nothing at all.

Spears had made his choice from the three women abducted from Alabama ten days ago and he'd vanished with her. Not one shred of evidence had been left behind. None they had discovered at any rate.

Nausea roiled in Jess's belly. She had to find a way to stop him.

Since her interview with Claudia Brown, the first of the two rescued victims, hadn't provided any additional information, Jess's only remaining hope was that Melaney Lands, the woman lying in the hospital bed a few feet away, would remember something useful. Jess shifted again in the uncomfortable chair. So far, she hadn't said anything at all.

Melaney, born and raised in Mobile and a nursing student at the University of South Alabama, adjusted her bendable straw with a shaky hand. She took a long draw of water from the plastic cup.

Enough time passed to have Jess's already strained nerves frayed completely. Melaney placed the cup on the tray-table extended across her lap. She clasped her hands on the white sheet tucked against the faded blue hospital gown she wore, but still she didn't speak. Jess wondered if she understood how very lucky she was to have survived a close encounter with Spears, the Player, a vicious serial killer who loved torturing his victims before ending their lives.

Of the thirty some odd cases of abducted women attributed to him by the Federal Bureau of Investigation, there had never been a survivor. *Not one.* Detective Lori Wells of Birmingham PD had met the monster and lived to tell, but then he hadn't abducted her. One of his reckless minions, Matthew Reed, had taken her. That was the last mistake Reed would ever make and, in all likelihood, the only reason Lori was still alive.

It seemed impossible that Lori's abduction had been scarcely more than a month ago.

The air stalled in Jess's lungs as her heart flailed like a fish swept onto the bank and then deserted by the tide. Everything about her life had changed and gotten far more complicated in those few short weeks.

God Almighty, what was she going to do?

She adjusted her glasses as well as her attention. Right now, she couldn't think about the other troubles stewing in her private life. There just wasn't time to linger and she couldn't afford the distraction.

"The man was smoking outside the Wash-n-Go where I do my laundry."

Startled by the sound of the woman's voice, despite having been on the edge of her seat in anticipation, Jess snapped to attention.

Melaney drew in a shuddering breath. "He was white, tall, kinda young—maybe twenty-five." She shrugged and then winced. During the final hours of the horror that had overtaken her life, her hands and feet had been tied behind her back with one end of the rope around her neck. She was sore as hell with plenty of bruises and abrasions.

"He had on jeans and a t-shirt," Melaney continued. "There was a logo but it was faded. I didn't look at him long enough to make it out."

Jess jotted a couple of notes on her pad. "According to the statements you gave earlier, this man didn't say anything to you as you exited the laundromat."

Melaney shook her head. "He didn't. When I glanced at him, he did one of those nods. You know, the one people do instead of saying hello or what's up?"

"Did you nod back?" Melaney hadn't mentioned a response, not even a gesture, in her statements to the other investigators. Hopefully, as the realization that she was truly safe now sank in and she relaxed, more details of the past ten days would surface.

Another negligible shrug prompted a second wince of pain. "If I did, I don't remember doing it. I think I just looked away."

For several more seconds she didn't speak. She was remembering. The horror of that night danced across her face as easy to read as the breaking news scroll on a cable channel.

"I put my laundry bag in the backseat and closed the door, that's when I noticed the tire was flat." She clamped her lips together and still they trembled.

"You drive a 1971 Toyota Corolla?" Jess knew the answer, but she needed to nudge Melaney past the shame she'd snagged on. For the rest of her life, she would question her every move from that night. Had she done this or that things might have turned out differently.

What Melaney Lands didn't grasp was that she had been chosen. Her hair color was the one he preferred. She had the right figure. She fit the profile of the women the Player selected. Nothing she did or didn't do would have made a difference.

"Yes."

"The flat tire was on the…?" Jess held her pencil poised to take down the answer. It was the mundane that most often prodded forth the notable.

"The driver's side. Rear tire. I said shit or something like that. When I looked up, he was standing right beside me. I jumped, and he apologized for scaring me. He offered to help. There wasn't anybody else around so I said okay." Tears slipped down her cheeks. "I did what anybody else would have done… I didn't—"

"If you had said no," Jess stopped her, "he would have taken a different approach, but the end result would've been the same." She held her gaze a moment more before moving on. "He fixed your tire and then what happened?"

"Damned thing wouldn't start." She knotted her fingers in the sheet, her eyes bright with the fresh tears brimming there. "It was running fine… before. I guess I must've been so upset I didn't lock the doors when I got in the car. Another stupid mistake. Then suddenly he was in the passenger seat next to me." Her lips trembled. "He used a hypodermic needle to inject a drug into my shoulder." She drew her right shoulder into her body. "When I woke up I was in a cage. There were two others… we were all in cages."

The ketamine, Spears's drug of choice, worked fast. There would have been little time or strength for a struggle. The story from both women was basically the same except for the setting. Claudia Brown, a graduate student at A&M College, lived in Somerville. She was taken by a different man from the alley behind her apartment. Her cat hadn't come in for dinner. At bedtime, Claudia had gone outside to look for the missing pet that, as it turned out, was alive and well ten-blocks away.

The woman Spears had kept, Rory Stinnett, was from Orange Beach. She was a student at the same university as Melaney, but the two hadn't known each other until they ended up in those cages in a white room with glaring fluorescent lights. They had described the cages as being made of heavy gauge metal wire, similar to the ones used to crate large dogs. The cages allowed the women to see one another and to communicate.

Some memory Jess couldn't quite grasp nudged her. Something to do with cages.

"Once you were in the cage," Jess asked, moving on, "you never saw anyone other than the masked man?" According to their statements, a man wearing a ski mask had checked on them daily.

Melaney shook her head, corroborating the answer Claudia had given. After viewing catalogs of mug shots, including photos of Spears, both women had confirmed what everyone else suspected: Spears was not one of the abductors and he wasn't the masked man. There was a strong possibility that he hadn't been anywhere near these women.

His presence was irrelevant, in Jess's opinion. This was his doing whether he was at the scene of the crime or not.

He had started a new game, and Jess was way behind the curve.

She blinked away the distraction. *Stay on the facts. You already know his motive.*

The women were dehydrated, bruised, and emotionally wounded but that was the extent of their injuries. During those ten long days of captivity, the man wearing a mask had dropped a bottle of water and a container of nuts and dried fruits into their cages daily. Not once had he attempted to touch the women or even to speak to them. But then torturing or murdering anyone at this stage in the game wasn't the goal—wasn't even on the agenda.

Spears had other plans.

"Since he didn't speak," Jess ventured, "how can you be certain the person wearing the mask was a man?" There were numerous reasons to make the assumption but she wanted to hear each woman's rationale for coming to that conclusion. The smallest new insight might make a difference.

"His hands." Melaney's brow furrowed as if she were concentrating hard on the question. "He had big hands with thick fingers."

"He didn't wear gloves?"

Another shake of her head confirmed he had not. Just went to show the level of confidence the man had in the hiding place used for holding the women. Claudia had mentioned his broad shoulders and muscled arms, as well as his hands. She'd also said he had dark eyes. Jess suspected Melaney had kept her gaze lowered whenever their keeper entered the room. Claudia, on the other hand, had studied his height, six feet at least, and his build—a little on the stocky side.

According to the descriptions provided by Melaney and Claudia, different men had abducted them at approximately the same time on the same night. Both insisted Rory had described yet a third man. All three women had received a phone call about winning a weekend getaway. That ruse had served a simple purpose, ensuring no one who knew the women grew suspicious when they disappeared. The abductions were a carefully choreographed series of untraceable steps in various locations for achieving the singular goal of a madman. The organized operation confirmed the

Bureau's theory that Spears had built a network of followers ready to do his bidding.

"What happened when you were finally moved from the cages?"

"He drugged us again." Melaney looked around the room as if searching for a safe place to rest her gaze. "When we came to, we were on the side of the road. Naked and all tied up so we couldn't go for help." Her lips trembled. "But we were alive."

She fell silent for a time. No doubt reliving the horrors and the relief.

"We started yelling for help. We kept screaming and crying, hoping someone would hear us. I don't know how much later—hours I guess—a trucker stopped. The guy was headed into the woods to pee when we managed to get his attention." She exhaled a shuddering breath. "Our voices were so weak by then it was a miracle he heard us."

Jess had interviewed the truck driver who discovered the women on that Tennessee mountain road. Otis Berry was short, bone thin, and sixty-eight years old. He had a bad knee that caused him to hobble and a bad back that kept him stooped over, making him easy to rule out as a suspect.

"Can you tell me anything else about Rory?" Rory Stinnett was the third woman, the one Spears had chosen to keep. *Victim number one.* Jess worked at calming another bout of churning in her stomach.

Something awful was coming. Spears had some twisted finale planned. She could feel it. And, dammit, she couldn't seem to do anything to stop it.

"We cried and talked a lot. Tried to figure out ways to escape but none of them worked." Melaney scrubbed at her tears with the backs of her hands. "We didn't know whether he was going to kill us or what. He never told us anything. Until Claudia and I were with the police we had no idea what was going on."

"I'm sure you'd seen the headlines about Eric Spears, the serial killer called the Player, before your abduction?" Just saying his name out loud changed the rhythm of Jess's heart. She tightened her grip on her pencil.

"I'm a nursing student. I don't have time for the news or anything else. But Claudia had heard of him and all those women he killed." Melaney's voice quaked on the last.

Not just women. Jess didn't bother correcting her. Eric Spears had murdered a federal agent who'd graduated from the Bureau's training academy with her. The truth was there were likely far more victims than they suspected. They might never know just how many lives Eric Spears had taken… or would take before he was stopped.

Just let me close to him one more time.

"A few more questions, Miss Lands." Jess resigned herself to the fact that she'd gotten all she was going to at this time. "Do you remember how the place where you were held smelled? If there were any windows? Any other furniture? Could you hear any noises from the outside?"

Melaney shook her head in answer to each question.

Okay, go back to the beginning. "Do you recall anything different or strange that happened in school or at home in the week or so before you were abducted? Besides the phone call about the weekend getaway you'd supposedly won?" Jess qualified.

The young woman stared at Jess as if she were completely overwhelmed and totally lost. Finally, she shook her head yet again, more tears shining in her eyes as renewed defeat clouded her face.

Enough. Jess stood and moved to the side of her bed. She placed a business card on the tray table. She wasn't usually the touchy-feely type but she gave Melaney's hand a gentle squeeze just the same. "Anything you remember or need, no matter when it is—day or night, tomorrow or weeks from now—you call me. Don't hesitate."

A jerky nod was her answer.

"Thank you, Melaney."

Jess turned and started for the door. She was thankful these two women were safe and unharmed for the most part. As grateful as she was, she wished something—anything—one or the other remembered could help them find Rory Stinnett.

How much time did they have before Stinnett became a statistic in the massive case file on the Player?

"Wait." Melaney's tinny voice resonated against the sterile white walls of the room.

Jess stopped, turned, and waited. Adrenaline pumped through her. There was something different in the other woman's tone now… a new kind of fear or desperation crammed into that one word.

Melaney visibly struggled as if she feared her words would somehow change what happened next. She toyed with the card Jess had left for her. "I wasn't going to mention it." She made an aching sound in her throat. "The drug was sucking me into the darkness, and I wasn't sure if I really heard what I thought I heard. Claudia said she didn't remember anyone saying anything. I figured maybe I imagined it."

Jess's thoughts, the very blood flowing through her veins, hushed.

Melaney moistened her chapped lips. "But, when you came in here and introduced yourself, I knew I hadn't imagined it."

A chill crept into Jess's bones. "You may have seen me or heard my name on the news." Her own voice sounded strained. Her chest seemed to be rising and falling too rapidly, yet she couldn't draw enough air into her lungs.

Melaney shook her head. "Told you I don't watch the news."

Jess moved closer to the foot of her bed. "All right. What do you think you heard?"

"He whispered… or maybe it was the drug that made his voice seem so low and quiet."

Holding her breath, Jess waited for the rest.

"He said, *tell Jess this is all for her.*"

Somehow, Jess managed a stiff nod. "Thank you, Melaney."

When she would have turned away, Melaney's voice stopped her again. "Are you the reason he did this to us?"

Jess would've given just about anything to be able to say no...

CHAPTER THREE

Sergeant Chet Harper waited at the drop-off area outside baggage claims. The somber face he wore warned it was going to be a long night.

During the return flight from Knoxville, Jess and Dan hadn't spent a lot of time talking. He'd made his thoughts on the matter perfectly clear: Jess should basically go into hiding. She had made her opinion equally clear: that was not happening. After the stalemate, she had prevented thoughts of Spears from intruding by fantasizing about the long, hot bath she intended to indulge in before climbing into bed next to Dan—even if he was frustrated at her—and shutting out the world for a few hours.

But that was going to have to wait now.

Her team had a new case.

The instant the plane had settled on the tarmac she couldn't take the not knowing anymore. She had checked her phone and listened to her messages. Dan had given her that look when she'd powered it on before the pilot announced it was okay to do so. She'd pretended not to notice and turned to stare out the window. The first message had been from Harper. They had a double homicide. A particularly gruesome one judging by the sound of her detective's voice. The two victims were both young and female.

Harper had said in the voice mail that he would pick Jess up at the airport. A reasonable call for her senior detective to make since Dan would need to retrieve his SUV from short-term parking and head home. There was no reason for them both to spend the next few hours, maybe the rest of the night, at a crime scene. At this point, Dan wasn't saying much. Having her rush off to a crime scene the minute they landed didn't exactly make him happy, but her team had caught this case. She had an obligation to her detectives and to the department. More importantly, she had an obligation to the victims.

It wasn't as if Chief of Police Daniel Burnett didn't fully grasp those facts. She glanced up at the man next to her. His face was grim. The lines of exhaustion told her just how worried he was about her and about Spears. She couldn't fault him for that. She was damned worried herself.

"Sergeant," Jess said in greeting as she and Dan approached Harper and his vehicle.

"Ma'am." He gave her a smile, and then nodded to Dan. "Chief."

"I'll keep you posted on my whereabouts at all times," Jess promised Dan. He didn't really want her out of his sight. Every move Spears made had him struggling harder to protect her. He was terrified he would fail. She wished she could make him see there was no way to fully protect her from what was coming.

There were no real choices in this deadlock. For this torment to ever end, she had to face Spears eventually.

During the past fifteen or so hours, she had come to terms with the reality that there was only one way to stop him. The tricky part was managing that feat without getting herself badly injured or... dead. A thread of unfamiliar fear wove its way through her. This time she wasn't the only one depending on whether she kept breathing or not. Having those pink lines appear on that pregnancy test this morning had changed everything.

"Sergeant, you know what I expect." Dan's voice drew her from the troubling thoughts. He glanced at the Birmingham Police Department cruiser waiting right behind Harper's SUV. "Don't lose your surveillance detail, and do not allow Chief Harris out of your sight even for a second. We have every reason to believe Spears or one or more of his followers are close. We can't take anything for granted."

Harper nodded. "I understand, sir."

Jess gave Dan's arm a reassuring squeeze. "I'll be fine."

Dan exhaled a heavy breath but finally gave her a nod. "Don't make me regret allowing you to stay on the job."

Regret was one thing she didn't want between them ever again. Whatever happened, no more regrets. They'd both spent far too much time lamenting the past as it was. They weren't kids anymore.

"No regrets," she reminded him. "Mutual respect and trust."

He held up his hands in surrender. "You win. Respect and trust." That ghost of a smile he managed couldn't have been easy but it warmed her heart.

"I'll be home as soon as I can," she promised.

Home. Jess moved toward the waiting SUV, keeping her back straight and her step purposeful. Strange as it seemed when she took the time to think about it, Birmingham was home again. She'd made a bit of a detour, spending most of her adult life far away from Birmingham, Alabama.

Far away from Dan.

But she was back. Spears had her rammed into a corner in many respects but she had no intention of allowing him to prevent her from living her life or doing her job.

Right now, two homicide victims were waiting for their killer to be found.

"Your weapon's in the glove box, Chief," Harper let her know as she settled into the front passenger seat and fastened her safety belt.

"Thank you, Sergeant." Jess claimed her Glock and held it for a long moment. Air travel restrictions and the lack of time to gain the necessary clearance had prevented her from taking her weapon with her. The Bureau had sent an armed escort to collect her and Dan from the airport in Knoxville, and then to shuttle them back for their return flight. Being armed hadn't really been necessary.

She drew in a deep, steadying breath. Her law enforcement career spanned more than two decades. First as a field agent and then a profiler for the Federal Bureau of Investigation and now as deputy chief of Birmingham's new Special Problems Unit, a modified Major Crimes Division. Not having her weapon with her was like forgetting to wear underwear. She just didn't feel comfortable.

"Give me a rundown on what we have." Jess stashed the Glock in her bag. Harper hadn't given her much in his voice mail. The sooner she was focused on the case the quicker she could push aside the pain of not being able to help Rory Stinnett, the woman Spears hadn't released.

"The two victims, Lisa Templeton and Alisha Burgess, were last seen at Chuck's Roadhouse after midnight last night." Harper merged onto I-20 west/I-59 south. "They closed the joint and left together."

Since the vics were last spotted in a public place, maybe there were reliable witnesses who would remember whether or not the women had left with anyone.

"The vics share a house in Homewood," Harper went on. "A couple hours ago a friend, Stacey Jernigan, who works with Lisa Templeton, dropped by to find out why she didn't come to work today. The front door was ajar and Jernigan went inside."

Even in B-rated movies, it was always the person who walked through the door left ajar or into the dark alley who ended up dead or who discovered the body. It was a miracle anyone who had ever watched a movie like that still took the risk. Morbid curiosity, Jess supposed.

"Chuck's is a restaurant? Bar?" She didn't recognize the name, but then she'd been gone for a long time. Most of the places she had frequented as a fake ID toting teenager were long gone.

"Popular nightclub over on Tenth. Detective Wells is there now interviewing the manager and the employees who worked last night."

Lori Wells was another respected member of SPU. Though Jess had only been away for the day, she was glad to be back at work with her team. She glanced at Harper's profile as he drove through the darkness. These people felt like family.

Her arms went around her waist. Being a part of a family was something she'd never been very good at. Her sister, Lily, would say Jess was too busy with work for family stuff. Frankly, it was high time she got the hang of balancing the two. The child she carried was depending on her.

The baby was a secret she had to keep for a while longer—or at least until she figured out how to prevent Spears from discovering what he would no doubt see as a new pawn to use in his evil game.

RALEIGH AVENUE, HOMEWOOD, 10:33 P.M.

The small bungalow sat on a corner lot in a neighborhood that had seen better days. The homes were older, the yards a little larger. The cars belonging to the victims were parked in the driveway. Four BPD cruisers were on the scene with two blocking the street, while the officers kept traffic and pedestrians clear of the area. The crime scene unit had arrived and, of course, the usual news crew suspects. Questions were shouted at Jess as she walked toward the house. She ignored the reporters. There was nothing to tell just yet.

"The ME en route?" she asked as she and Harper ducked under the yellow tape officially proclaiming the property as a place where bad things had happened.

He nodded. "Dr. Baron's heading this way now. She's sent me three," he glanced at his cell, "make that four text messages wanting to know what was taking us so long. She didn't want to show up until you were on the scene."

They were all waiting for Jess to arrive and take charge. Murder was her specialty. Typically, she considered that an asset, somehow tonight she just felt tired.

As tired as she was, she was surprised Deputy Chief Black wasn't here insisting his division work this double homicide. He and Jess had issues when it came to who was assigned what case. Maybe Black was resigned to having her around.

If he wasn't, he might as well get that way. Jess was here to stay.

"Officer Cook is taking statements from the two uniforms that were first on the scene." Harper gestured to the official BPD car parked in the driveway behind the victims' vehicles. "Jernigan's waiting in the cruiser. She didn't want to stay in the house."

"Can't say as I blame her." Jess looked from the cruiser to the home now filled with official personnel. "I'll come back to Jernigan after I've had a look inside." The sooner she examined the scene, the more quickly she could start to form an assessment of the killer. His every move told her something about him and his reason for committing murder. Uncovering the motive was key in finding the killer.

The uniform guarding the front door stepped aside as Jess approached the stoop. Harper passed her gloves and shoe covers. "Thank you, Sergeant."

"I know you've seen a lot in your time with the FBI," Harper was saying as he tugged on the required protective wear, "but this is damned bizarre. Whoever killed these women is one sick puppy."

Jess reminded herself to catch a last big breath before entering the house. "Lead the way, Sergeant."

The odor of coagulated blood hung thick in the air. Not that it had far to go in the small home. Forensic techs were snapping photos and dusting for prints in the main living area. There were no immediate indications of trouble. The space was sparsely furnished, with little of the usual clutter of everyday life. If the home had air conditioning, it wasn't working very well. It was as hot and humid inside as it was out, making the smell all the more overwhelming.

"No air conditioning?" Jess dabbed at her forehead, perspiration forming on her skin already. If she didn't know better, she would swear she was suffering with hot flashes. *Did pregnant women get hot flashes?*

"On the fritz," Harper explained. "Windows are painted shut. Doesn't look like anyone's tried to open them in the last couple of decades."

Jess wondered how the women had made it through the long, hot summer. And there were still another three or four weeks to go.

"We believe the killer washed up in the bathroom," Harper gestured to the kitchen side of the living area, "and then exited through the back door."

Jess followed him across the room, studying the details that painted a picture of how the victims had lived. Unwashed cups in the sink and paper plates in the trash suggested busy women on the go. Cabinets were mostly bare but there were grapes, yogurt, and vitamin water in the fridge. She opened the freezer door, found one unopened bottle of Vodka and a carton of chocolate ice cream, a girl's best friends after a bad date.

She turned to the open back door. "Maybe that's what he wanted us to think." If he'd gone to all the trouble to clean up, why not close the doors? Why leave the front door ajar and go out the back? Were one or both open while he went about his heinous business?

Was he just arrogant enough not to care? Or was he driven by emotions fierce enough to prevent him from thinking logically? Then again, someone or something may have interrupted him, forcing him to rush away.

Jess considered the room once more. "No indication the locks were tampered with?"

"None."

"Seems unlikely the killer was a stranger." Either that or the ladies failed to lock up when they came home. Had the killer followed them home or was he invited? Were the victims' actions compromised by excessive amounts of alcohol or some other drug?

"The bodies are this way, ma'am."

Jess's stomach did a little quiver and she hesitated. "Let's see where our perp washed up first." She couldn't remember the last time she had put off her assessment of the victim—victims, in this instance. The ME wasn't here yet so she had some time. Still, she didn't like this unexpected need to hesitate.

Had pregnancy hormones overridden her usual unflappability?

As she followed Harper, she hoped all the fatigue and turbulent emotions she was experiencing were limited to the first trimester. Otherwise, she might just have to take that vacation Dan wanted so badly for her to consider.

Like that was going to happen with Spears setting the agenda.

Keep your mind on the business at hand, Jess.

The main living area flowed into a cramped hallway. Harper stood to the side of the bathroom door on the right so Jess could have a look at the tiny space. Bloody footprints led from the hallway's hardwood floors to the usually white tile of the bathroom floor. More blood was smeared on the white walls, the sink and the tile in the shower. The hand and footprints were too small, in Jess's opinion, to be a man's. She crouched down and had a closer look. Size seven, she decided. Same size she wore.

"There are an awful lot of prints here for one perp," she noted absently. Either the killer had done a lot of going back and forth or there was more than one, both about a size seven. And a hell of a lot of blood. What had the perp done, used it for body wash? The blood was dry now. The killer or killers had been gone for a while.

"There's a lot of smearing," Harper pointed out. "Makes lifting a good print more difficult."

Just their luck. Jess pushed to her feet. "The killer certainly didn't appear to care about leaving behind possible evidence." There was no visible attempt to clear the endless impressions away.

"We could be dealing with perps who were strung out on something," Harper offered. "Too messed up to think straight."

She examined the footprints once more. "Could be teenagers."

"Definitely someone of a smaller stature," Harper agreed.

Jess turned away from the bathroom. "Possibly female."

"That would explain a lot," Harper said, rather mysteriously. "This way, Chief."

There were maybe six steps between the bathroom and the first bedroom. The stench of decomposition grew stronger but the room was clear of any visible blood. There was a single bed and a dresser. An art easel with a half finished scene on the canvas waited on one side of the room. Jess leaned close to the unfinished art and sniffed, smelled the oil in the paints. She touched it. The paint was still a little tacky. Recent work. The closet in the room was empty, and so were the dresser drawers.

Back in the hallway, a few more steps brought them to the second of the two bedrooms. It was this slightly larger room where the final act in two lives had played out. Jess braced herself.

"No one's been in here yet except for the responding officers and then me."

Harper's voice sounded far away as Jess stared at the scene, her mind centering completely on the grotesque images.

Both victims were naked and restrained. Jess moved toward the first. She lay supine on the bed. Braided nylon ropes secured her wrists and ankles to the brass bedposts. A sex toy intended for giving a partner pleasure was fastened across her pelvis. Around her neck, a leather strap was pulled tight. The way her eyes bulged and the open mouth suggested asphyxiation. Then there was the pièce de résistance—a gapping hole in the center of her chest.

"Alisha Burgess, twenty-six. School teacher." Harper waited at the foot of the bed. "No criminal record."

Burgess had dark blond hair. She was tall and thin. Her finger and toenails were well manicured. Her body was lean and toned.

Jess shifted her attention to the final act of depravity committed by the killer, the one that told far more about him or her than anything else in the room. The victim's chest had been opened in a savage, primitive manner. A number of tools—hammer, box cutter, hatchet and pry bar—had been used to hack open her ribcage and then abandoned haphazardly around the room. Was this killer just careless or totally arrogant?

The lack of arterial spray confirmed the damage to the chest had been done after the heart stopped beating. At least the vic hadn't suffered that horror before taking her last breath.

Leaning closer, Jess's stomach did a warning flip-flop even as her throat tightened. "Her heart is missing."

"Yes, ma'am. If either one is here, we haven't found them."

A generic list of motives for removing a victim's heart immediately cataloged in Jess's thoughts. Jealousy. Regret. Hatred. She moved around the bed and to the other side of the room to get a better look at the second victim whose body hung in front of the the closet doors. The doors were a set of bi-fold louvered ones about four, maybe five feet wide. Wrist shackles had been mounted to the wood facing on either side.

At least one of the two women was no novice at sex games.

To each her own.

The second vic was tall and slender as well, with long auburn hair. She hung by her wrists, her head lolled to one side and dropped back as if she were staring heavenward.

"Lisa Templeton," Harper said. "Twenty-seven. She was a manager at an adult entertainment shop over on Valley Avenue."

Whatever her cause of death, which wasn't readily discernible, Templeton's heart, like her roommate's, had been excavated from her chest. There was more blood but not arterial spray. Gravity had drained a good portion from her body. Blood had spread across the hardwood floor.

That tightening in her belly warned Jess again. She hadn't barfed at a crime scene in twenty years, but being pregnant wasn't going to make this part of her work easy.

Templeton's wrists didn't bear the markings of a prisoner who had attempted to escape her bonds and her feet were unrestrained. What had prevented her from fighting her killer? Jess scanned the body for some indication of cause of death. The state of rigor and visible lividity in both bodies indicated death had occurred more than a few hours ago.

Templeton's eyes bulged and her mouth was open but there were no ligature marks on the neck or any other indication of strangulation on the throat or face. Jess dug a penlight from her bag. She needed a look into Templeton's throat, but that wasn't possible without a stepladder.

"I'll grab a chair from the kitchen," Harper offered, recognizing her problem.

"Thanks, Sergeant."

While he hurried back to the kitchen, Jess worked at calming her stomach's reaction to the scene. These two women needed her on her toes. No one deserved to die in such a vicious manner.

Harper returned with the chair. "ME's here."

"Just in time," Jess muttered as she climbed up onto the chair's wooden seat. The victim was in full rigor, but her mouth was wide open. Jess aimed the light into her throat and immediately spotted what she imagined would prove to be the cause of death. Something neon pink and possibly plastic or rubber had been jammed deep into the woman's throat. "Well that explains the asphyxiation."

Harper helped Jess down. However experienced these women were at sex games, their ménage-a-trois or whatever it was, had taken a wrong turn.

"Sergeant, check with Detective Wells and see if we know yet who these ladies left the club with last night. We need names and descriptions, if possible, of anyone who left about the same time they did." Jess considered the room again. "We need to know who they partied with on a regular basis."

She exhaled, wished she could exorcise the smell of rotting blood from her lungs. "Let's start with Templeton's coworker."

"You want to question her here?"

By now neighbors would be gathering near the police blockade. Reporters would be growing impatient. "Let's take her downtown. Also, locate the landlord and find out how long the ladies have lived here and if there's been any trouble."

"Yes, ma'am."

Even in the bedroom there were few personal touches in the home. No family photos on the walls. Had these two just moved in?

"Well this is interesting," a female voice announced from the door.

Jess turned to greet the medical examiner. No matter the hour, Sylvia Baron never showed up to the party looking anything but her best. Tonight she'd outdone herself. Black sheath and glossy pearls. Maybe she'd had a date.

"Sometimes dating can be hell." Jess presented the medical examiner with a smile.

"That's why I only date men I've properly vetted." Sylvia entered the room and prepared to do her part for the victims. She would provide a preliminary time and manner of death—not that there was much question as to the manner.

"I'll make that call to Detective Wells," Harper said before making himself scarce.

Sylvia had a reputation for rubbing folks the wrong way. Most cops preferred to steer clear of

Jefferson County's deputy coroner. Jess had sort of gotten used to her, considered her a friend. Kind of.

"Did you learn anything in Knoxville?" Sylvia asked as she set to her task of examining Alisha Burgess.

"Not as much as I'd hoped." Unfortunately, that was the ugly truth. They were no closer to catching Spears than before. Just because he'd been in Birmingham three days ago didn't mean he was here now. And just because one of his minions had held three women captive for more than a week near Gatlinburg, Tennessee, didn't mean he'd ever been there.

What they had boiled down to nothing except a missing woman and a freak show of followers who had been talking about Jess on the Net and stalking her from a distance. She'd only picked up on one stalker but judging by the photos of her all over the Net, there were a whole lot more than one.

"That's a shame," Sylvia remarked.

Jess couldn't agree with her more. "The Bureau still has nothing. Feels like we're all just running around in circles." Worry gnawed at her again.

"That's too bad, but I meant it's a shame for you," Sylvia explained. "I heard Mayor Pratt's received several requests from concerned citizens who think you should be run out of town before your obsessed serial killer can murder anymore of Birmingham's citizens."

"Aren't you sweet to keep me informed like this?"

Sylvia sent her a look. "What're friends for?"

CHAPTER FOUR

Jess arched her back as she tugged the zipper of her dress into place, then she studied her reflection. The turquoise dress she'd had for ages still fit the same. She didn't look any different, not really. Well, other than the glaring dark circles under her eyes from working until two this morning and managing less than three hours sleep.

Slogging through murder scenes and interrogating witnesses and killers alike was her job. Her body rebelled regularly at her consistent abuse. Just as regularly, she ignored the nuisance. After all, murder rarely stuck to a nine-to-five schedule or selected the most convenient places to occur.

But everything was different now.

She pressed her hand to her abdomen. "You really messed up this time, Jessie Lee."

Her chest felt suddenly too heavy. What was she thinking? Dan Burnett was the only man she had

33

ever really loved. How could she equate carrying his child with messing up?

She couldn't. It was that simple.

"Bad timing. That's all." She ran the brush through her hair, then stepped into her Mary Jane pumps and swung her bag onto her shoulder. She turned to the bathroom door but hesitated before opening it.

Dan was in the kitchen preparing breakfast. He'd insisted she stay with him for now. Nothing new there. He'd been nagging at her practically from day one to move into his place. He wanted her near. He wanted to protect her and, she smiled, he loved her. So she'd grabbed a couple outfits and here she was.

At any other time she would have fought him tooth and nail on the issue. Not because she didn't want to be with him, she did, but his need to protect her spilled over into the workplace and that was a problem. At work, she needed him to treat her the same as he did the other deputy chiefs. How was she ever going to earn their respect otherwise?

She had wrestled her way out of foster homes and through college to be an independent, capable woman who could take care of herself—who never again had to depend on anyone else for survival. Years of hard work and dedication to the career above all else had accomplished that goal. She needed him to respect her strength and ability as a woman and a cop.

Though, she had to admit, lately she'd started to wonder if a good strong shoulder to lean on occasionally might be a good thing. Why fight the inevitable? She wanted this relationship, as long as they could juggle the personal and professional boundaries. So here she was living with the boss. She imagined every cop and staff member in the department had heard the news. Eventually, someone would complain, citing fraternization and unfair workplace practices. It could turn ugly.

Jess groaned. Not even two months after leaving the Bureau her fresh start was already meandering down a bumpy road. As if that wasn't head spinning enough, years of hard work at ridding herself of her southern vernacular had gone out the window. Just went to show the adage that you can take the girl out of the country but you can't take the country out of the girl was painfully true.

Oh well, there was just no keeping her life tidy.

Lifting her chin and squaring her shoulders, she reached for the door and headed for the kitchen before she could lose her nerve. She couldn't stay holed up in the bathroom, there was work to be done and people counting on her.

First, however, she had to get through breakfast and telling Dan they were pregnant. She'd needed a little time to recover from the shock of learning the news. Frankly, she was still reeling just a little but she had no right to keep this news from him any longer. He deserved to know he was going to be a father.

That persistent ache deep beneath her sternum eased as anticipation fluttered in her belly. They were in this together. He'd told her in no uncertain terms that he loved her. Dan wanted to move to the next level in their relationship, as did she. She had no right to keep him in the dark… if she could just work up the courage to squeeze the words past the massive lump expanding in her throat. What she needed was a good dose of steaming hot coffee.

Her steps slowed. Was it okay to drink coffee? Should she be on a special diet? Even she knew alcohol was off limits for the next seven or so months. What about avoiding things like touching up her roots and working out—wait, she avoided that last one already. What about prenatal vitamins? Shouldn't she be taking those already? Heaven's sake! She needed an assistant to figure this all out. More importantly, she needed a competent doctor… *soon.*

The scent of bacon had her walking a little faster. When she'd first come back to Birmingham—had it only been six weeks ago—after more than two decades away, she'd accused Dan of buying this big old house in the elite Mountain Brook neighborhood just for show. She would've bet her measly savings he had never cooked in this gourmet kitchen. She paused in the doorway and watched as he deftly portioned scrambled eggs from a nonstick pan onto two plates. Had she been that wrong or had he suddenly decided he wanted to use all those high-end appliances for something other than proof of his income bracket?

Maybe they'd both decided they wanted more now that they were together again. Until very recently, she had expected to spend the rest of her days in the Behavioral Analysis Unit at Quantico. The prospect of marriage—much less children—hadn't been penciled into her ten-year plan. At forty-two, she'd pretty much decided she didn't have time to be a mother. *So much for ten-year plans.*

She watched as Dan pulled biscuits from the oven. A mental harrumph accompanied the conclusion that those two perfectly round, fluffy cakes of bread had either come from a twist open can or a freezer bag. No way had he made those from scratch. But judging by the tempting aroma, they were going to be delicious either way.

"Smells wonderful," she announced. She might just nab both those biscuits. After all, she was eating for two, right?

Dan looked up as she crossed to the island. A smile lifted his lips. Her heart did a little dance that made her feel all giddy. The first time she'd seen that smile, back in high school, she'd reacted the same way. The man had the most amazing smile. When those blue eyes lit up, any woman in the vicinity still breathing swooned. This morning he wore a pale blue shirt and navy tie, both of which highlighted his eyes and made him look all the sexier even wielding a potholder and baking sheet.

Would their child have his midnight black hair and beautiful blue eyes? Or the plain old blond hair and brown eyes she stared at in the mirror every morning? She hoped this baby had Dan's patience and his innate ability to be charming and kind.

He was going to be an amazing father.

Her shoulders sagged. How in the world was she going to hold up her end? Being a mother was a big deal. A huge commitment. What if she was a terrible mother? She'd lost her mother when she was just ten. God knew her drunken aunt hadn't provided any sort of role model. She'd moved away before Lily started her family. Her sister was a wonderful mother. Maybe she inherited some special nurturing gene that Jess hadn't.

What if this baby didn't like her? Suppose the baby sensed somehow that she was no good at being a parent?

The idea of her impending motherhood shook her all over again. *This poor child was doomed!* She could just see him sitting on the bleachers alone at the soccer field because Jess was caught up in a case and forgot to pick him up. If they had a girl, it would be even worse. What did she know about little pink dresses and hair bows? Her experience with dance classes and dance mothers proved without doubt that she would not do well in that environment. She'd never worn a tutu in her life. Mothers carried all manner of emergency essentials in their purses. Jess carried a Glock, latex gloves and M&Ms.

She couldn't breathe.

"Eat while it's still warm." Dan tugged off the mitt and pointed to a stool on the opposite side of the island. "Coffee? OJ?"

Jess blinked. Somehow, she inhaled a breath. *Calm down before you start hyperventilating. You can do this.* She forced a smile. "How about both?" The coffee was for her, the OJ for the baby. A reasonable compromise.

Breakfast wasn't usually her favorite meal, but her stomach rumbled as if she hadn't eaten in days. The scents alone had her appetite revved into high gear. She scooted onto a stool and plopped her bag on the one next to her as he settled a plate on the granite counter in front of her. Her mouth watered. She might not even bother with a fork.

"Butter?"

No was on the tip of her tongue but instead of saying it she licked her lips and confessed, "Absolutely. Maybe some jelly, if you have any."

He quirked an eyebrow at her. "This is Alabama, Jess, jelly is a staple of every kitchen."

She'd bet her beloved Mary Jane pumps this southern boy had only recently stocked his pantry with traditional staples. A shiver went through her as she pondered the concept that Daniel Burnett was nesting. A few months older than her, he had the successful career, the power of his family name and the respect of the community. Even after three failed marriages, he was ready for a wife and family.

Careful what you wish for.

As she slathered butter and jelly on her biscuit, all thought of her big news and of murder cases vanished. She dug into the meal, the rejoicing of her taste buds overriding all other brain activity. Orange juice and coffee appeared in front of her and she barely stopped chewing long enough to say thanks.

When she'd scraped the last morsel from her plate, she realized he was watching her.

"Glad you enjoyed it." He munched on a strip of crisp bacon.

Jess patted her mouth with the napkin that had landed next to her plate at some point. "You sure you didn't hire someone to sneak in here and make breakfast while I was in the shower?" Maybe he'd been taking some of those cooking classes his friend Gina Coleman raved about.

Stop being petty, Jess. Gina was Birmingham's hotshot TV news reporter. She was gorgeous and she and Dan had once been an item.

Something else Jess had struggled with since returning to her hometown—all Dan's ex girlfriends and wives. All rich. And all gorgeous. She sighed, feeling frumpier with every passing minute.

Stop putting off the inevitable. No matter that she was confident he would be thrilled about the baby, she also understood his need to hover would increase exponentially.

Complicated. So, so complicated.

Jess cleared her throat. "I wanted to discuss—"

The old fashioned clang of her cell phone's ringtone echoed from deep within her bag. The rattle of Dan's cell vibrating on the counter joined the cacophony.

Their gazes met and for one instant she wondered what it would be like to have a few days away with Dan. No work… no Eric Spears. *Was a little time for themselves with no interruptions too much to ask for?*

A break would give her the chance to tell him about the pregnancy and for them to figure things out.

But that wasn't going to happen today.

BIRMINGHAM POLICE DEPARTMENT,
INTERVIEW ROOM 2, 9:50 A.M.

Jess smiled at the young woman seated across the table. "Stacey, before we go on, I want to be clear—for the record—you've waived your right to have an attorney, is that correct?"

She nodded. "I didn't do anything wrong. I don't need an attorney."

"I understand," Jess said patiently. "But, I need a yes or no."

"Yes. No attorney." The young lady was caught. She knew it and so did Jess. Now she was working extra hard to be cooperative in hopes of making herself look a little less like a suspect.

"All right. Now that we have that behind us, why don't we go over this once more?"

Stacey Jernigan had cried throughout the interview this morning just after midnight. She had talked on and on about how she cared so much for her dear friend and coworker, Lisa Templeton. Then, around six this very same morning, she posted a photo of the crime scene and the victims on a private Facebook page. It was a tribute, she'd announced, to her friend and the true heart of art.

How ironic since the victims' hearts were missing.

Too bad dear old Stacey hadn't stopped to consider that the BPD would be checking all social media sites belonging to the two victims, including emails and such discovered on the laptop in Lisa Templeton's home.

"You said," Jess began, Stacey jumped as if a weapon had been discharged in the room, "you and Lisa shared a love for art. This private page on Facebook you and your friends created is for sharing things that inspire you the way folks do on Pinterest, is that right?"

"Lots of people do it," Stacey said quickly, her voice quavering just a touch. "Writers, readers, dog lovers, lots of people. It's not unusual."

Jess might not have a Facebook page but she was quite familiar with the purpose of the social media outlet. She also knew the rules. "You and I both know photos like the one you shared this morning are not allowed on Facebook."

"I…" She shifted in her chair. "I didn't go in the room or touch anything. I just went to the door and took a pic with my cell phone. I wasn't thinking."

No doubt. "The members of this private page are friends you met in one of the classes you took at a local art school, is that correct?" Jess intended to get all she could while the young woman was feeling guilty and worried about staying out of trouble.

Stacey nodded. "The Art Academy. It's an exclusive private school. The owner spent most of his life in Europe. He was schooled in the ways of the Old Masters. We're very lucky to have him in Birmingham."

"Really?" Jess might have been gone from Birmingham for two decades, but if this school was so exclusive she would've heard about it from some of Dan's Mountain Brook friends. The *Brookies* in his neighborhood would all have their offspring enrolled before birth. "I need his name, phone number and address, if you have it."

Jess readied to take down the info, her pencil was dull from the lists of folks who could vouch for Miss Jernigan's character. Her alibi for last night had checked out. Despite this morning's allegedly thoughtless act, she hadn't killed her friends.

Stacey chewed at her lip a second. "His number and address are private."

Laying her pencil aside, Jess removed her glasses and rubbed at her eyes. She was far too tired this morning to beat around the bush. With a deep breath, she replaced her glasses and tapped her pencil on the desk. "Let me be clear, Stacey. You have thirty seconds to give me his name and address or I'll arrest you for obstruction of justice. Oops," she checked the big clock on the wall, "make that twenty-five seconds."

The woman blinked but couldn't conceal the fear in her eyes. At least she had the good sense to be afraid. "His name is Richard. Richard Ellis. We call him Rick. He prefers to stay out of the limelight. He funds the school and teaches there because he loves art not because he's looking for accolades."

Stacey spouted his phone number and address from memory. Jess added both to her notes. "This Mr. Ellis taught you that scenes like the one at your friend's home represent art?"

About ten seconds of squirming had the woman's chair squeaking. "He teaches us that real life is true art. I guess I was in shock or something when I found my friends murdered." She closed her eyes and shuddered. "I was so upset. Maybe I went a little crazy. I haven't slept all night. I don't know what I'm doing even now."

How convenient. The shock may very well have caused her to behave erratically but snapping a pic of her murdered friends didn't quite qualify, in Jess's opinion. Particularly since she'd waited more than four hours to post the photo. "So, Alisha Burgess was your friend, too?"

This morning Stacey had insisted she hardly knew Alisha.

"I… mean…" Stacey shrugged, glanced nervously around the room for several more seconds. "I suppose she was. She was Lisa's roommate so…"

Now she was just outright lying. Stacey Jernigan had been in this room for better than an hour. There was absolutely nothing noteworthy in any of the department's interview rooms. Certainly nothing warranting more than an initial look around. Yet, Stacey surveyed the space as if seeing it for the first time. Sterile white walls, plain metal table and stiff plastic chairs. Not one thing interesting or inspiring. The big clock with its second-hand ticking off every trauma-filled moment was intended to twist the tension a little tighter. As a general rule, it worked. Like now.

"Were Lisa and Alisha lovers?" Jess had a feeling that was where the conflict existed between these three young women. Jealousy could turn violent very quickly.

"No!" Stacey shook her head adamantly. "None of my friends are... like that. We like guys... men."

"I didn't ask if either preferred women over men," Jess clarified. "I asked if they were sexually intimate."

"I don't think so." Stacey shrugged. "I can't say for sure."

Stacey Jernigan was an attractive young woman with long black hair, gold eyes and perfect skin. She dressed well, if a little provocatively. Her academic resume was admirable despite her current occupation at a sex toy shop. Jess would also lay odds that she was well informed in the ways of the world. She might not have been out with her murdered friends last night but she had been before. There were things Stacey believed based on her experience with the two victims. Things she obviously didn't want to share.

Jess's continued silence did the trick.

"Lisa liked trying out the toys," Stacey murmured.

The words were spoken so softly Jess barely heard them. "The sex toys? From the store where you work?" Like the neon pink object shoved down her throat. *Not a pretty way to die.*

A nod this time. "There are bonuses for pushing certain items. Lisa didn't believe in promoting anything she hadn't tried."

Like any good businesswoman. "So she and her housemate may have tried out the toys together on more than one occasion."

"Guess so."

"I need you to think long and hard, Stacey, about anything you may have forgotten to tell me." Jess slid a notepad and a pen across the table. "Then I want you to write it all down."

Stacey stared at the notepad. "I already told you everything."

Time to shake things up. Jess opened the plain manila folder on the table in front of her. "Do you understand how posting that photo of your dead friends makes you a person of interest in a double homicide?" She pushed the folder and the stack of crime scene photos it held across the table, and then fanned out the close-up images of the victims like a poker hand. "I'd hate to see you become an accessory to these murders."

"Oh, Jesus!" Stacey twisted in her chair and vomited on the floor.

Now Jess had her attention.

"I'll have someone bring you a bottle of water." Jess plucked the travel size box of tissues from her bag and dropped it unceremoniously on the table. "Make that list, Miss Jernigan. Someone will be in to follow up shortly."

When Jess had tucked the photos and folders into her bag, she exited the interview room.

Detective Lori Wells joined Jess in the corridor. Lori had watched the interview from the observation room. "I called for a janitor. Cook's on his way with a bottle of water to finish up with Jernigan."

"Thanks." Jess appreciated her quick work. Her detectives were particularly good at anticipating her needs. "Let's track down this benevolent benefactor Richard Ellis."

"Already on it." Lori checked the notes she'd made on her smart phone.

Jess decided she must be one of the last people on the planet who still used a spiral pad and plain old pencil for note taking. As much as she loved her cell phone, she'd barely mastered texting much less anything else.

"Ellis has a gallery on Broadway." Lori tapped a few more keys. "He's scheduled to speak to a group from Montgomery this morning so he should be there right now."

Why in the world was Jess worried about handling whatever the future held? She had the best team in the department supporting her.

CHAPTER FIVE

Dan waited for Lieutenant Clint Hayes to make himself comfortable. He chose not to consider that what he was about to do could be problematic in the future on a number of levels, legal and otherwise. If the detective now seated before him wanted to create complications this would certainly give him the ammunition. But it was a chance Dan was willing to take.

"Thank you for making time to see me this morning, Lieutenant."

Hayes grunted a laugh that carried far more disdain than amusement. "You're the chief of police. Not making time wasn't an option. My superior insisted I stop what I was doing and come here immediately. How could I say no?"

So this was how it was going to be. "I'm well aware of your issues with authority, Lieutenant, but let's set that aside for the moment."

Hayes turned his palms up. "It's your nickel, Chief. We'll talk about whatever you want to talk about."

Dan tamped down his irritation. As much as he'd like to give this cocky SOB a reminder of just who the hell he was addressing, this wasn't the time for egos. This extra measure he needed to put in place was too important. Dan leaned back in his chair and went for broke. "It's come to my attention that you're interested in moving out of Admin and into the field, is that correct?"

Another burst of curt laughter. "I've made about a dozen requests over the past three years only to be turned down each and every time. Did my chief finally run out of excuses to deny my requests?" Hayes shook his head, his expression blatantly indifferent. "Wait, I get it. He needs my spot to bring his niece over from Traffic. She's bitched about the heat all summer."

A new wave of fury blasted Dan. He gritted his teeth and let it pass. "This isn't about Chief McCord or any of your previous requests, Lieutenant. This isn't even about what you want. It's about what *I* want."

Hayes actually showed some interest for the first time since walking through the door. "I'm listening."

"I appreciate that, Lieutenant." Dan worked at keeping his impatience in check. There was no other choice. He had to make this option work. He'd done his research on the detective. Jess had already mentioned him and Dan was well aware just how badly Hayes wanted out of Admin. "I'm certain you're familiar with the department's new Special Problems Unit and Deputy Chief Harris."

"I am." The lack of defiance in his voice now confirmed he was paying considerably more attention.

"There's an opening in SPU." The detective sat up a little straighter, and the smug expression vanished completely. Maybe they'd get through this without Dan having to kick his ass. "I believe you'd be a good fit with the team already onboard—if you're interested."

"I'm interested."

He was more than interested. The anticipation that flashed in his eyes told Dan what he needed to know. "I'm prepared," Dan went on, "to make that happen, effective immediately."

Wariness slipped into the lieutenant's expression. "I sense a condition or two somewhere in that offer."

The voice of reason railed at Dan, but he ignored it. There was nothing rational in any of this and absolutely no need to pretend. "You're aware of the situation with Eric Spears?"

Hayes gave a nod of confirmation.

"I have grave concerns about Chief Harris's safety. She and her team are close." Dan shoved aside the guilt that attempted to intrude. "I recognize they have Chief Harris's back but—"

"You need someone who isn't emotionally involved," Hayes guessed, "to keep you apprised of the situation. *A spy.*"

Dan wasn't going to deny the assertion or mince words here. "That's right. I want someone who will do whatever needs to be done to protect Chief Harris. Someone who isn't compromised by emotion."

"Someone like me."

Dan nodded. "Someone who reports directly to me and only me where her safety is concerned."

"Just so we're clear," Hayes said, "define the parameters you have in mind for protecting Chief Harris."

Dan hesitated for a moment. He was about to cross a line from which there would be no going back. "There are none." His voice seemed to reverberate in the room.

Hayes inclined his head and considered the proposition. "If I accept and excessive force is required to protect her, who's going to protect me from the fallout?"

"You know the law, Lieutenant." Dan cast aside the last of the reservations still loitering around the fringes of his conscience. "I expect you to do whatever's necessary, even if you have to skirt it. I'll take care of the fallout."

"Is this assignment a temporary one?"

A reasonable question. "How permanent this move is depends upon you, Lieutenant. Chief Harris has set high standards for her team. Meet those and I'm certain you'll find your place there permanently, if you so choose."

Hayes studied him for a long moment, setting Dan farther out on that edge he'd dared approach. Finally, the detective said, "I accept."

As profound as his relief was, Dan couldn't deny the other feeling—he was betraying Jess's trust. He could lose her over a move like this, and yet, it had to be done. "You'll start this afternoon. I'll handle the logistics."

Hayes rose from his chair. "I presume Chief Harris won't be aware of this additional duty."

"This stays between the two of us." Dan stood, putting them back on equal ground. "You will be cooperative and respectful to Chief Harris and the other members of the team, but I expect you to remember at all times where your orders come from for now, are we clear on that as well?"

Hayes gave a nonchalant shrug. "No problem. I'm just glad I'm not the one sleeping with her at night."

Dan stilled. Outrage roared inside him. With tremendous effort he held it back. "Do not presume to understand my motives, Lieutenant. I'm doing you a favor. That's all you need to understand." Dan held his thumb and forefinger about an inch apart. "You are this close to being out of here. I'm giving you an opportunity to prove you're as good as you think you are. Have I made a mistake?"

"No, sir."

"Good." Dan ignored the twitch in his jaw. "That'll be all."

Dan watched him go. Despite the anger and frustration raging through him at the man's insubordinate attitude he almost laughed. If Hayes gave Jess any grief, she would take him down a notch or two. No worry there. She could hold her own with any cop in the department.

If she learned about his deal with Hayes, she would see the move as exactly what it was—a planned and executed deception. They were just beginning to make headway on the trust thing. He couldn't afford for this to backfire on him.

Dan swallowed back the uncertainty that rose in his throat. There simply was no other course for ensuring her safety. Somehow he'd find a way to make it up to her when this was over.

His cell vibrating on his desk pulled him from the troubling thoughts. He picked it up and checked the screen. It was Gant.

More uncertainty trickled into Dan's veins. He took a breath and tapped accept. "Tell me you have a break in the case." Supervisory Special Agent Ralph Gant had been Jess's superior when she was with the FBI. He was the lead agent in charge of the Spears investigation by virtue of the fact that no one, except Jess, knew Spears better.

He wouldn't call unless there was a break in the case or bad news, either one or both could spell trouble for Jess and the Stinnett woman who remained missing.

"I wouldn't call it a break," Gant said, squashing any hope of good news. "We have nothing new on Stinnett, but we have found the hellhole where the three were held."

Dan would lay odds Spears was never even there. The bastard was too good for such an elementary misstep. "You have a team on the ground already?"

"Our people arrived half an hour ago."

Which meant the team hadn't been on site long enough to make any sort of determination on what they did or didn't have at this point. Dan raked his hand through his hair. "So what've you got for me?"

"We've narrowed down one geographic location from last week's internet traffic related to Jess."

Dan grabbed a pen. "You have an address?"

"No specific address yet, but this one suddenly became active again. He's bouncing between Nashville, Atlanta, Birmingham and various smaller towns in that tri-state region. He's good but we're inching closer."

For two weeks chatter about Jess and photos of her had been floating around the Net. Eric Spears had a surprisingly dedicated following. Whether there were two or twenty supporters at his beck and call, they were doing a damned good job of using up FBI resources. That was likely the goal. Spears wanted the feds distracted.

He wanted a clear path to Jess.

Over Dan's dead body.

Then the chatter had suddenly stopped and they had nothing. Hopefully this time the outcome would be different.

"What kind of timeline are we looking at before you narrow this lead down to a specific location?" Hell, Dan tossed the pen aside, they needed the names and locations of the perps involved in this not more talk about how the investigation was inching closer. A new twitch started in Dan's jaw.

"We're doing all we can, Burnett. Spears clearly handpicked the people carrying out his wishes. They know what they're doing, and all we can do is follow their tracks. He's been several steps ahead of us for years."

"Meanwhile, the body count keeps rising." Dan threaded his fingers through his hair again. Damn it! They were getting nowhere.

"Just be aware," Gant said, his tone indicating the conversation was over, "we are closing in on at least one element of these unknown subjects. That's something we didn't have twenty-four hours ago."

"I can't tell you how reassuring that news is, Gant." Dan ended the call and slung his phone across the desk.

Damn Eric Spears.

He was a coward who watched from a distance, allowing others to do the dirty work. It wasn't until his prey was captured that he bothered to come close. He loved torturing and murdering women once they were disabled.

And yet, Dan's blood ran cold, the bastard had deviated from his usual MO and walked right up to Jess on Friday… close enough to touch her.

Dan clenched his jaw against the new blast of outrage. He and Spears had been face to face once. He hoped to have that opportunity again… *soon.*

CHAPTER SIX

Jess surveyed the street as she emerged from Lori's Mustang. Nothing like having Spears show up for a press conference attended by nearly every cop in the department to put a woman on edge. Arrogant bastard that he was, he'd not only dared to set foot in Birmingham again but he'd appeared in the crowd at last Friday's press conference just to prove he could.

He'd touched Jess. She shuddered even now.

Lori joined her on the sidewalk. "He's not here."

Jess blinked. "Ellis?" He was supposed to be here speaking to a group of visiting art lovers from Alabama's esteemed capital.

Lori held her gaze. "Spears. No one followed us here except our assigned BPD escort." She inclined her head toward the cruiser parked across the street. "I kept an eye out for the Infiniti his friend drives and any other potential tails. We're okay for now."

That transparent, was she? Emotion welled so fast inside Jess it was all she could do not to sway with the weight of it. The urge to tell Lori just how high the stakes were now was nearly overwhelming. But she couldn't. Lori was already too close. The first real friend Jess had had in a long time. But that friendship made Lori a target. She'd almost lost her life once already.

Spears could still be here, and the dark haired man who'd been following Jess for days in that damned Infiniti could be lurking somewhere close. Those possibilities disturbed her more than she wanted to admit, even to herself.

"Good to know." Jess gave her friend a nod. "Let's go meet this enigmatic Mr. Ellis."

The vintage storefront windows on either side of the entrance to The Gallery were filled with lovely framed art pieces and sleek sculptures. A bell jingled overhead as they entered the elegant shop. The cardboard 'open' sign flopped against the glass in the massive wood door. The gallery turned out to be an unexpectedly generous space, but not very well lit. Smelling of oil and age, it reminded Jess of the library at the middle school she'd attended. The art classroom had been next door and the smell of wet oil paints wafted into the library and mingled with the scent of old books.

That library had been Jess's favorite place to hide out when she wanted to skip class. Not because she'd particularly loved reading, it just felt safe and smelled comfortable, the way a home should.

Ellis's gallery didn't have that same comfortable vibe. The décor was too chic with that museum hush about it. Seating areas filled with graceful furnishings flanked the entry, making a corridor down the center of the space that led deeper into the building. Art hung along the walls, each piece spotlighted with a soft glow. Sculpted pieces sat on pedestals beneath their own spotlights.

The sound of a deep voice resonated from somewhere beyond Jess's line of sight, interrupting the quiet.

"I guess he's still with that visiting group." Lori checked the time on her cell.

"Let's give him a few minutes. Have a look around." Jess wanted to get a better feel for the place and maybe some perception of the man.

Lori nodded and headed left. Jess went right. She moved from painting to painting studying the work. New work, she decided. The color layers were distinctly vivid, not dulled by time. The unique smell of oil lingered stronger near the paintings. Maybe Ellis preferred to focus on up and coming artists, local ones perhaps. Whatever the case, his gallery features were new and bold. The colors were strong, vibrant. Most of the work appeared to be landscapes or local landmarks. A few were renderings of people, mostly women.

As if she had nothing else in the world to worry about, she suddenly found herself trying to recall the last time she'd been to a gallery. Strange thing to have come to mind when her life was about as sideways as it could get.

The National Gallery of Art with Wesley. That was it. Felt like a lifetime ago.

Wesley Duvall, her one and only ex-husband, had been another life. She'd hit forty and suddenly marriage seemed necessary. She and Wesley had married on a Saturday and were back at work on Monday. The marriage lasted barely longer than the senseless celebrity wedding debacles that made the news. Sooner, rather than later, Wesley transferred to the west coast where he was needed since Jess didn't seem to need him after the initial ceremony.

Looking back, she understood now she'd only needed to prove to herself that someone wanted to marry her. Wesley just happened to be in the wrong place at the wrong time. At least they had remained friends.

"That masterpiece comes from the admirable imagination of a local artist."

Jess turned from the commendable rendering of Sloss Furnaces, a local landmark, to the man who'd spoken. He stood medium height with broad shoulders and a kind face. Late forties, maybe fifty, she estimated. Nice silk jacket, very expensive and a stark contrast to the comfortable jeans and gray t-shirt that sported the Crimson Tide logo. The man looked nothing at all like she'd pictured the owner of an art gallery or a master teacher of one of the fine arts. He looked more like a firefighter or football coach.

A stealthy one considering he'd walked right up to her and she hadn't sensed his presence until he spoke. *Where was her mind?*

"She's quite talented," Jess agreed. The artist's signature read Leah J.

"Quite." He extended his hand. "Richard Ellis at your service, Chief."

So, he knew who she was. My, my. Jess shook his hand. His palms and fingers weren't as smooth as she'd expected. Evidently, nothing about this man was to be what she'd anticipated. "Do you have an office where we can discuss an ongoing case?"

He gestured to the room at large. "This is my office."

Visitors, those who had come from Montgomery, she supposed, filed out the entrance. Jess counted ten. He was a popular guy. "I was thinking of some place a bit more private, Mr. Ellis."

"Please, call me Rick."

Before Jess could respond, he strode to the entrance, made a parting comment in French, no less, to the exiting visitors, and then closed and locked the door. He rotated the 'open' sign to the closed side and released the Roman style shade so that it dropped down over the glass in the door.

"Now." He glanced at Lori, and then turned back to Jess. "Would you and your friend like coffee? Water?"

"No thank you, Rick." Jess moved to the nearest sofa and took a seat. She settled her bag next to her and removed her pad and pencil. "I hope we're not catching you at a bad time."

Lori continued to wander the gallery.

Ellis relaxed in the stylish sofa stationed on the other side of the marble and glass coffee table. "Not at all. What may I have the privilege of doing this morning for Birmingham's newest deputy chief?"

"One of your former students, Lisa Templeton, was murdered." Jess didn't hear any sign of a European accent in his voice. What she heard was a northeastern one, most likely Massachusetts.

He nodded, his expression shifting from congenial to somber. "Stacey called me. She was horribly upset. Lisa was a dear friend of hers." He shook his head. "I'm continually amazed at the evil one human can do to another. Lisa was a lovely young woman."

Jess was amazed at what dear friends like Stacey could do as well but she opted to keep that to herself. "When did you last see Lisa?"

He inclined his head and flashed her a knowing smile. "Are you asking me for an alibi, Chief?"

"Do you have one?" Charm wasn't going to buy him an ounce of slack.

"Let's see. Sunday night I went to dinner with friends who will gladly corroborate as much. By midnight I was tucked in for the night."

"Alone?"

He smiled again. "Unfortunately."

Jess decided not to point out that he actually didn't have an alibi for the time of the murders since the ME had estimated time of death at between two and four Monday morning. "When did you last see Miss Templeton?"

His brow furrowed in careful concentration. "She took one of my classes last spring. Until two weeks ago, I hadn't seen her since the class ended in April."

"How did you come to see her two weeks ago?"

He leaned forward, propped his elbows on his knees and folded his hands together. He had blue eyes. His hair was close cropped and brown, she decided, with a scattering of gray. No wedding ring. No jewelry at all.

"She'd completed a new painting and she wanted my opinion."

"Did Miss Templeton hope to become a full time artist one day?"

Ellis laughed. "Many have that hope. It's the misery all artists suffer, I'm afraid."

"What was your opinion of her work?"

"Lisa beautifully captured the emotions she kept bottled up for most of her life. In fact, I was so enthralled I purchased the painting for the gallery." He shook his head sadly. "Would you like to see it?"

"I would." Jess shoved her pad and pencil into her bag and followed Ellis deeper into the gallery. Lori, who'd apparently already spotted the painting, had paused to admire the work.

"Breathtaking, isn't it?" Ellis said.

"It is," Lori agreed, stepping aside for Jess to have a closer look.

Jess adjusted her glasses and considered the work. Nude lovers, women, in the midst of a sexual act. The affection and ecstasy captured was undeniably compelling. The crisp colors and perfect brushstrokes conveyed the sensual moves and setting as if the scene were in motion. But it was one of the faces that told Jess more than anything else. Stacey Jernigan had been wrong about her friend.

"It's lovely." She turned to the man whose pride for his pupil's work literally beamed from his face. "Is this the first painting you've purchased from Lisa?"

"I rarely purchase a painting from a student." He shrugged. "Most are just learning to put their feelings on the canvas. The work, though perhaps fairly well done, isn't generally extraordinary enough to fit in here."

"But this one did?" Jess indicated Templeton's painting. "Because she needed money?"

"I don't make a habit of buying art because the artist needs money," he chided. "I made an exception with this one because for the first time, Lisa allowed all the emotion she'd kept inside to spill onto the canvas. She was in love with another woman and she wanted the world to know. She wasn't hiding anymore. That decision elevated her work from the so-so to the remarkable. It's that ability to convey ones deepest emotions that defines a master artist."

"Do you know who the other woman in the painting is?" The profile was not clear enough for Jess to be certain. The long flowing dark blond hair could have been Alisha Burgess's, Templeton's housemate, but the eyes were closed and there just wasn't enough facial detail to make that determination. The other woman was obviously Lisa Templeton.

"Lisa had a secret lover," Ellis explained. "She opened up to me after class one evening. She didn't want anyone to know. I urged her to stop hiding her true feelings and this was her way of coming out, so to speak." He turned to Jess. "But the answer to your question is no. I have no idea who the other woman is."

"Did Lisa have any enemies that you know of? Anyone who gave her trouble at her shop or in your class?" Templeton had moved here almost three years ago from northern Tennessee. Neither she nor Burgess had any family in the area. They were still working on a list of the women's friends.

Ellis crossed his arms over his chest and tapped his finger against his chin as if giving the questions a great deal of thought. "Lisa struggled mightily with who she was. Like most artists, she had difficulty accepting her lot in life. She did what she had to do to earn a living, but she wanted more. She moved to Birmingham to escape her family. They have very strong religious beliefs that, shall we say, hampered Lisa's lifestyle. She wanted to be who she was. After moving here, she started to open up, like a tiny bird just hatching. I watched her grow in my class this past spring, spread her wings. This," he indicated the painting, "was the real Lisa."

But did that decision cost Lisa her life? "Did she mention any family problems at all? Had anyone come to Birmingham to try and persuade her to come home?" Or repent? The idea made Jess think of Wanda Newsom, her aunt and only living relative besides her sister and her sister's family. The aunt who'd let Jess and her sister down as children when their parents were killed but who had suddenly found religion and wanted to make it all right.

Jess banished the painful memories.

Ellis shook her head. "Lisa had been estranged from her family for over two years. They never called or visited."

"Any trouble with work?" Jess prompted.

"There are those, even in a city as progressive as Birmingham, who didn't agree with Lisa's business choices. This is still the Bible Belt. There was the occasional protest outside her shop. I read about the incidents in the paper but she never mentioned them to me."

"Are you aware that several of your students maintain a closed Facebook page where they feature some pretty graphic art?"

Ellis frowned. "I am not. The inspiration, however, could be a result of my classes. I encourage them to share their art and their feelings with those they trust. Life is about exploring one's world, inside and out. Sometimes it's difficult to share the discoveries with those who might not understand."

How nice. Jess scrounged around in her bag for a business card. One of these days she had to get better organized. She handed the card to Ellis. "I really appreciate your time, Rick. If you think of anything else that might help us find the person responsible for this tragedy, I hope you'll give me a call. We'd like to give the folks who cared about these women closure."

He read over the card before tucking it into his jacket pocket. "Of course. Anything I recall, you'll be the first to know."

Jess started to turn away but hesitated. "You're not from Birmingham, are you?"

He chuckled as if he recognized she'd been trying to figure out the answer to that question from the moment he said hello. "I came to Birmingham ten years ago after spending two decades in Europe, primarily in Paris, surviving as an artist."

"But you hail from Massachusetts originally?"

"Indeed." He grinned. "There are some things we can never escape."

Jess knew a little something about that. She'd spent twenty years trying to rid herself of her southern accent only to have it reemerge in full form barely a week after returning to Birmingham.

Some things were just destined to be.

Ellis escorted them to the door and insisted they should come again under more pleasant circumstances, and then he wished them a *bonne journée*. Outside, Jess considered her impressions of the man. "I didn't get anything from him, you?"

Lori vigilantly scrutinized the street. "Only that he was quite taken with you."

Jess moved toward the Mustang. "I think he just wanted to see my badge."

Lori grinned at Jess across the roof of the car. "Face it, you're a celebrity, Chief."

Jess rolled her eyes. "Lucky me."

When they'd settled inside, Lori hesitated before starting the engine. "You're okay, right?"

Her team—no, her friends—recognized she was not herself. How could she be? Her hormones were focused on gestation. Her emotions were scattered all over the map. She was a mess.

"I'm okay." Jess faked a smile.

"You know you can talk to me," Lori ventured, "if you need to."

Jess nodded. "I absolutely do."

But I may not be able to protect you…

That stone cold reality haunted Jess incessantly.

BIRMINGHAM POLICE DEPARTMENT.
12:50 P.M.

"I have a list of Templeton's and Burgess's friends and close acquaintances to interview, Chief." Harper grabbed the massive steak and cheese sub sandwich he'd ordered and tore off a bite.

Cook tossed back the last of his soft drink and wiped the back of his hand across his mouth. "Stacey Jernigan remembered all sorts of things after puking all over the interview room."

Jess nibbled at her sweet potato fries. She had to eat, she knew this, but her appetite apparently wasn't interested. "Anything more than the names of friends and acquaintances?" A couple of scenarios were drifting around in Jess's head but none had anchored just yet.

"A couple details." Cook hopped up and strode over to the case board. He tapped the photo of Alisha Burgess. "She and Templeton were lovers. Jernigan admitted the two women had been keeping the relationship secret."

Evidently not secret enough. Jess sipped her apple juice and shuddered. It was awful. Why would people drink this stuff much less force it on their kids? "Why keep it a secret? She didn't have any family here. Birmingham isn't exactly L.A., but we have our share of non-traditional couples." The bigger question remained, was the other woman in the painting Burgess? "Did she mention the painting?"

"She did not," Cook said.

Photo in hand, Lori scooted back her chair and joined Cook at the case board. "Templeton kept the relationship a secret because she didn't want her boyfriend to find out her roommate was also her one true love." Lori added the photo of a twenty-something male beneath Templeton's and announced, "Meet Rod Slater. He owns the building where Templeton managed the sex toy shop, along with half a dozen other small commercial buildings in the city. Since she lived in the apartment above her shop until two weeks ago, he was also her landlord. Slater and Templeton were in a relationship for about a year. Nothing serious. More like friends with benefits."

Cook pointed to the photo. "Except, this guy wanted to be her only friend. Jernigan says Slater roughed Templeton up a couple of times. He kicked her out of the apartment and threatened to cancel the lease on the shop she managed. The next day Templeton moved into the Homewood house and took Burgess with her."

Jess pushed her lunch aside. "Any witnesses to these violent episodes?"

"Not specifically the ones with Templeton," Harper explained, joining the conversation. "I checked his record. Slater's one of the possessive-aggressive types. He thinks the women he dates belong to him. They have to be faithful even if he's not. His rap sheet confirms Jernigan's allegations. Five counts of intimate partner violence over the past three years."

"Pick him up." Jess had no tolerance for men or women who abused their intimate partners or anyone else. Strength and power were not excuses to be a bully.

Harper grabbed the remains of his lunch. "On my way now, ma'am."

"Detective Wells, why don't you give Sergeant Harper a hand," Jess suggested. If this guy Slater put up a fight, he would need someone to protect him from his bad decision. Harper was typically a quiet man but, like Jess, he had no patience with jerks.

Lori grinned. "Love to." She grabbed her purse.

Harper waited for her at the door. They shared a secret smile. After they were gone Jess stared at the closed door for a long while. Lori and Chet were very lucky. They'd found each other and seemed to be on the right track for making their relationship work. So far, their personal lives hadn't interfered with work. Jess was thankful. She wouldn't want to part with either detective.

Cook cleared his throat and settled at his desk. "I'll just keep going through the reports from the neighbors."

Jess reined in her wandering thoughts. "As soon as I finish my lunch we'll pay a visit to the ME. See how Dr. Baron's coming along with the autopsies."

Cook's face brightened. "Awesome—I mean, yes, ma'am."

What was that all about?

A firm knock on the door drew her attention there. Jess fully expected to see Dan walk through the door just to check up on her. He was keeping extra close tabs. The door opened and the man who strolled in was a stranger. Well dressed and reasonably handsome, but a stranger nonetheless. Before she could stop the automatic reaction, she was reaching for her bag and the Glock tucked there.

Cook was suddenly on his feet and in front of Jess's desk, between her and the potential danger. She appreciated the move. It prevented her from doing something ridiculous like drawing her weapon. What was wrong with her? She was overreacting. This man had passed through security. The department's security guards were on alert for trouble. There was no need for melodrama in her own office.

And she worried about Dan overreacting.

"Can I help you?" Cook asked, demanded actually.

"I'm here to see Chief Harris."

While Cook continued his interrogation, Jess moved around her desk. The man looked to be in his early thirties. He had dark hair and eyes and carried himself like a businessman.

So did Spears. Appearance alone was rarely a measure of a man's heart.

"You have a name?" Cook pressed on with his interrogation.

"Lieutenant Clint Hayes," he said to Cook. "I'm here about the vacancy on your team." The last he said to Jess.

Hayes. He was the detective Lori had said would make a great addition to their team. Jess had briefly reviewed his personnel file. Her preliminary assessment was that the man was vastly over qualified for his current assignment. A wasted resource she could certainly use in SPU.

She stepped forward and extended her hand. "Nice to meet you, Lieutenant."

Cook still eyed him warily.

Hayes gave her hand a firm shake. "The pleasure's mine, Chief."

Though she hadn't found the time to set up an interview with Hayes, maybe Lori or Harper had passed along the word that Jess was interested in speaking to him. However he'd heard, she was glad he was here. SPU could use the help.

"I'm glad you took the initiative and dropped by, Lieutenant." Jess turned to the youngest member of her team. "This is Officer Chad Cook."

The two men shook hands, visibly sizing each other up.

Jess gestured to the chair in front of her desk. "Have a seat, Lieutenant."

Cook sauntered back to his desk, dragged out his chair and collapsed into it. He was feeling a little outranked and Jess wanted that to change. They had to prepare him for the detective's exam as soon as someone around here could catch their breath.

Hayes waited until Jess was seated before taking his. *Manners too. Nice.*

Clint Hayes could be a high-powered executive. The suit was no everyday off the rack purchase. Reminded her of Richard Ellis's taste for the finer labels, but Ellis's taste had run more to the eclectic. From the lieutenant's manner of dress to the way he carried himself he seemed the type who would have gone to school with Dan and all his rich friends. Only Clint Hayes hadn't come from a rich family. Based on what Lori had told Jess about him, he'd come from the same side of Birmingham's tracks as she had. He'd worked his way through college as a gigolo. His secret occupation had cost him his chosen career as an attorney.

If the guy was a good cop, Jess could care less how he paid his way through school. He'd cashed in on the one asset readily available.

Necessity is the mother of invention. Something else they had in common.

Hayes cleared his throat. Jess blinked and scolded herself for letting her thoughts drift. She just couldn't stay focused today. "You have uncanny timing, Lieutenant. We're in the middle of a double homicide and we could certainly use some help. Did Detective Wells mention we have a vacancy on our team?"

Hayes smiled, the kind of flirtatious expression that made the ladies sit up and pay attention. "Actually, I heard the rumor and thought I'd get the jump on any official posting."

Ambitious too, Jess admired that in a cop. "You're acquainted with Detective Wells, do you also know Sergeant Harper?"

Hayes dipped his head. "I'm familiar with his reputation. Wells and I have run into each other from time to time socially."

Do tell. Jess would be asking Lori about that one. She never mentioned having socialized with the man. Not that Jess could blame her. "You've been in Admin for years, Lieutenant. Moving directly to a major crimes team could be challenging."

"My marksmanship score is perfect, every time. I have buddies in SWAT and I routinely take part in their training drills. I enjoy a challenge, Chief."

Cook cleared his throat and then coughed. Hayes ignored him.

"Physical prowess can bring down the bad guy," Jess allowed, opting not to permit him to see just how impressed she was even if Cook wasn't, "but it won't provide you with the instincts to find a killer. Close attention to detail and understanding the motives that drive those who commit acts of violence are the skills you need to be a part of this team, Lieutenant."

"I'm a quick study," he pressed. "We all have to begin somewhere."

Well, he had her there. "When can you start?"

"Is now too soon for you?"

His answer surprised her. "Your chief won't have an issue with you leaving without sufficient notice?"

"I cleared the move with him this morning."

Confidence was another admirable trait, but too much was not.

"If you would have me," he said as if reading her mind, or maybe her cocked eyebrow, "Chief McCord was agreeable to an immediate move. Admin is a bit overstaffed so a loss in manpower isn't an issue."

Making the decision without having an in-depth look at his personnel file and a proper interview, including a discussion with her team, was not how she'd planned to do this. Lori seemed to think he was a good guy. Harper hadn't mentioned any complaints or misgivings. SPU desperately needed another warm body. He was here and anxious to start.

"Would you be open to a six-month trial period?" Jess offered. "This is a tight group, Lieutenant. The work we do requires a certain level of trust and cohesiveness."

"I have no objections to a probationary period," he assured her.

"Excellent." She stood and reached across her desk. "Welcome to the team."

Hayes followed suit and gave her hand another hearty shake. "Thank you, Chief. You won't regret the decision."

The obnoxious ringtone Jess despised called out from her bag. Most days she wanted desperately to change the damned thing but it made hers different from everyone else's.

"Officer Cook, show the lieutenant around," Jess suggested. They were crammed into one reasonably good-sized room for now so there wasn't much to see.

While Cook grudgingly gave Hayes a tour, Jess fished around in her bag for her phone. It had stopped ringing by the time she dug past the M&Ms and the other stuff to find it.

"Dammit." The call was from Virginia but it wasn't Gant. Patricia Lanier, her realtor. Anticipation had Jess's nerves jumping as she returned the call. This could be the news on her house she'd been waiting for.

Jess needed the sale on her house in Stafford closed and any equity after all was said and done in her bank account. The last she'd heard the only glitch was narrowing down a workable closing date for both parties. "Hey, Patricia, this is Jess Harris returning your call."

"Thank you for calling back so quickly, Jess. All is in order and I'm just trying to coordinate the buyer's schedule with yours. Would Thursday, September thirtieth, or Friday, October first, work for you?"

Jess checked her calendar. Since most crimes weren't scheduled with the police in advance, the dates appeared to be clear. "Either one works for me. Can we do this in the early afternoon?" Flying to Virginia and back in the same day would be optimal.

"I'm certain we can arrange an afternoon closing. I'll confirm with you soon."

The call ended and Jess was grateful she could check that one off her need-to-do list. Though she was in no hurry to buy another house, it would be a relief not to be paying for a place where she no longer lived.

Her apartment here pretty much fell into that same category at the moment.

As much as she appreciated Dan wanting her at his house with him, she missed her little garage apartment. She even missed Mr. Louis. He was a bit strange but a very attentive landlord. Jess liked him. The poor man had to be wondering what the heck was going on with his tenant. She really should stop by today or tomorrow.

There were a million things she needed to do. Like go shopping. The same five suitable work out-fits wouldn't do forever. Her hand went to her belly. How long would it be before she would need maternity clothing? She bit her lip. Her sister would have all kinds of ideas about that. Jess cringed. Their styles were totally different. Lil was happiest in comfortable flats and cotton dresses with lovely flowers. She hated high heels. Jess loved them. She'd kicked them off more than once to chase down a bad guy. Not that the need to give chase happened very often in her current position or in her last decade with the Bureau.

Still, she stared at her shoes. How much longer would she feel comfortable in her beloved Mary Jane pumps? A lot was going to have to change.

Her cell vibrated and she checked the screen. A text from Wells. Jess opened it.

On the way with Slater. He's a little banged up but he was that way when we found him.

A photo of Rod Slater followed the text.

"Ouch," Jess muttered. Apparently, Mr. Slater had been up to no good. Whatever he'd gotten himself into, it looked very much like he'd come out on the losing end. He had a nasty black eye, a bruised and swollen jaw, and a split lip. With all those injuries maybe he'd behave himself in the interview and Jess wouldn't have to unleash Harper's bad cop side.

Her gaze drifted across the room to the newest member of their team. Taking Hayes on without due consideration was out of the ordinary for her. Like buying a pig in a poke. She wondered if Hayes had a bad side. Certainly he'd had a colorful one in the past.

Time would tell.

CHAPTER SEVEN

"Mr. Slater, you have a history of domestic violence." Jess gave the man a moment to think about her statement. "I'd be remiss in my duties in this case if I didn't consider you a suspect, wouldn't you agree?"

"I have an alibi." He might have pulled off the look of insolence to go along with the tone if not for the one eye being swollen shut. "That's why I don't need a lawyer. I got nothing to hide."

Rodney Slater sat directly across the worn table from Jess. He looked like hell, smelled like cigarettes and cheap bourbon. His clothes were wrinkled and his hair was mussed. Evidently, the bender he'd started over the weekend had continued into the workweek. One of the perks of being self-employed, Jess supposed. He was his own boss, as he'd so proudly proclaimed when the interview started.

Unfortunately, daddy had entrusted his only son with the family business. Dear old Rod hadn't worked for a single thing he owned. It gave him a bad attitude, in Jess's opinion. The entitlement mentality was not attractive on anyone over the age of five.

Harper sat next to her. He silently stared at Slater. Didn't seem to faze the cocky guy. He was one self-centered piece of work.

"You claim you were at Chasers, a pool hall, from eight Sunday night until the manager locked the doors just after midnight," Jess read from her notes.

"That's right. Ask my friends if you don't believe me."

"I most certainly will." Jess tapped her pencil against her pad. "There's just one thing that keeps bugging me, Mr. Slater. I'm having trouble believing your story about how you came to have all those nasty bruises. Why didn't you call the police after two Hispanic males attempted to rob you? They didn't take your cell phone, did they?"

"They didn't get anything. Like I told you," he ran his fingers through his tousled hair, "I beat the crap out of 'em and they ran. Calling the cops wasn't necessary. Don't you have better things to do, like hang out at the donut shop?"

The joys of interviewing idiots. Jess adapted an expression of concern that was about as fake as the story he'd just confirmed. "You must be in serious pain, Mr. Slater. Your hands and forearms are all scratched up. Men don't usually fight openhanded. You use your fists." She balled her fingers. "Makes me wonder if you had a physical altercation with your girlfriend."

He worked up the energy to pull off a listless shrug. "What can I say? Mexicans fight like girls." He tossed a look at Harper. "It's nothing. Hydros make sure of that."

Next to her, Jess felt her detective stiffen. Harper's Hispanic heritage was obvious, and Jess knew for a fact there was nothing girlish about the way he handled himself in a physical altercation. She'd take Harper as her backup any time, any place.

"I assume you have a prescription for those," the detective tossed at the arrogant man. Hydrocodone was one of the most abused pain relievers on the market.

"Wouldn't've mentioned 'em if I didn't." Slater snorted a laugh. "I'm not that stupid."

Jess wouldn't touch that one with a ten-foot pole. "Did you have a physical altercation with your girlfriend, Mr. Slater? Remember, we're recording this interview. You need to be very careful how you answer."

"Don't have a girlfriend."

"Is that right?" Harper countered. "Several witnesses saw you coming and going from Lisa Templeton's home on numerous occasions. She wasn't your girlfriend?"

Slater made a face then winced. "She managed a shop in one of my buildings. Your witnesses must've seen me dropping by her place when she rented the apartment over the shop. She was just a tenant. Not my type at all."

Harper made one of those male sounds that were more grunt than anything else. In Jess's experience, it meant he'd had enough of this guy. She was right there with him.

Jess opened the folder in front of her and removed a series of photos that had been printed from the ones saved on the victim's cell phone. "If this is what you do with the women who aren't your type, I'm confident there are laws against what you save for those who are."

She fanned the photos in front of him. Most of them showed Slater and Templeton in various forms of sexual activity. His face wasn't visible in all the photos, but the tattoos on his chest and shoulders were and that was sufficient to identify him. With Slater this close and his partially unbuttoned shirt revealing a good portion of the Phoenix inked on his chest, denial would be just a little difficult.

He lifted one shoulder in another of those uncaring shrugs. "We had sex. Often. Big deal. She needed lots of favors and this is how we settled things."

Outrage started a resolute climb up Jess's spine. "But Lisa didn't worship you the way you prefer your women to." The statements made by the victims of his prior arrests had one allegation in common: *He wanted me to worship him.* "In fact," Jess went on, "Lisa Templeton was in love with another woman. I imagine that was quite a blow to your manhood."

He snorted. "She was a dumb bitch. Couldn't make up her mind what she wanted. I was done with her anyway."

"Is that why you kicked her out of the apartment over the shop two weeks ago?" Jess folded her arms over her chest and eyed him with blatant suspicion. "You found out you weren't the love of her life and that made you angry."

"That was business," he argued. "She didn't pay her rent on time."

"Had she always paid it on time in the past?" Jess countered. Templeton had lived over the shop she managed for two years. Had one failure to pay on time justified her eviction?

"Doesn't matter. I wanted her out and she got out."

"There are laws that protect tenants, Mr. Slater." Jess leaned forward so he'd know she really wanted to hear his answer to the next question. "Did you break those laws?"

He had the guts to smile even with his split lip. "Didn't have to. She understood what I wanted."

"So the two of you settled that situation too," Jess surmised.

He leaned back in his chair. "That's right."

Jess gathered another stack of photos from the file and spread them on top of the first ones. "Is this how you settled things, Mr. Slater?"

"What the—?" He shoved back from the table, his chair scraping across the tile.

"Did you murder her?" Jess demanded. "Did you crack open her chest and dig out her heart just to feel its warmth in your hands? Or was it a symbolic gesture about the loss of her love?"

Slater shot to his feet. "I had nothing to do with that! I didn't kill nobody!"

Jess stood but Harper was already on the other side of the table with a warning hand on Slater's arm. "You need to sit down, sir." Though spoken quietly, Harper's words carried a distinct promise of what Slater should expect if he did not comply.

"Is this," Jess snatched up one of the photos and shoved it toward Slater, "how you settle the issues in your sex life?"

Whatever Rod Slater had done or not done, he went still as stone and glared at Jess with his one good eye. "That's all I got to say without a lawyer present."

"You waived your right to an attorney, Mr. Slater," Jess reminded him, not that it mattered if he'd now decided otherwise.

"I changed my mind." He looked around the room, found the camera high on the wall in one corner and stared directly at it. "I want a lawyer! Now!"

Jess shuffled the photos back into her folder and tucked it into her bag. "You calm down, Mr. Slater." She gave him a sugary smile. "Sergeant Harper will make sure your attorney is notified."

"Take your seat, sir." Harper ushered Slater back into the chair. "Write down your attorney's name and number and I'll get him on the phone for you."

Jess gave Harper a nod and left the room. Lori and Hayes waited for her in the corridor. Both had observed the interview.

"We'll be holding Mr. Slater for a few hours as a person of interest. If he's smart he'll agree to let forensics take a few samples." Jess drew in a big breath. "Meanwhile, Detective Wells, I'd like you and Sergeant Harper to continue questioning the friends and coworkers of both victims. If we can put Slater anywhere near those women on Sunday night, we can push harder for him to agree to submit the samples necessary to eliminate him as a suspect."

"On it, Chief," Lori said.

Before the detective could ask the question Jess knew would be next, she went on, "Officer Cook and I are going to the ME's office to see what Dr. Baron has for us." Probably not very much but anything would be better than nothing. And that was what they had right now, a little speculation and a whole lot of nothing.

"I'd like to accompany you, Chief," Hayes piped up.

He was standing right there and still she'd forgotten to include him. Where was her mind? "That's a good idea, Lieutenant. Go back to the office and let Cook know we're heading out. I'll be right there."

When Hayes was on his way, Lori said, "I did some follow up on Ellis's background and found some interesting facts from his past."

"In this country or another?" Something about the man bothered Jess. Whatever it was, he'd camouflaged it too well for her to get a handle on it, but it was there. The way he balanced his rough edges with all that elegance didn't ring true. Twenty years in

Europe certainly would have influenced his speech, and possibly his overall manner. Maybe that was what she was picking up on.

"This one," Lori clarified. "He had a friend whose older sister was murdered by her father who then turned the gun on himself. Ellis was visiting the friend and apparently saw the whole thing. The mother of the murdered girl insisted she had no idea why her husband would have done such a thing. But one reporter maintained throughout the investigation that there was a cover up."

"Is the reporter still alive?" If so, Jess wanted to speak to him.

"He died a few years ago."

"What about the mother?"

"She still lives in the family home in Boston with her son."

A trip to Boston might be in order. The image of Spears elbowed its way into her thoughts. Not that she was going anywhere, but she could send Harper. The outrage that had camped at the base of her skull started to tighten her muscles, making her want to scream. Spears had her right where he wanted her. She was virtually his prisoner. She couldn't go to her apartment. She couldn't go anywhere alone.

Take a breath. Focus on the case.

"Keep digging. The tragedy in Ellis's past might not be connected—he may have nothing to do with these murders, but at least one of our victims was close to him. We need to know all we can about him if for no other reason than to eliminate him as a suspect. Find out what he did with these *Old Masters* in Europe."

"Will do." Lori glanced down the corridor and then grinned. "I guess you like Clint."

"He's motivated," Jess said, "I'll give him that much. As long as he works hard and fits in with our team, I'm happy." A frown creased her brow. "I was surprised he just showed up at the office. I guess he wanted a transfer badly enough to keep tabs on the comings and goings of department personnel."

Lori made a face. "Probably. He's been pretty unhappy for a while."

"Well." Jess hefted the straps of her bag higher onto her shoulder. *Was it her imagination or was it heavier today?* "Maybe SPU will be able to change that for him. He agreed to a probationary period to see how things work out."

"He's a good guy," Lori said, almost to herself.

Jess started not to ask but her curiosity got the better of her. "Did the two of you have a… thing?"

Surprise, then amusement sparkled in Lori's green eyes. "We'll talk about that sometime. Over a margarita." She glanced past Jess to the interview room. "I should give Harper a hand."

Jess hoped they could have that chat without the margaritas otherwise they would be waiting about seven months or so.

As she headed to her office, she wondered if Clint Hayes had ever attended an autopsy. She would soon know if he had the stomach for the business of murder.

"This took some patience," Dr. Sylvia Baron said as she surveyed first Lisa Templeton's body and then Alicia Burgess's.

To her utter frustration, Jess's stomach had started that annoying churning again. She breathed through her mouth and prayed she would get through the next few minutes.

Okay. Baron mentioned patience. *Focus, Jess.*

She couldn't argue the point the ME made, but patience wasn't a word Jess would have used when describing this killer's work. Vicious and relentlessness was more what she'd call it. The evil that committed violence this savage against another human was determined to accomplish some goal only he understood. The real question was: what was his or her motive?

"Both women were intoxicated based on the alcohol levels in the vitreous humor," Sylvia continued. "I won't have the full tox screen results for a day or two. No traces of semen or male pubic hair. Neither had eaten for several hours prior to their death. No other health issues so far." She gestured to the damaged torsos. "The wounds on both bodies are consistent with the hand tools found at the scene."

"Has your estimate on time of death changed for either victim?"

Sylvia met Jess's gaze. "Are you asking me which one I believe died first?"

"If one killer did this," Jess wasn't convinced that was the case, "one victim had to die first. If not, we may be looking at two killers working in concert." The sheer number of prints, however smeared and possibly unreadable, seemed to indicate more than one killer. When Jess had more evidence back from the crime scene unit she might be able to make that call, but not yet.

"If I had to pinpoint TOD that precisely—unofficially, of course—I would say Burgess died first. But it's too close to call. We're talking four or five minutes max between the murders. I can tell you that after a close examination of the wounds inflicted, if two killers were involved, they're both right handed."

It wasn't much, but it was a starting place. The killer or killers were right handed and wore about a size seven shoe. *It was a beginning.*

"If," Jess moved back to the timing, "Burgess died first, that would mean Templeton watched the woman she loved be murdered." Holding her breath, Jess leaned down to study the woman's wrists with the aid of the bright lights. The lighting at the scene had been less than optimal. "And yet there's no indication she fought her restraints." Jess straightened away from the body and dared to breathe. "Was she that intoxicated?"

Sylvia considered the question for a moment. "Not in my opinion. I have a scenario I'm working on, but what are you thinking?"

"That both victims were unable to struggle," Jess suggested. "Burgess didn't fight her restraints as the belt tightened around her throat. Templeton didn't react physically while her lover was being murdered or when it was her turn. How could you have an object pushed that far down your throat and not fight back? Any bite marks on the," Jess shrugged, "object?"

"You mean the neon pink dildo?"

Jess rolled her eyes. Couldn't Sylvia just answer the question? Hayes cleared his throat and stared at the floor. Cook shifted from foot to foot but didn't take his eyes off the pretty medical examiner.

Sylvia surveyed her audience. "Is there a problem, gentlemen? We're all adults here. Professionals. A woman has needs, and sometimes she has to get creative to fill those needs."

Hands in his pockets, Hayes rocked back on his heels as if he might have several pertinent responses for the ME's comment. Cook, however, just stared at Sylvia. Maybe stared wasn't the right word. He gawked like a teenage boy who'd never seen a naked woman before.

The trouble was, Sylvia was fully dressed in one of those sleek, stylish sheaths she always wore beneath her lab coat. She looked like a million bucks and Jess imagined that Cook was enthralled. But this wasn't his first visit to the coroner's office. Why was he suddenly infatuated with the ME? Most cops were ready to clear the room when they heard her coming. Or maybe it was the talk of sex toys. Jess certainly hadn't taken Cook for a guy so easily flustered.

"Is that a yes or a no?" Jess asked, hoping to maneuver the conversation back on track. She needed fresh air... soon.

"No teeth marks," Sylvia confirmed. "She deep throated without resistance."

If a pin had dropped, the sound of it hitting the floor would have boomed like an explosion.

"So it's possible both victims were paralyzed," Jess proposed, her patience thinning. "They may have been aware of what was happening on some level but unable to struggle?"

"That's my thinking," Sylvia said. "I'm looking for drugs in that category. Most of the date rape drugs are hard to detect, but if one was used, I'll find it."

"He wanted them to see death coming," Lieutenant Hayes chimed in.

The deep sound of his voice startled Jess. She had to keep reminding herself they had a new man on the team. She was glad he hadn't taken one look at the two dissected bodies and made a run for the nearest sink.

"Or she," Jess countered. "Either way, the killer knew the victims and wanted them to suffer as much horror as possible before they died."

Cook stepped forward, pausing closer to Sylvia than to Jess. "We may be looking for a former lover."

"Bad choices can certainly come back to haunt us," Sylvia agreed.

The way Cook watched Sylvia as she spoke clarified the situation for Jess. The much younger man was smitten with the sophisticated ME. Jess needed to have a talk with him. He was on the verge of biting off way more than he could chew. Sylvia Baron was way, way, way out of his league.

"Officer Cook, drop by the lab and give them a push," Jess said, breaking the awkward silence. "We need whatever new evidence they may have discovered."

He snapped out of his lust coma. "Yes, ma'am."

He took one last lingering gaze at Sylvia before stumbling off. The ME smiled. When she turned to Jess, her face was a little flushed. For Pete's sake, was she actually interested in Cook or just flattered? Sylvia should have learned her lesson about relationships with cops after the unpleasant split with her ex. Jess did a mental double take. Didn't say a lot for her and Dan rushing back into that minefield. But, then again, they had extenuating circumstances.

Don't go there, Jess.

Sylvia turned off the spotlights over the bodies. "I see you have a new shadow, Harris. Is this your bodyguard?" She sized up Hayes, her approval written all over her line free face.

Had the ME had Botox injections? Next time Sylvia was in friend mode, Jess intended to ask her. She resisted the urge to reach up and smooth her own lined brow with the back of her fingers. Getting old was no fun. She was going to be really old by the time this child graduated college. That rolling in her stomach took an extra deep dip.

"Harris?" Sylvia repeated. "I was asking about this tall, dark and silent type you brought along."

Jess gave herself a mental kick for getting distracted. The distraction was immediately replaced by frustration. "He is not a bodyguard." What was with all the flirting? Maybe Sylvia Baron needed a man in her life. Before Jess stuck her foot in her mouth and said as much, she reminded herself of all the things *she* needed. Like a baby carriage. *Oh God.*

Jess wished her mouth weren't suddenly so dry. "This is Lieutenant Hayes. He joined SPU today."

Stripping off her gloves with far more fanfare than usual, Sylvia said, "Aren't you lucky to land a spot on the department's new dream team, Lieutenant?"

"Yes, ma'am. Very lucky." That smoky voice of his oozed with charm.

Men. They were all alike. Or maybe Hayes always used a suave tone when speaking to women. Maybe old habits were hard to break.

"You know your new boss has a fan club." Sylvia tossed her gloves. "You should watch your back, Hayes. One of the world's foremost serial killers is her biggest fan. His followers are always watching her."

"So I've heard." Hayes moved to Jess's side. "I'm a dedicated fan of Chief Harris myself. Those with the wrong intentions should be forewarned, Dr. Baron. I am very, very good at handling trouble."

Jess didn't know about Sylvia, but she was impressed. No matter how he'd worked his way through college, she liked this guy.

"I'm glad to hear that, Lieutenant," Sylvia announced. "Harris is growing on me. I'd hate to see anything bad happen to her."

So maybe they were friends. Jess was weary of trying to figure it out.

"You have my word. The chief is in good hands." Hayes flashed a smile even Jess had to admit was more than a little appealing.

This meeting had gone way, way off course and Jess was ready to be out of here. "Call me if you can find the drug the killer used, Dr. Baron."

"The screenings may take a while, but I'll let you know as soon as I find it."

Jess thanked the ME and headed for the door. If she hurried, she might just get out of here before it was too late. Which only reminded her that she needed to pick up a couple more pregnancy tests to ensure the first one wasn't a false positive. Just because there was only a minute chance of a false positive didn't mean it couldn't happen.

Yeah right.

The truth was she needed confirmation for her own peace of mind.

She thought of all the unanswered questions in this case and decided her peace of mind would have to wait. First, she needed a second look at the crime scene. Things always looked a little different in the light of day. She glanced at the man next to her. A new perspective couldn't hurt either.

"Lieutenant, I'd like to have another look at the scene before calling it a day." She hesitated at the building's main exit, ignored the scrub-clad tech that hurried out around her. "Give you a chance to share what *you* see."

Hayes stepped past Jess, pushed through the exit and surveyed the parking area before holding the door open for her to follow. "Is this a test, Chief?"

She gifted him with a smile. "Nothing you can't handle, Lieutenant."

RALEIGH AVENUE, HOMEWOOD, 5:05 P.M.

As soon as he parked, Jess wasn't surprised the lieutenant rushed around to open the car door for her. He was on a mission to keep her impressed.

So far, he was doing an exemplary job.

The neighborhood was quiet. Most of the residents were either still at work or caught up in the commute home. Kids squealed and chased after a basketball in a yard at the far end of the block. No dogs barking. Too hot, she decided, and the humidity was stifling. Jess blew out a big puff of air and wished for cooler days.

"The Tide's first game is next weekend. Which side do you stand on, Chief? Alabama or Auburn?"

"I prefer staying neutral when it comes to sports." Jess considered her newest team member. "I didn't take you for the college football type, Lieutenant."

"Looks can be deceiving." With that, he motioned for her to lead the way.

Valid point. Just because the box was pretty didn't mean what was inside would be. Eric Spears was proof positive of that adage. She booted Spears out of her head. The Bureau was focused on finding him and the Stinnett woman. Jess had a job to do here. Staying on track was tantamount to getting that job done.

At least that was what she told herself every few minutes when he tried to strong arm his way into her head. She was here and this was her case. As much as Jess wanted to, she could not help Rory Stinnett. But maybe, just maybe, she could find justice for Lisa Templeton and Alicia Burgess.

The forensic techs had already made the second sweep, inside and out. On the stoop, Jess slipped on shoe covers and gloves while Hayes did the same. He finished first and opened the door. The stench of death lingered in the air, mingled with the humidity and filled her lungs. She stepped inside and moved through the house, taking her time despite the sickening odor. A second look always provided a few more details.

"No signs of forced entry," Hayes commented.

"The front door wasn't locked. In fact, it wasn't even closed." She perused the few magazines and other items on the coffee table. *Cosmo* and *Glamour*. A couple of Red Box rentals lay near the small flat-panel television. Templeton's purse had sat on an end table, right where she'd left it when she came home that last night. Nothing had appeared missing. Not even the twenty bucks in her wallet had been taken. Burgess's bag had been found in the bedroom on the dresser. Her credit cards and forty dollars in cash remained in her wallet. A couple of old cocktail napkins with names and phone numbers littered the bottom of both bags. The lab was analyzing the purses and contents, along with anything else from this house that might yield useful evidence.

The laptop that had been found on the counter had provided some insight to the victims' social calendars. The perp or perps hadn't bothered to take any of those items on the way out the back door. Told Jess the killer or killers either left in a hurry or weren't interested in fast cash.

No cigarettes or ashtrays lying around. Both vics went to the gym four or five times a week, according to the personal trainer Cook had interviewed. No close family. Lots of friends. Two happy, beautiful, adventurous women.

The back door had been left open, whether by the victims or the killer was irrelevant. The point was breaking and entering hadn't been necessary. Jess added too trusting to her list of adjectives about the victims.

The killer was most likely female. Small footprints and the lack of seminal fluid or other trace evidence indicating a male presence pretty much solidified that scenario in Jess's mind.

She turned to Hayes. "Give me your impressions, Lieutenant."

"No empty beer cans around. No drink glasses." He surveyed the kitchen side of the living space. "The party ended here but it didn't start here.

Whatever alcohol the victims had consumed, they did it some place else and they brought trouble home with them."

"Very good." Jess headed toward the bedrooms. "Chuck's Roadhouse was where the evening started. They closed the place down. According to witnesses, they drank a lot and danced a lot. The party was moved here for fun of a more intimate nature." She paused at the bathroom. "The killer or killers showered off before leaving. Hair was removed from the shower drain as well as the sink. Forensics is still working on separating what belongs to the victims from any that doesn't."

"When the party arrived they didn't spend much time in the front part of the house," Hayes offered.

"They came straight here." Jess moved on to the bedroom where the women had been murdered. "There are boxes of sex toys in the closet. Handcuffs. Whips." Her attention shifted to the bed. "They wanted to play hard and rough."

The tools the killer had used to remove the victims' hearts had been analyzed. "Prints were found all over the tools used to remove the hearts, but no matches in any of the databases."

"Why do you think their hearts were removed?" Hayes walked slowly around the room.

Good question. "Since we know Templeton and Burgess were lovers, jealousy would be at the top of my list."

"You think Slater had anything to do with this?"

Jess shook her head. "He's a jerk. A taker. But he's not this kind of killer."

"What is this *kind* of killer?"

"All of us are capable of evil, Lieutenant. Maybe even murder." Jess ventured to the closet and slowly rifled through the clothes, picturing the women in the racy outfits. These were women who kept in shape and liked showing off their bodies. They enjoyed the dangerous side of pleasure. "You," she glanced at Hayes, "or I could commit an impulsive act. An act of rage that was driven by pure emotion at the spur of the moment, without premeditation."

"But this was premeditated." He paused at the foot of the bed.

"Absolutely. The tools confirm the killer thought out what she wanted to do before committing the murders. Even if murder wasn't the intent when she arrived, she retrieved the tools from somewhere. Maybe from her car or maybe she went to a store and bought them. Either way, they were brought into the house with a certain intention. There is nothing here to suggest the residents kept or owned any sort of tools."

"If the vics were drugged," Hayes turned to Jess, "our killer had the run of the place. No worries about screaming or any noise associated with a struggle. He could do what he wanted and take what he wanted."

"They were drugged." That was the other part of this tragedy Jess felt confident in deducing. "Nothing, as far as we can see, was taken from the home except the victims' hearts. The other organs were untouched suggesting it wasn't about the black market. We can, I believe," she moved to where he stood, "accurately conclude our killer planned the event to some degree. She intended to kill these two women. What we need now is to know why."

"Hearts go for a nice price online for the discriminating palate."

Jess had considered that avenue as well. "If that was the intent, the technique for removal was rudimentary and risky." Even those who ate human organs preferred their purchases to be in good condition.

"I guess that leaves us with a more personal motive."

"And when we find the motive, we'll find our killer."

Lisa Templeton had only just learned to pour her emotions into her art. Ellis's comment about the victim sifted through Jess's mind. Since Templeton had her coming out, was her murder, as well as her lover's, a hate crime?

Jess needed air. The smell in here was beginning to overwhelm her. She sure hoped this queasiness didn't last the duration of the pregnancy.

"I have to make a couple of stops before going back to the office, Walmart and my apartment. Will that be a problem?"

"I'm available for as long as you need me."

"Good answer, Lieutenant."

CHAPTER EIGHT

Hayes insisted on going in first.

Jess carried a badge and a gun too, but apparently that was irrelevant.

Thankfully her place was just one big room, not counting the bathroom, so his look around didn't take longer than the allotted time she had to enter the security code before the cops were summoned. Like she didn't have enough cops around already.

As soon as the system had stopped singing its annoying tune, she produced a smile for the man standing in the middle of her space. "I realize it's late but I'll be a few minutes more, Lieutenant. Feel free to call home. Check in with your girlfriend." She waved her hand in dismissal. "Whatever you need to do."

The idea of going to pee with nothing but a thin wall between them just didn't work for her.

As if he'd abruptly realized she needed some privacy, he came to attention like a soldier falling into formation. "I don't have anyone waiting for me at home, but I'll step outside and check in with Detective Wells." He started backing toward the door. "I'll see if there's anything new."

Jess kept her smile tacked in place until he was on the landing and closed the door behind him.

"Finally." She took a deep breath, closed her eyes and savored the smell of home. It was funny how fast this little garage apartment had become home to her. She stared longingly at her bed before letting go another sigh.

One day her life would be peaceful and normal. Ha! Now she was delusional. She hugged the over-filled Walmart bag a little tighter. Any hope of normalcy in the next couple of decades was long gone.

The bathroom made her smile again. She loved this little bathroom with its antique fixtures. After shutting and locking the door, she shouldered off her purse and let it drop to the floor. Hands shaking she dumped the array of feminine products she'd purchased on the floor and picked out the three test kits from the pile.

"Okay. Let's do this."

One by one she opened the three boxes, removed the test sticks and placed them side-by-side on the sink. She stared at the seemingly harmless plastic sticks for a whole thirty seconds. It wasn't as if she didn't know the answer already. This exercise in futility was totally pointless.

"Just get it over with."

She assumed the position and did the required business, returning each stick to the sink ledge as she finished. Accomplishing the job was a little awkward, but she managed. Then she washed her hands and waited.

Three minutes felt like a lifetime sprawling before her.

She bent down and fished her cell from her bag. She might as well do something while she waited. Thumbing through her contact list, she paused on Buddy Corlew's name and gave him a tap. During the three rings that followed, she shoved the test boxes and pamphlets back into the bag. That reminded her, she'd hidden the first test she'd used in the toilet tank. She should dispose of it, too.

As she reached for the tank lid Corlew croaked a hello. "What's wrong with you?" she asked. He sounded sick or like he had a hellacious hangover.

"Flu or some such nonsense." He coughed. "What's up, kid?"

As she stood there holding the evidence of her latest secret, she had a moment of déjà vu. She'd called Corlew yesterday morning just before she'd had to make that unexpected trip to Tennessee. She wondered why it was that her first instinct was to call him. Definitely not because she trusted him... not by a long shot. Maybe because they'd known each other since grade school and he was from the same neighborhood as her. As kids they had lived a world away from Mountain Brook and Dan's crowd.

"Did you go to the doctor?" She sank onto the toilet seat. If Corlew was sick, he probably hadn't been able to look into that other business she didn't want to talk about.

"Vanessa took care of me."

Another coughing jag echoed in Jess's ear. She made a face. He sounded terrible! "Who's Vanessa?"

"Quincy. We went to school with her. She's a doctor."

Oh yes. Jess remembered her. "The girl who stole my pink purse in sixth grade." The one her mother had given her for her tenth birthday. "The same girl who poured paint in my hair before the sophomore dance!" The freshman class had been tasked with painting a backdrop for the dance. The guy Vanessa liked had asked Jess to be his date. Vanessa had not been amused. Jess couldn't believe that pesky girl was a doctor.

"That's the one. As a matter of fact, she asked me about you."

Jess peered at the test result windows. She frowned, wished they would hurry. "Why would she ask about me?"

"She wondered if you were married and had any kids. Pediatrics is her specialty."

Twisting away from the incriminating evidence, Jess made a sound of disbelief. "Did you tell her no on both counts and that my career has kept me busy?" But that was all about to change. Jess chewed her lip. "Does she have any?"

His laughter turned into another coughing jag. "I told her all about you and, yes, she has four kids."

Jess's jaw dropped. "She's a doctor and she has four kids?"

"Yep."

If Jess was lucky he didn't hear her scoffing sound. "More power to her." Her frown deepened. "Why in the world did you call a pediatrician?"

"She's the only doc I know who makes house calls."

"For you maybe." Every female in school had been enamored with Buddy Corlew. Except Jess. She had been in love with Dan. Most of the time. She and Buddy had their moments. But nothing ever came of a single one. Thank heavens.

"What's up, Jess? I know you didn't just call to see if I was still breathing."

She stood, put her hand on her hip. "If you're trying to make me feel guilty for not rushing over with chicken soup you can forget about it, Buddy Corlew."

"A guy can hope."

Jess rolled her eyes. Why the heck had she called him? Oh yeah. Stop skating around the issue. "I guess since you're sick you haven't had a chance to look into the accident that killed my parents?"

"I started some preliminary searches," he said, surprising her. "But it'll take some time, Jessie Lee. You only asked me to do this yesterday, you know."

The past twenty-four hours felt like half a lifetime. She understood what she was asking him to do would take some time. Her parents had died in a car crash more than thirty years ago. Jesus! Why had she even opened this Pandora's box? Whatever her Aunt Wanda's agenda, Jess should never have allowed the woman to burrow under her skin with her claims about the past. Wanda Newsom had probably killed most of her brain cells with drugs and alcohol. She'd never done one good or kind thing for Jess or her sister.

"I can give you one shocker, though."

In spite of her tirade to the contrary, Jess held her breath in anticipation.

"Your Aunt Wanda filed a report claiming her sister had warned her there was trouble with her husband. Did you know about that?"

The world shifted and Jess had to reach for the sink. Pregnancy test sticks clattered to the floor. "Are you certain?"

"Got a copy of it this morning. As soon as your folks were buried, Wanda went to the BPD. She insisted your mother told her that if anything happened to her, Wanda should tell the police to look into it. I have a pal in records who's searching for any investigation into the accident."

"Thanks, Corlew. Call me... when you have more." Jess tried to wrap her head around this news. The fact that Wanda had filed that report just like she said meant nothing. Had to be the drugs. Wanda probably suffered bouts of paranoia back then. Who knew what had prompted her to file the report.

"See ya, kid."

The call ended. Jess dropped to her knees on the floor, set her phone aside and gathered up the test sticks.

She had no idea how many minutes had passed but pink lines had formed on each one. *Positive. Positive. Positive.*

A rap on the door made her jump.

"You all right in there, Chief?"

"Yes." Jess reached up and turned on the sink faucet. "I'm fine. I'll be out in a minute."

She waited until she heard his footsteps retreating. Scrambling to her feet, she snatched up the Walmart bag and shoved the test sticks into it. After herding the pile of feminine products she'd dumped on the floor into a little stack in the corner next to the pedestal sink, she stood. She still felt a little lightheaded. Probably just needed to eat. Lunch had been a long time ago.

She set the Walmart bag in the sink and, as quietly as possible, removed the toilet tank lid to retrieve the first test she'd hidden there. With Dan in the other room yesterday morning when she'd taken the first test, she'd had no choice but to hide it. All she had to do now was stuff it into the Walmart bag with the others and take the whole thing to the trashcan outside.

Inside the toilet tank, the bag she'd carefully tied and tucked away there was open and the test stick floated next to it. "What in the world?" Had she not tied it tightly enough? She groaned and fished the test stick and bag from the toilet tank. The pink lines in the little window were no longer readable. She crammed the wet mess into the new bag, tied it up tightly, and shoved it into her purse.

She washed her hands again and smoothed her hair. *Stay calm.* There were a few things she needed to round up and then she was going to Dan's. Then, over dinner tonight, she would tell him the news. Her nerves jangled. Nervous or not, she couldn't keep finding excuses not to tell him.

Jess opened the door and exited the bathroom. Hayes waited at the front door. She mustered up a smile. He returned the smile but she didn't miss his quick inventory of her condition. Evidently the others had already warned him to keep a close eye on her.

"I have to round up a few things and then we're off."

She grabbed the new suit her sister had bought for her. Jess smoothed a hand over the herringbone tweed blazer with its notched lapel and lightly puffed sleeves. The charcoal color was classic. The pencil skirt was her favorite style. Lily might not like to wear suits, but she'd done a stellar job picking this one out. As foolish as it was, doing something as normal as selecting her clothes for work soothed Jess's nerves.

She decided to take the red suit and the ivory one as well. That was about it. She really did need to do some shopping. Everything she owned had been destroyed in the motel room she'd rented when she first came back to Birmingham. She'd been meaning to put together a new wardrobe, but there just hadn't been time for more than a quick fix to her immediate needs.

"Can I help you with those?" Hayes asked, as she headed for the door.

Jess thrust the hanging garments at him. "Thank you. I'll lock up."

After setting the security system to away, she closed and locked the door. Hayes started down ahead of her. Jess smiled when she noticed Mr. Louis waited at the bottom of the stairs. She'd expected to see him. He surely wondered what had become of her the past twenty-four hours.

"Jess, I'm so glad to see you," George Louis said, looking past Hayes who had planted himself between the older man and Jess as she descended the final steps. "I was getting worried."

"I'm sorry, Mr. Louis, I—"

"George," he reminded gently.

"George," she repeated. "I meant to call you, but I've hardly had a chance to catch my breath."

Her landlord frowned at the garments Hayes carried. "Are you moving?"

"Oh no. No." Jess turned to Hayes. "Lieutenant, this is my landlord, George Louis."

Hayes dipped his head in acknowledgement. George looked the taller man over thoroughly before allowing an answering nod.

"Lieutenant, would you give me a moment, please?" Her landlord deserved an explanation for her abrupt departure yesterday morning.

With a final look at George, Hayes strode off to his stylish Audi. His was one of the newest models. Jess's twelve-year-old Audi waited sadly in the drive for her attention. She had no idea when she'd get her freedom back. For now, she was escorted every- where she went.

Just like a celebrity. Ha!

"Are you all right, Jess?" George moved closer, concern shadowing his face. "I saw you on the news at the scene of that terrible murder."

"Murders," Jess corrected. "Two young women were murdered."

He shook his head and pressed his palms together as if he intended to pray. "How horrible. I keep thinking about that awful man who came here to hurt you."

The Man in the Moon. George Louis had saved her. Sort of. "I feel bad about that, George. I hope you're okay after all the excitement." He'd seemed okay the last time Jess spoke to him.

He stared at the ground, shuffled his feet in that shy manner of his. "I'm fine." He looked up at Jess then, his eyes appearing huge behind the thick lenses of his glasses. "You must be exhausted. Have you had dinner?"

"I'm going to dinner now," she assured him. If Daniel Burnett knew what was good for him, he'd have dinner waiting. She was starving!

"Will you be coming home tonight?" her land- lord asked hopefully.

If Louis hadn't looked so genuinely worried Jess might have been annoyed by his nosiness. But it was nice to know someone cared. Missed her. "Unfortunately, I might not be home for a few days more. This case is keeping me busy night and day. You have my cell number so you can reach me if you need to."

"Yes, I have your number." He reached out and patted her shoulder, the move awkward. "You should have a good dinner and just rest. You work too hard, Jess. One of these days you're going to have to take a vacation."

She couldn't remember the last time she'd taken anything that even resembled a vacation. A memory from the past intruded on her thoughts. Unless she counted Christmas ten years ago when she'd come back to Birmingham to spend the holiday with her sister. She'd had a promotion to celebrate, not to mention she'd solved the biggest case of her career to that point.

She'd run into Dan at the Publix on Christmas Eve, and they'd ended up still in bed together the next morning.

Here they were a decade later… together again. *And pregnant.*

Her head did a little spinning and the ground shifted again.

"Here now!" Louis reached for her. "You might need to sit down."

Jess regained her balance and held up a hand to ward off his concern. "I'm fine. Really."

Hayes was suddenly there and Jess felt her cheeks burn with mortification. "I'll call you in a day or two, George," she promised.

She really did have to go. What she would give for an enormous glass of wine right now. Since wine was off limits maybe chocolate would do the trick. Mostly she just needed to get out of these clothes and to relax.

"Take care, Jess!" Louis called after her.

She managed a smile and a wave as she settled into the passenger seat of her new detective's luxury automobile. Hayes closed the door and rounded the hood.

Eyes closed, Jess dropped her head against the seat and tried to stop the ridiculous swaying sensation keeping her off balance. She should see a doctor this week. No putting it off. Calling Lily was on that same urgent list. But first she had to talk to Dan. Where did *relaxing* fit into all that?

Hayes slid into the driver's seat and started the engine. When he'd backed onto the street and headed toward Mountain Brook, she felt her tension receding. Dan was waiting for her.

Whatever else was wrong in the world, she glanced in the side mirror and noted the BPD cruiser on their tail, being in Dan's arms felt right.

"If I'm out of line just say so," Hayes said, his voice making her flinch after the minutes of silence.

She turned to the driver. Was her new recruit disenchanted with the job already? "Go on, Lieutenant."

"I don't know much about your personal life, Chief. But I do know there are some things a person doesn't need to do alone."

She set aside all the other worries troubling her long enough to mentally review every step she'd taken in Walmart as she'd collected and purchased those tests. "Do you have a point?"

"I do." He sent her a look that said he wouldn't be making any apologies for where he was headed. "You have a serial killer determined to get to you. He has all manner of freaks watching you. Your latest case is a damned creepy double homicide. This is not the time for secrets."

Well damn, she was busted. "What gave me away?" Evidently, the old I-need-feminine-products bait and switch hadn't worked on the perceptive lieutenant.

His attention remained on the street as the sun slowly lowered, drawing this too long day to a close. There was a lot she didn't know about this cop, but her instincts said he was a good one.

"Women," he explained, "whatever their choice in feminine products, most, particularly those over thirty, have a preferred brand." His lips quirked. "It was obvious you snatched up the handiest ones. Your cover might have worked otherwise."

Why hadn't she thought of that?

"I'll remember that, Lieutenant." Despite a new blast of tension, she almost laughed. So he knew. She was his superior. If she gave him an order, he was supposed to follow it. Hopefully, that formality wouldn't be necessary. "I assume this will stay between us for now."

No one could know. Not yet. Dan had to be first and she had to find the time to tell him.

"I'm not about to make my new boss unhappy the first day on the job. I'm very good at keeping secrets, Chief. You have nothing to worry about there."

Easy for him to say.

He slowed for the turn onto Dunbrooke Drive. Jess stared at the stately homes they passed. If Hayes let this slip to Lori or Harper, both would be upset that she hadn't shared the news. Jess closed her eyes. Her friends couldn't know yet either.

The smoke rising in the backyard signaled that Dan had decided to grill their dinner. He was thrilled to have her staying here with him and it showed. If he had his way she would never return to her little apartment. She would stay right here in his big house in this upscale neighborhood where she felt so out of place.

Reality sank deeper, making it hard to breathe. *You are still not one of them, kid.* Corlew had warned her that just because she had the right job and wore the right clothes didn't mean a thing. She would never be like Sylvia Baron or Annette Denton, Dan's most recent ex-wife.

"Why don't you leave that bag in the car? I'll take care of it for you."

Jess turned to the man behind the wheel. There were things she probably should say, but she didn't know this man well enough to explain herself. "Thank you, Lieutenant."

She left the Walmart bag in his car, grateful for one less thing to worry about. He carried her clothes.

Dan came around the corner of the house and Jess barely restrained the tears. It took every ounce of strength she possessed not to run into his arms. Weepiness was, apparently, another part of being pregnant.

"It's about time." He smiled. "Thought I might have to send out a search party." He glanced at Hayes. The two exchanged those nods that only the male species understood. Women, being far more evolved, didn't communicate in nods and grunts.

"Lieutenant Hayes moved over to SPU today," Jess announced. The entire day had passed and she and Dan had scarcely had a minute to carry on a real conversation.

"I signed off on the transfer." Dan reached for the garments the detective carried. "I see Chief Harris is working you overtime already."

"Not a problem, sir." Hayes relinquished the load. "See you in the morning, ma'am."

Jess managed a smile. "Thank you, Lieutenant."

While Dan and Hayes discussed his new car, Jess went inside. She grabbed a bottle of water from the fridge and went in search of something more comfortable to wear. Sweat pants and a tee and bare feet sounded good about now. She slipped off the Mary Janes and peeled off her dress. It would be nice just to sit and close out the world—at least to the extent possible.

With the sweats and tee on she sighed. "Way better."

She brushed her teeth and finger combed her hair. Nothing in her bag of tricks was going to camouflage those raccoon eyes.

As she padded back to the kitchen the scents of whatever Dan had been grilling had her stomach rumbling. He turned from the fridge, a bag of mixed salad greens in his hand. He smiled and her heart reacted.

"Can I help with anything?" She felt a little guilty that he seemed to be doing all the domestic duties.

"Thanks, but I have it under control."

She should feel even guiltier that she'd been hoping for that answer, but she didn't. Besides, this was as good a time as any to just spill it. No need to wait until the first course was out of the way. She braced herself, opened her mouth to say the words but he spoke first.

"By the way, my parents are coming for dinner." He winced. "I apologize for the short notice, but Mother only called a little while ago. I had to run to Publix for more steaks."

Jess bit back a groan. "That's nice." *What a lie.* Nice and Katherine never, ever went together.

Dan gifted her with a lopsided grin. "I can see by your pained expression just how nice it is."

She should be ashamed. These people were his parents. Daniel senior was terrific. It was the mother who drove Jess crazy. Nonetheless, she couldn't expect Katherine to just stay away forever… no matter how appealing. "Sorry. I'm just tired. I was hoping to relax and," she shrugged, "I don't know, talk about things."

Telling him the news tonight was out for sure now. They needed time to discuss the subject at

115

length. She had no desire to just blurt the announcement and move on. The absolute last thing she wanted was for Katherine to waltz in here and sense something was wrong. She could not know about the pregnancy—at least not for a few more months.

Oh God. She was going to have a baby and Katherine was the grandmother.

Dan came around to her side of the island and lifted her off the stool. He settled her on the granite counter, put his arms around her and moved in close. "I know you're exhausted and I appreciate your patience with my mother. I realize she doesn't make it easy."

Now there was the understatement of the century.

"It's fine. Really. I'm glad they're coming." *She was going to hell for sure.*

He kissed her lips. "Thank you for being a good sport."

Jess hugged him hard. She blinked back the tears that rose unbidden. How would she ever keep the evil chasing her away from this man and the child she carried?

CHAPTER NINE

His heart beat faster and faster. He had to close his eyes or risk having the organ burst from his chest.

Too much beauty to take it all in at once.

He inhaled deeply, relishing the scent of fresh, warm blood as it oozed forth, spilling across the flesh. He shivered.

"Isn't it beautiful?"

He opened his eyes. His breath caught. Crimson trailed down her forearms as she reached out to him. The precious blood speckled her breasts… slipped down her smooth, pale skin.

"Almost as beautiful as you," he murmured, emotion blurring his gaze.

She smiled. Holding the still warm heart in her palm, she danced around the room to the rise and fall of the music.

The other one joined her… dancing and bathing in the rich blood still teeming with life just as they did in paint as they created their works of art.

How long had he waited for this? *Decades.* Finally, the ultimate triumph was his for the taking. The consummate vengeance for the most agonizing of injuries was before him. She had taken everything from him, even the will to live.

She should have paid attention. Her selfishness was her ruin. Now she would know the pain and the emptiness. She would be devastated. She would scream and gnash her teeth and tear out her hair when she learned what he had done to her precious ones.

What a shame he wouldn't be here to watch.

CHAPTER TEN

DUNBROOKE DRIVE, WEDNESDAY, AUGUST 25, 5:48 A.M.

A soft sound woke Jess.

She opened her eyes and blinked, tried to focus. The room was dark. Her pulse sputtered into a faster rhythm.

Dan's house.

His warm body was spooned against her backside. His arm tucked protectively around her waist. The idea that a few months from now they would be able to feel the baby move terrified her just a little. But it also made her wish she could stay right here in his arms all day and never leave the house. She could pretend the evil beyond these walls didn't exist.

A pale glow flashed from the nightstand. Her phone vibrated again.

Damn. She wasn't ready to face the day yet.

Dan's parents had stayed through the ten o'clock news last night. Jess had humiliated herself by falling asleep on the sofa. Katherine would find a way to make being exhausted an etiquette felony.

Jess had never been good enough for Katherine Burnett's only son. She hadn't been twenty odd years ago and nothing had changed. *You are still not one of them, kid.*

Stifling a yawn, Jess kicked Corlew out of her head and reached for her cell. She checked the screen. Text message. The number wasn't one from her contact list. Her heart started to pound. She hadn't heard from Spears this week. Was he finally reaching out to her? Bastard. She snatched her glasses from the nightstand and slid them on as the text opened.

Video.

Could be a proof of life on Rory Stinnett or a message related to her. Holding her breath, Jess tapped the play arrow.

A young man, early to mid twenties, stared into the camera. Classical music played in the background. It was something familiar, Beethoven maybe?

"I will not take off my clothes on camera." The guy in the video laughed. "No way."

Dan roused. He peeked over Jess's shoulder, squinted at the screen. "Who called?"

Jess sat up, Dan's arm and the covers falling away from her. "It's a video." Not about Stinnett and maybe not from Spears. Jess didn't know whether to be relieved about that or not. She watched as the handsome young man with the rich chestnut colored hair and glittering brown eyes shook his head again.

The symphony in the background grew louder. He grinned. "Still not doing it," he shouted above the concerto of strings, brass and percussion swelling around him. He wore a University of Auburn t-shirt. He stared directly into the camera. "Not unless you take yours off, too."

The video went silent, his smiling face frozen on the screen.

"What the devil was that all about?" Dan wanted to know.

He sat beside Jess now. His hair was mussed and every bare inch of him above the waistband of his boxers made her want to throw her phone across the room and put those earlier thoughts about staying right here into action. Her heart constricted at the idea that, unless it was a mistake, the man—boy really—was in danger. Why the hell else would she receive the video?

Maybe the sender entered the number wrong. In her heart she knew that wasn't the case.

"I don't know." She played the video again. The wall behind the young man was white. There was the occasional glimpse of a bed, the linens tousled, behind him.

Her cell rang. She jumped, almost dropped the damned thing. An image of Chet Harper appeared on the screen.

Dan cursed under his breath. "I'll go make coffee."

They both knew what a call from Harper at this hour meant.

Jess cleared her throat and steadied herself. "Good morning, Sergeant." She stood and headed for the closet. Might as well get dressed. She had a feeling she was going to miss breakfast with Dan today.

"Morning, ma'am. We have another homicide. The heart was taken from this one, too. Vic's name is Logan Thomas. Twenty-four. Bioengineer. I notified Lieutenant Hayes. Detective Wells is en route to pick you up. Officer Cook is already here, knocking on doors."

Jess stilled, her hand on the closet door. It took every ounce of courage she owned to ask the next question. "The victim," her blood went a little cold with certainty, "does he have dark hair and eyes? An Auburn t-shirt?"

The hesitation gave Jess the answer before Harper spoke.

"Yes, ma'am. How did you know?"

Fury started to smolder deep in her belly as she grabbed something to wear from the closet. "I'll explain when I get there. Is the crime scene unit on the way?"

"Yes, ma'am. Officer Cook called Dr. Baron and she's also en route."

Cook made that call? Really? Jess was going to have to keep an eye on him. Maybe she should speak to him about Sylvia. Then again, maybe she was making too much of the sparks she'd seen flying at the morgue yesterday.

"I'll be there soon, Sergeant," she promised before ending the call. Braced against the closet door she watched the video again. Was this someone else Spears had invited to play games with her?

Though she had not one single piece of tangible evidence to corroborate her theory, she was certain he'd resurrected the Man in the Moon to taunt her.

We have to go outside where he can see.

Fergus Cagle, aka the Man in the Moon, had said that to her. Then, his last words before being shot were about his daughter. Obviously he'd gone over the edge. The fact was, nothing he said was reliable. Still, in her gut, she sensed the Man in the Moon had started sending those remains to her because of Spears. Otherwise, how would Spears have known the location of the rest of the victims? But that alone wasn't proof he'd directed Fergus Cagle's actions. It only proved Spears had been watching.

Whatever it showed, Jess had a feeling the Man in the Moon and, after seeing that video, this case were somehow related to Spears. She stared at her cell phone. If that was true, it meant three people had been viciously murdered just so Spears could send her a message.

Hot, bitter bile rushed into Jess's throat, and it was all she could do to avoid throwing up on Dan's expensive carpet before she made it to the toilet.

Another sign that nothing about her future was going to be easy.

FIRST AVENUE NORTH, 6:50 A.M.

Jess stared at the building. Her stomach had only just settled down, and now it was threatening another rebellion. "This is the address?"

It wasn't like the two official vehicles and the crime scene unit van parked at the curb wasn't a dead giveaway.

Couldn't be.

"This is it," Lori assured her.

It had to be a coincidence. The building was the one where Dan had lived ten years ago when they'd run into each other on Christmas Eve. Birmingham was a relatively large city, the biggest in the state of Alabama, but the downtown area was a small world. There was bound to be crime in places she and Dan had frequented in the past.

"You ready?"

Jess reached for the door handle. "As ready as humanly possible with only one cup of coffee." She faked a smile.

Lori studied her a second too long, but kept whatever she was thinking to herself. Jess readied to face what would no doubt be another horrific murder scene. *Logan Thomas.* His image, big smile and eyes twinkling with mischief, kept playing in her head.

The officer shadowing Jess's every move this shift was propped against the side of his cruiser watching the official chaos.

For a change, she was thankful for the added precaution. Distraction was a dangerous enemy, and lately distraction had been her constant companion.

"There's a security camera in the lobby," Lori said. "A representative from the company that maintains the building is on his way."

"Maybe if we're lucky the killer didn't notice the camera." Most criminals missed the little details. Though she had to admit, a surveillance camera was a considerably major item to miss.

The uniform at the building's entrance opened the door that, under normal circumstances, would have required a code for entry. Security measures wouldn't have stopped this killer. Judging by the video she received, Logan's killer had been his guest.

Inside the small lobby was another uniform, this one monitoring the stairs and elevator. Between the elevator and the door leading to the stairwell was a wall of mailboxes. Above the mailboxes was a surveillance camera.

Jess distinctly remembered this lobby from ten years ago. The camera hadn't been there then. Otherwise, the place looked the same. Not that she'd paid much attention that long ago night. She'd been caught up in something that refused to let go. Desire, need, and the desperation to feel alive after the case she'd just solved.

"Eighth floor." Lori hesitated. "Elevator or stairs, Chief?"

Jess dragged her head out of the past. "Did you say the eighth floor?"

Lori nodded, a frown forming across her brow.

Another of those little shots of adrenaline fired through Jess. This just got creepier and creepier. Dan's apartment had been on the eighth floor. She swallowed, trying to loosen the emotion caught in her throat. "Let's take the elevator."

Why was it nothing in her life came about in a routine manner? Just when she'd reached a major pinnacle in her career, a serial killer latched onto her like a bad rash and refused to go away. She couldn't marry and have children the way her sister had. Was she forever destined to have the unusual and the bizarre crammed into her existence at the most inopportune times?

Maybe this was fate's way of showing her who was in charge.

Closing her eyes, Jess leaned against the back wall of the elevator as it bumped into upward motion. She tried her very best to ignore the queasy feeling in the pit of her belly. Maybe the stairs would have been the better bet. Hopefully the feeling would pass. Soon.

"I don't mean to push," Lori said quietly.

Jess opened her eyes and turned to her.

"But I'm here when you're ready."

Lori was a good friend as well as a great detective, and they did need to talk. "I appreciate that."

Thankfully the elevator jolted to a stop at their destination. Jess pushed aside her personal worries and stepped into cop mode. Nature was taking care of the rest for now. Pregnant women all over the world went about their lives without freaking out or falling apart, she reminded herself.

Lori led the way, taking a right out of the elevator. Jess followed. The carpet along the corridor softened their steps, lessening the likelihood of disturbing residents. Four apartments, two on each side, lined the corridor in this direction. Another uniform waited at the door where a young man's life had ended.

Jess stalled a few yards away.

Apartment thirty-One.

"This is it." Dan grinned at her as he shoved the key into the lock. "It's not where I hope to be in a couple of years but it's home for now."

"This was Dan's apartment."

Lori came to her side. "Chief Burnett's?"

Jess hadn't realized she'd spoken aloud. "Yes." She accepted the gloves and shoe covers Lori offered her. Hands shaking, she tugged on the protective wear. By the time they walked inside the apartment her heart was racing. This couldn't mean anything.

Just a coincidence.

The thick odor of coagulated blood had her breathing through her mouth. The main living area was one big space with a nice view of the city that she recalled vividly. The room was sparsely furnished, a typical bachelor's apartment with a big sofa, an even bigger television and a table and chairs. An iPad sat on one those docks with speakers. Nothing appeared disturbed.

Ten years ago it had been much the same. Dan had been working his way up in Birmingham politics and a downtown apartment was all he needed. She had admired the view of the city. She'd been gone so long that staring out at the lights had mesmerized her. Even now something wistful swelled inside her. Then Dan had kissed her and thoughts of the view as well as the pie she'd purchased at Publix for Christmas dinner with her sister's family had vanished completely, taking all semblance of good sense with them.

"This way, Chief."

Jess blinked away the past and met Harper's concerned gaze. He'd walked right up to her and she hadn't even noticed. Lori had already moved across the room and was speaking to one of the forensic techs.

Breathe and focus.

She gave Harper a nod and followed him to the small box of a hall that separated the one bedroom and bath from the main living space. The entire apartment had been carpeted before. Now it was hardwood or something that looked like hardwood.

"Our perp used the same MO this time. Washed up in the bathroom, leaving a hell of a mess and dozens of smeared prints."

Like the previous scene, bloody hand and foot prints marred the tile. No discernable attempt to clean up the scene. The killer was daring them to catch him... or her.

Four or five feet away the door to the only bedroom stood open. Inside, a tech videoed the place where Logan Thomas's life had ended. Feeling numb, Jess took the steps necessary to enter the room. For the first few seconds she stared at the window on the other side. The drapes were open, giving an inspiring glimpse of downtown. In the middle of the floor a pair of jeans, boxers and an

Auburn t-shirt lay in a pile. Smudged footprints, made in the victim's blood, were tracked all over the floor. The tools the killer had used, hammer, hatchet, screwdriver, pry bar and box cutter, had been cast aside.

The walls were white, uncluttered and untainted by the ugliness that had occurred within them. A single dresser stood on one side of the room facing the king size bed where the victim waited for her assessment. The sheets beneath the body were twisted and soaked with blood.

"Vic doesn't appear to have been strangled or suffocated," Harper said quietly. "The wounds all appear to be post mortem."

"Something stopped his heart before it was taken from him." Jess ignored the tossing and turning in her stomach. The same brutality and crudeness utilized to pry open Lisa Templeton's and Alisha Burgess's chests and to remove their hearts had been used on this young man.

"Drug overdose, maybe?" She stepped closer, searched his cold, marbled skin for any signs indicating cause of death. There were plenty of ways to end a life that might not be readily visible.

"That's my thinking," Harper said in answer to her question.

A puzzle best solved by the medical examiner.

"He's been dead for five or six hours anyway." Jess turned to the detective. "You haven't found any messages or notes of any sort?" She steeled her body to stop the trembling. Whoever committed this murder wanted to share the experience with her—at least the before part.

But why send her a prequel to this murder and not the other two?

Harper shook his head before searching her face. "How did you have a description of the vic and the Auburn t-shirt?"

She passed him her cell. "I was sent a preview via text just before you called. Submit the video into evidence, would you?"

The ability to breathe grew more difficult as Harper played the video and the victim's voice echoed in the room. Had he been murdered because he lived here? If so, how was that connected to the murders in Homewood?

Jess swallowed the bitterness climbing back into her throat. And how was it that the perp sent her the video only moments before Harper's call? Another coincidence? She didn't think so. He or, more likely, she had been nearby, waiting and watching for the police to arrive.

"Who called this in?" Jess glanced at the body of the young man whose life had been wasted.

"Neighbor. Some sort of symphony was blasting from the victim's iTunes playlist." He handed the cell back to Jess. "First on the scene turned it off in deference to the neighbors."

"You certainly have a way of attracting the genuinely weird, Harris."

Jess turned to find the medical examiner waiting in the doorway, assessing the situation before jumping in.

Dr. Sylvia Baron shook her head sadly. "There always seems to be at least one encore to every case that lands in your lap."

"I'm a regular creep show magnet." Jess didn't bother attempting a smile for the ME. She just didn't have it in her. "No visible cause of death this time."

Sylvia Baron searched for a clean spot on the floor to leave her bag. Finally she gave up and shoved it at Harper. "Let's see what we have here."

Taking her time, she studied the victim, and then she glanced at Jess. "Let's turn him over."

Harper passed Sylvia's bag to Jess. "Let me do that, ma'am."

Jess couldn't decide whether to hug the detective or to scold him for presuming she was unable to do the job. Truth was, at the moment she felt completely incapable of the task.

The gurgling sound of gases moving around inside the victim as he was rolled to his side had her gritting her teeth. Holding her breath was the only way to keep the urge to heave at bay. She'd seen, heard, and smelled this dozens of times. Didn't seem to matter to her confused body.

"I can't tell you if this is cause of death," Sylvia announced, "but I can tell you how the killer most likely disabled him."

Jess spotted the marks. "A stun gun."

Sylvia nodded. "More than one hit." She pointed to the sets of red marks. "One, two… three. We may be looking at the cause of death."

"Time of death?" Jess hated that her voice squeaked. Sylvia glanced at her. She hated even worse the ME noticed.

"Give me a minute." Sylvia reached for her bag.

While the ME measured body temperature, Jess ushered Harper out of earshot. "Have Cook go down to the property assessor's office as soon as it opens and dig up the names of the owners for the house on Raleigh Avenue. I want to know every tenant who's lived there since," she shrugged, "I don't know. Have him go back as far as he can. I need that list ASAP."

"Do you have reason to believe location is the link between these murders?"

Jess hesitated but only for a second. "I don't know, Sergeant, but I'd like to rule out a scenario that's nagging at me. It's probably nothing but—"

"I thought this place looked familiar." Sylvia turned to Jess. "Didn't Dan live here before he bought his house?"

"You know," Jess looked around as if she hadn't noticed, "I think you might be right. Since I was in Virginia I really can't recall."

Sylvia accepted the lie and went on about her business. Jess had a sinking feeling whatever was going on with these murders wasn't about whether Dan had lived here or not... it was about that evening a decade ago when he brought her here. They'd made love all night in this very room. The sun had come up the next morning through that massive window while the city's first snow of the year started to fall.

Jess had left that Christmas morning without saying good-bye. Not once in ten years had she allowed herself to look back. Until a few weeks ago…

Sylvia was right about what people were saying. The evil that intended to destroy Jess had followed her to Birmingham, and clearly had no intention of leaving before the job was done.

How many people would die before he achieved his goal?

CHAPTER ELEVEN

"We have two killers." Lori posted the updated information on the case board. "Or, at least, two people participating in the kills. Two distinct sets of prints—not belonging to the victims—were lifted from the tools found at the scene, but no hits in any of the databases."

"We believe the perps are female based on the size of the prints collected, but we can't confirm that conclusion by the prints alone," Harper said as he perused the report he'd just received. "Analysis on the hair collected from the shower drain at the Homewood house shows two distinct Caucasian specimens besides those of the victims: one brunette and one a pale, bleached blond."

"The killers are reasonably organized," Hayes spoke up. He'd propped against his desk, legs crossed at the ankles. "They bring the tools, new ones, they need with them. I'm running down where the particular brands are sold locally. Depending on what I find, there's the potential for security videos or a sales person who might recall the buyer."

Lori flashed a smile for the newest member of the team. Jess had a feeling Lori had news that would take this investigation from going nowhere to getting somewhere.

"None of the neighbors noticed anyone coming or going in Mr. Thomas's building." Lori waltzed over to her desk and picked up a folder. "However, a few minutes ago, I reviewed the surveillance video." She returned to the case board and posted more photos there. "Two females left the building at one-fifty. Dr. Baron estimated time of death between midnight and two this morning." Lori gestured to the photos. "Ladies and gentlemen, I think we have our killers."

Jess reached for her glasses as she moved around her desk. Slipping them on, she stepped closer to the board to inspect the images of the two women. "What kind of bag or sack is the one in front carrying?"

Lori tapped the photo. "With those blue cinch ties, I'd say Hefty trash bags. You know, the big black ones used for yard cleanup."

The brunette kept her face turned from the camera. Both wore sweats but they were too clean to have been worn during the murder. The female with pale blond hair had on a hoodie but she hadn't bothered to wear the hood up. The photo had captured her as she turned to look directly at the camera and smile.

Not afraid of getting caught.

"Their clothes are in the bag," Jess said, mostly to herself. "In addition to the tools, they bring a change of clothes and shoes to the scene."

"After they strip off their bloody clothes and clean up," Harper picked it up from there, "they put on the clean clothes and shoes they left near the door. Anyone who saw them on the street wouldn't think twice. Just a couple of residents taking their garbage to the dumpster in the alley."

Jess studied the blonde's face. "What about the heart?"

"Since they're not carrying anything else," Lori answered, "we have to assume the heart's in the bag, too."

"Unless they ate it at the scene."

Jess turned to Hayes. "You think this is some sort of cannibalistic ritual? We have no evidence to support that conclusion."

"We don't have any rumblings about black market organ sales either," he offered. "That doesn't leave many other options."

"Not to mention," Harper cut in, "if they were looking to make money, they left a whole hell of a lot at the scene. Like kidneys."

Jess turned back to the board. The woman who dared to show her face looked young, early twenties maybe. "Templeton and Burgess may have been their first kills."

"What makes you lean in that direction?" Hayes asked.

"Their work was sloppier the first time," Harper explained, obviously enjoying the opportunity to show up the lieutenant. "The crime scene looked somewhat the same, but a closer inspection of the way they butchered the chests of the two female victims indicates they had a harder time removing the hearts that first time. With Thomas they knew what they were doing. The work was a little cleaner."

"That only suggests they hadn't removed a human heart before," the lieutenant countered, "not that they hadn't taken a life."

Jess and Lori exchanged a look.

Harper crossed his arms over his chest. "When you've worked as many homicide scenes as I have, you'll understand."

Jess hoped these two weren't planning to waste time in a pissing contest.

"What's to understand?" Hayes folded his arms over his chest in a mocking manner.

"The killers hurried from the scene," Jess interjected. "They didn't close the door much less lock it." She turned back to the photo. "They were excited and terrified at the same time. They couldn't believe they'd done it. But they weren't in a hurry after last night's murder. Now they're feeling brave. Cocky. This time they enjoyed all the excitement without the fear."

Harper's lips twisted in a little smirk of victory.

Hayes would learn this wasn't as easy as experienced detectives like Harper and Wells made it appear. "What kind of motives are we looking at?" Jess asked, moving on.

"Since we don't know the identities of the killers, we can't prove a personal connection," Lori said.

"Even without a distinct personal connection," Harper added, "could be envy or revenge."

Hayes pushed off from his desk and moved toward the case board. "But isn't the personal nature of these murders right in front of us?"

"The objective may have been to humiliate the victims," Lori pointed out. "When I was abducted by Matthew Reed, Eric Spears's protégé, he wanted to scare me… to humiliate me the same way he did the other women he abducted. To anyone analyzing his actions, what he did to us appeared very personal but it wasn't. We were the pawns he used to make a statement. Humiliating and scaring us was just for his personal entertainment."

"One of the women," Jess said, the images Lori's words prompted playing rapid fire in her head, "was a federal agent. When she tried to escape, he cut off her hands and feet. She died as a result of those injuries."

Silence thickened in the room.

"Some people are just screwed up," Harper muttered.

Jess shifted her attention back to the case at hand. She glanced at the window beyond her desk. "What about all those cameras the mayor had installed? Any chance we can pick up these two suspects on any of those?" The cameras had certainly helped save Jess a couple of weeks ago.

Lori shook her head. "I already checked. There's one in that area, but the angle isn't right."

The door opened, breaking the tension, and Cook strolled in. "It took a while," he said as he waved the pages in his hand, "but I dug up the names all the way back to when the house on Raleigh was built."

"Leave it on my desk," Jess instructed. She didn't want to discuss her theory with the team until she'd had a look at the list herself.

Cook dropped most of the pages on her desk, and then waved the one he'd held onto. "I also picked up some preliminary results on our latest vic from the ME."

"You went by the morgue?" Harper asked the question on the tip of Jess's tongue.

Cook's head moved up and down, his expression full of enthusiasm. "She called me. Told me to come by and pick it up." His face fell. "Was I not supposed to do that?" He looked from Harper to Jess.

"You did the right thing, of course." Jess reached for the report. "I'm just surprised Dr. Baron had anything to share this quickly." She and Sylvia needed to talk. It was one thing for Cook in his foolish youth to lust after the ME, but Sylvia was old enough to know better. *What was going on in that woman's head?*

Jess scanned the preliminary report. Nothing Sylvia couldn't have passed along over the phone as she had many times before. "No indication Thomas engaged in sex before his murder," Jess said, passing along the results. "His alcohol levels show he was considerably intoxicated at TOD. Dr. Baron does not believe the stun gun caused his death and more results are coming."

Jess passed the report to Lori. "Let's check with neighbors at both scenes and see if anyone recognizes the blonde. Run her photo past the friends of the victims. Maybe someone will recognize her."

With her team divvying up the tasks, Jess took her seat and reviewed the list Cook had dug up for her. The names were in reverse chronological order, starting with the present owner.

The first few pages were listings of tenants. Poor Cook had had his work cut out for him. He'd contacted each landlord for the names of their tenants, and he'd still turned the task around in record time. Not one name on the list was familiar to Jess. Fifteen years ago the house had been owner occupied rather than a rental. That same scenario proved the case from that point all the way back to when it was built.

Jess reached the name of the family who'd built the house and her stomach took a dive.

Paul and Wanda Newsom.

Her aunt and her husband had built the house where Templeton and Burgess were murdered?

For several seconds Jess could do nothing but allow the information to digest. This was exactly what she'd hoped Cook *wouldn't* find.

More than a little shaken, she stood. "I think I'm going out for lunch." She shoved the page into her bag and readied to go. She needed to speak to her aunt. There had to be a mistake.

It wasn't until Jess looked up that she noticed everyone staring at her.

Ignoring the questioning looks, she said to Hayes, "Lieutenant, it's your turn to play chauffer."

Jess felt Lori's eyes on her as she left the office. She couldn't look back. Couldn't say anything to her friends. If what she suspected was true, any friend of hers was in far more danger than they could possibly comprehend.

DRUID HILLS. 12:20 P.M.

"That's the one." Jess stared at the house where her aunt had lived for more than thirty years. The house was clad in dingy white siding. At least the lawn was freshly mown. The last time Jess had driven by the grass was ankle deep.

How she had hated this place. For months she and Lily had been angry with their parents for dying and leaving them with nowhere to go but this hellhole with an aunt who spent what little money she had on booze and most of her nights on her back under a different John. Not once had she done a single thing to help two young girls devastated by the loss of everything they knew and loved. The aunt the court had relied upon to see after Helen Harris's children had already spiraled so far downhill that she'd hit rock bottom.

Not any more. Now Wanda Newsom had God.

"Do you want to go in?"

Jess flinched at the sound of the lieutenant's voice. For the life of her, she couldn't stay on point with a damned thing. "Yes." She steeled herself for the battle with her newest team member. "I'll need you to wait out here, Lieutenant."

"I'm afraid I can't do that." He reached for the door handle.

"I wasn't asking you, Lieutenant." She was not debating this with him or anyone else. "You can watch me from here." *Damn Spears.* Damn this whole damned situation! People were dying and she couldn't stop it. The weight on her chest multiplied by a thousand. She felt like the guy in that commercial with the elephant on his chest. "Just like the uniform sitting in that cruiser ten yards behind us."

She was so sick of this!

"How about I walk you to the door, have a look inside, and then I'll wait on the porch." He sent her a sideways glance over the top of the Ray-Bans he wore. "Does that work for you?"

She bit her tongue. Jess reminded herself that he was right and she was wrong. Her emotions were controlling her instead of the other way around. They were keeping her distracted and hampering reason. She needed someone watching her back. He was here to do that.

"Fine."

Hayes emerged from the car, surveyed the neighborhood, and walked around to her side. He opened the door and she got out. As difficult as it was to admit that she wasn't fully capable of protecting herself at the moment, it was true. Her detectives intended to keep her safe. She appreciated their efforts.

Somehow that admission didn't make her feel one iota better.

"Thank you." Jess braced herself again, only this time for facing her aunt. She ran a hand through her hair and smoothed the front of her skirt. The sooner she had this over with the better. Since Wanda's ancient Toyota was in the drive, Jess presumed she was home.

Hayes knocked twice before the door cracked open. Jess leaned toward the narrow opening. "I need to speak with you." Her voice sounded thin and a little high pitched.

"Jessie Lee?" Wanda drew back the door. She looked up at the man beside Jess. Her forehead furrowed in confusion.

"Lieutenant Clint Hayes, Ms. Newsom," he announced. "I'll just need to come inside with Chief Harris and have a look around."

How did he know her aunt's name? Maybe Lori had told him. That was another feeling Jess didn't like—the one where you knew everyone was talking about you and not to you.

"Come on in." Wanda shuffled back, drawing the door open wide. "There's nobody here but me."

"It's just a precaution, ma'am."

"Well, all right." She closed the door after them and stood in the middle of the room wringing her hands.

Jess waited impatiently as Hayes walked through the small house. She wasn't saying a word until he was outside. If there was nothing to this, then there was no need to share it with the world.

The smell of fried chicken lingered in the air, invading Jess's senses. Her stomach rumbled. Wanda glanced at her. Jess wished the floor would open and swallow her. She didn't know why she cared what this woman thought of her or her stomach.

"The house is clear," Hayes announced as he reentered the room. "I'll be right outside, Chief."

Jess waited until he closed the front door behind him and then she turned to Wanda. "I have a few questions."

"Here." Wanda hurried to move the newspapers spread across the sofa. "Sit down, Jessie Lee. Anything you want to ask is fine by me. Would you like a glass of water?"

"Thank you, no. I don't have a lot of time."

"You don't have time to sit for a minute?"

Jess looked at her aunt. Really looked at her for the first time since returning to Birmingham. Until recently, she hadn't seen the woman in over thirty years. Wanda Newsom looked old, far older than her sixty-some years. The drugs and alcohol had taken a toll. Not to mention she'd probably suffered every STD known to man.

Jess's stomach started that frustrating churning again. Her knees felt weak. If she didn't sit down she would likely regret it.

"I guess I have a minute." She perched on the edge of the sofa. Wanda took a seat in a well-worn chair to Jess's right.

"What is it you want to talk about? Is it about your father and what I told you? It's the God's truth. I—"

"It's not about that." The anticipation in the older woman's eyes made Jess look away. Whatever hopes Wanda had that one day Jess would forgive her and they could be friends was a waste of energy.

"When did you move into this house?" Jess asked, turning back to the woman once more.

"After my Paul died, I couldn't afford the payments on the house we built. I wandered from pillar to post for a few years. Eventually I got this place." She glanced around the room. "It's not much but it's home."

Dread coiled in Jess's belly.

"We didn't have any children so at just twenty-two I wasn't entitled to social security benefits. I didn't know how to do a thing. I'd never had a job besides being a wife." She shook her head and made a sound that might have been a laugh. "I was a mess. The good Lord is the only reason I survived those years."

Marshaling all her powers of restraint, Jess managed to not roll her eyes or say anything unpleasant.

"We had all these plans," Wanda went on. "He was going to build me a white picket fence. My job was to stay at home and have babies." She blinked rapidly at the moisture shining in her eyes. "But I guess it wasn't meant to be."

"Life can be that way sometimes." That was the closest thing to sympathy Jess had to offer. "Where was this house you and your husband built?" She held her breath.

"It was over on Raleigh Avenue in Homewood. It was the neatest little thing. There were just two bedrooms but it was all we needed. At the time there were lots of other young couples just starting out in the neighborhood."

Jess needed to breathe but somehow the air wouldn't go into her lungs. Her eyes burned but she refused to cry.

"You wouldn't remember, but your mother and Lily were staying with me when she went into labor with you."

Air rushed into Jess's lungs. "Why were they staying with *you*?"

"Your father was out of town." Wanda shook her head. "He was always out of town. Anyway, Helen knew her time was close. Since she'd delivered Lily so cotton pickin' fast she didn't want to be alone that night. She had a feeling you were coming."

Emotion flooded her and Jess licked her lips to conceal their trembling. "So, you drove my mother to the hospital?"

Wanda wagged her head side to side. "No sirree. Once you started coming you didn't want to wait. I called an ambulance but by the time they got there, you were already in my hands." Wanda brushed back tears even as she laughed. "Popped right out of there with your eyes wide open and screaming at the top of your lungs in indignation."

"I was born in that house?" Jess knew the answer, for Pete's sake. The woman had just told her but somehow the reality of it wouldn't sink into her brain. Her body had gone ice cold.

"You most certainly were. In the bigger of the two bedrooms, right there on the bed your Uncle Paul worked an hour overtime every day for months to pay off."

Jess pushed to her feet, the air she'd managed to drag in rushing just as quickly out of her. "Thank you for your time. I have to get back to the office."

Her head was spinning. Spears had found a new way to use her as a catalyst for murder. Selecting people based on locations and events in her life.

"What's this about?" Wanda asked. "Is something wrong?"

As if he'd had one ear to the door, it opened and Hayes walked in. "We ready to go, Chief?"

"Has she had lunch?" Wanda asked. "I think she needs to eat. She looks a little pale."

"I'm fine." Jess cleared her throat. She really could use a cold glass of water. *Anywhere but here.* "I'm ready, Lieutenant."

"I hate to see you run off like this," Wanda persisted. "I just fried a whole chicken. Cooked up mashed potatoes and green beans. I'll never be able to eat all that myself."

"I'm sorry—"

"I love fried chicken," Hayes said, abruptly cutting Jess off. He flashed that charming smile of his at Wanda. "I don't know about the chief, but I'm starving."

Jess wanted to kick him. She just wanted out of here! What the hell did he think he was doing?

Wanda grinned. "Well good. Come on into the kitchen and I'll pour up the iced tea."

Jess shot the lieutenant a glare. He had the audacity to smile.

Still steaming, Jess settled at the table that looked as worse for wear as the ones in the BPD interview rooms. She considered the many ways she could make Hayes pay for this. All the while he kept the conversation going with Wanda.

No wonder the man had done so well as a gigolo, he could charm anyone. Or maybe the two felt a kinship since Wanda had spent most of her adult life as a low rent prostitute.

Guilt overwhelmed Jess. One of these days she was going to have to give the woman a break whether she wanted to or not. Maybe she had done the best she could. Jess banished the crazy thoughts whirling around in her head. *Some other time she could sort all that out.*

A glass appeared in front of her. Jess managed a smile for her aunt even though she felt like running out of the room screaming. The iced tea cooled her throat, and as much as she didn't want to admit it, tasted good.

"You should like this chicken, Jessie Lee," Wanda placed a drumstick on Jess's place, "your mother taught me how to fry chicken. All these fancy cooks you see on TV got nothing on Helen Harris."

Maybe it was the idea that the chicken was her mother's recipe, whatever the reason Jess found herself nibbling on the chicken leg. The breading was amazingly crisp, but the meat beneath was tender and juicy.

"Told you it was good."

Jess looked up. Wanda and Hayes were watching her, smirks on their faces. "It is." Jess dabbed at her lips with a paper napkin. Whether she had moaned out loud, or just the fact that she was devouring the chicken that drew their attention, she couldn't say. "Delicious. Really... delicious."

By the time Jess pushed away from the table, to say she was stuffed was putting it mildly. "That was—"

"Incredible," Hayes finished for her. "I don't think I've eaten that much since the last time I had Sunday dinner at my grandmother's house."

Wanda insisted the lieutenant was welcome to have Sunday dinner with her any time. "You too, Jessie Lee." The hope in her expression was undeniable.

Jess didn't have to work too hard to present a smile. As much as she hated to admit it, she did feel better now that she'd eaten. "Thank you. I'll remember that."

Not anytime soon, but there was no need to mention that part.

"You tell your sister, too," Wanda urged as they moved back into the living room and toward the front door. "I'd love to have y'all over so we could catch up."

Jess clenched her jaw to hold back the retort that came immediately to mind. She'd put the past aside for a moment, but she couldn't hold it at bay for long. There was nothing between her and this woman except hurt. Why in the world would she pretend otherwise? She appreciated her efforts—or at least she tried to—but no amount of fried chicken and potatoes was going to change the past.

What was with all this waffling back and forth?

"When you have more time," Wanda went on, oblivious to Jess's irritation, "I'll show you the photos I have from when you were a baby." She literally beamed. "I didn't realize I had so many. But when your friend dropped by, we started talking about those days and the next thing I knew I was digging out all kinds of family photos."

Uncertainty made it impossible for Jess to move. "A friend of mine stopped by?"

Wanda nodded. "He did. A very nice man. He said he was doing a feature on you and all the work you're doing to keep Birmingham safe."

"Was his name Gerard Stevens?" Jess didn't know the man but she disliked him immensely for trying to make Dan look bad in a recent interview with Corlew, of all people. The thought made her mad at her old friend all over again.

"Oh no. It wasn't that reporter fella," Wanda assured Jess. "It was your old friend from the FBI in Virginia. His name was Ross. Ross Taylor. Said he was retired now and doing some writing for some big newspaper in Washington D.C."

Fear blasted through Jess. Special Agent Ross Taylor was dead. Eric Spears had murdered him.

"When was he here?" It took everything Jess had to keep her voice from shaking. She wanted to scream. She wanted to hunt Spears down and rip him apart with her own two hands.

"Must've been about two weeks ago. Right about the same time that policeman's wife killed his partner's wife. That case was all over the news."

Jess quieted the storm of emotions whirling inside her. "Wanda, I need you to start at the beginning and tell me everything you told him."

CHAPTER TWELVE

Dan signed the last requisition form and closed the folder. It was already half past one and he hadn't heard from Jess or anyone in SPU. Hayes should have checked in with him already. He scrubbed at his eyes and exhaled a weary breath.

The idea that Jess was out there on the streets—an open target—was driving him out of his mind. He understood her reasoning for staying on the job. She needed to be working. Hell, he needed her on the job. But the reality that any one of the warped fans Spears had watching her could so easily reach her was killing him.

Add to that the undeniable reality that the FBI was getting nowhere on the Spears investigation. They had no idea where the bastard was. He could be right here under their noses. Dan closed his eyes and forced away the images that came with that thought. Spears had touched Jess at Friday's press conference. He had been close enough to hurt her—or worse—with cops all around him.

How the hell were they going to protect her if they didn't know where the son of a bitch was?

He stood and walked to the window that overlooked the city. Ensuring the safety of the citizens of Birmingham was his responsibility. Taking care of Jess was his responsibility. He'd never felt more helpless.

With everything that was going on, he hadn't even managed time for lunch with Andrea before she went back to college for the fall semester. So much had happened this summer, starting with his stepdaughter's abduction. Those had been some scary days. But Jess had come when he'd called and she had found those girls. No one else could take credit for that incredible feat. She was a hero.

He wanted to be hers.

If anything happened to her—

The intercom on his desk buzzed and was followed by, "Chief, Mayor Pratt is on line one for you."

"And the day just gets better," he grumbled. Mayor Joseph Pratt wanted Jess gone. He was just itching to find a good reason to try and force Dan's hand. "Thanks, Sheila."

Dan blew out a breath and took the call. "Afternoon, Mayor."

"Why is Harris working this investigation? Logan Thomas's uncle called me. He, like everyone else in this city, is worried sick about Harris's ability to somehow draw these devils into our community.

How long do you plan to pretend she's an asset, Dan? It's time to look past your personal feelings and do the right thing."

For a moment Dan was lost as to how to respond to such ridiculous accusations. It took no time at all for the mayor and his cronies to forget all Jess had done for the city. Dan was well aware of Pratt's problem. The mayor's family had come under scrutiny during the 'Five' investigation. Pratt wasn't going to let that go easily.

"Joe, I understand that Jess's work to find the truth has made your family uncomfortable at times," Dan told him straight up, "but she's the best thing that's happened to this department in a very long time. Furthermore, the murders Jess is investigating at this time have nothing to do with her or Eric Spears or any damned thing else that you can logically complain about." He hadn't meant for his voice to rise as he uttered that last statement but he was sick to death of Pratt's jabs at Jess.

"That may very well be," Pratt argued, "but I'm maintaining a close watch on this situation. I will not ignore my responsibilities to this city. I would suggest you follow my example."

"Always nice to hear from you, Mayor." Dan slammed the phone down. "Narrow minded old bastard."

A rap at his door hauled his attention to yet another intrusion. "What?" Damn, he was on a roll here. If his secretary was on the other side of that door, he'd probably damaged his relationship with her permanently.

Harold Black poked his head in. "You have a minute, Chief?"

Dan took a second to find control over his frustration. "Sure." He waved in the deputy chief of the department's Crimes Against Persons Division. Harold was also working closely with Gant on the Spears investigation. Maybe they'd just gotten lucky and there was good news for a change.

Harold paused at Dan's desk, a folder tucked under his arm. "I thought I'd bring you up to speed on the Allen case."

Captain Ted Allen, head of the Gang Task Force, had gone missing almost three weeks ago. His personal vehicle had been discovered abandoned, but no other trace of him had been found until last week when his cell phone appeared in Dan's garbage. An internal investigation into Allen's activities was ongoing. No cop wanted to accuse another of wrongdoing but it was looking more and more as if that were the case.

Another sticking point in the investigation was the very public disagreements between Allen and Jess. According to his cell phone carrier, Allen had last used his cell near Jess's apartment. The fact that the same phone was found in Dan's trash made both him and Jess look suspicious. It was an uncomfortable situation, but all they could do was ride it out. Truth was on their side. Eventually that truth would come to light. Allen was either dead for things he had or had not done when dealing with one of the biggest gang leaders in the country or he'd taken a handsome payoff and disappeared for parts unknown. Either way, his return was unlikely.

"Have you uncovered new evidence? Found a witness who saw him after the night he disappeared?" If Allen hadn't gone rogue, hope of finding him alive was pretty much nonexistent at this point. For the man's family's sake, Dan wished the case was solved, one way or the other.

Harold shook his head. "Nothing like that." He opened the folder he held. "We did discover some documents in his office that are quite troubling."

Seemed a little sudden, or perhaps convenient depending upon what these documents showed. What dirty cop kept damning evidence in his office? Whether he was dirty or not, Allen was smarter than that.

Harold passed a handwritten report across Dan's desk. "Apparently, Captain Allen was planning to file a complaint against you."

"Against me?" Dan snatched up the report and skimmed it.

"He claims in that statement that you threatened him on two occasions in regard to his interactions with Chief Harris."

"This is absurd." Dan tossed the report aside. "I assume you've had the handwriting analyzed."

Harold nodded. "It's his handwriting."

Dan flatted his palms firmly on his desk and fought to hold back his outrage. The best way to handle this was to keep his cool—unlike the way he'd handled the situation with Pratt. "This is getting old, Harold. First it's the cell phone. Now this."

"I agree. But these documents were found in the due course of the investigation. I can't exactly dispose of them, Dan. Detective Roark brought them directly to me before turning them into evidence. No one wants to set this kind of nasty business in motion, but we simply have no choice. We must treat you the same way we would any other person of interest on a case."

"Don't patronize me, Harold. I know what we *must* do. But that doesn't mean I have to like it."

Harold nodded. "No one likes it, Dan. We're working as hard as we can to solve this mystery."

"You do what you need to do," Dan reminded him. "But along the way, remember that this," he gestured to the report, "is pure fiction. If Ted Allen wrote that report he was either out of his mind or lying."

"I agree." Harold stood. "I'll keep you apprised of any new developments."

"Thanks. I appreciate the update." Better to be aware of potential trouble than to be blindsided.

When Harold was out the door, Dan picked up his cell. He couldn't wait any longer. Jess should have checked in with him by now. He needed to hear her voice as often as possible.

The idea that Spears could be watching her every move from right here in Birmingham had him on edge. His phone vibrated with an incoming text.

"It's about time." He tapped the screen expecting to see Jess's image along with a text.

He stilled. Not Jess. The number wasn't one he recognized. He opened the text.

Want to know how this story will end? Oak Hill. Near Linn Mausoleum. Cheers, ES

"Son of a bitch!" Dan shoved his phone into his pocket and rushed around his desk. He stormed out of his office. "Have Chief Black and someone from the crime scene unit meet me at Linn Mausoleum at Oak Hill Cemetery," he said to Sheila.

His secretary was already passing along the order before Dan was out of earshot. He bypassed the elevator and took the stairs.

At least Spears was playing his game with him today and not Jess and that suited Dan just fine. If Spears made the mistake of getting close again, Dan planned to be the only one walking away this time.

OAK HILL CEMETERY, 2:33 P.M.

Dan strode through the gates of Birmingham's oldest cemetery. Many of the city's pioneers were laid to rest here, including Charles Linn. The park where the press conference had been held last Friday was named after him. Spears apparently wanted to remind Dan that he'd missed his opportunity there.

"What's going on, Dan?" Harold Black hurried to catch up with him. "A tech from the crime scene unit is on the way."

"Shortly after you left my office I received a text from Spears. He said there was something here that would tell me how this story is going to end." He glanced at Harold. "I guess he doesn't want to keep me in suspense."

"Have you called Gant?"

"Not yet. Let's see what we're dealing with first." There was no need to have the FBI over here until they had confirmation this was more than a wild goose chase.

Harold surveyed the headstones, statues, and mausoleums that dotted the hillside. "What is that monster up to now?"

"We'll soon know." Dan paused long enough to find his bearings. He hadn't been in this cemetery in ages. He spotted his destination. "There. The Linn Mausoleum."

"Did he give you any indication of what we're looking for?"

"No. Just that it was here." They reached the mausoleum but if Spears had left anything it wasn't readily apparent.

Dan turned all the way around, scanning the hillside. "It could be a setup."

"I considered that," Black said as he, too, looked around. "I figured you would be too angry to think of it before showing up here."

The uniforms came into view. Cops were heading their way from every direction.

"Thanks." Dan railed at Jess all the time for doing this very thing. He'd acted on impulse, without thought as to the danger. "Let's have a look around the mausoleum."

Harold went one way and Dan took the other, circling the stone house that stood as a monument to one man's contributions to the Magic City. On the other side of the mausoleum, beneath the shade of a big oak tree, was a headstone. This one wasn't aged by time and the elements.

"Oh my," Harold murmured. "I think we're going to need a forklift to take this chunk of evidence to the lab."

The date of birth was chiseled into the stone, month, day and year. Where the date of death should have been were two words: *Very Soon.*

The name inscribed in large, sweeping letters across the front was *Daniel T. Burnett.*

CHAPTER THIRTEEN

Harper stretched a map of the city on one end of the case board. Lori added new notes beneath the photos of victims and the persons of interest they had so far. As of now, the video was all they had on the Thomas murder. Not one soul in the building had seen or heard a thing until the music woke the closest neighbors. Evidently the two women, if they were indeed the killers, had set the timer on the iPad for the music to go on at just the right time. Neighbors would be roused and the cops would be called. All accomplished long after they were gone.

Officer Cook was still interviewing the young man's coworkers. No forensic reports were back yet. Hayes was coordinating the surveillance details. Wanda and Lil's homes were on the top of his list. Jess had called her sister as soon as they'd left Wanda's. Lil assured Jess she hadn't seen any strangers in her neighborhood, and she promised to cooperate with the detail assigned to her. A call to

Mr. Louis had been next. He needed a detail, too, though he insisted the extra trouble wasn't necessary. Jess had added one to Dan's parent's home as well. They couldn't take any risks with the people closest to them. Corlew outright refused to have a cop following him around. Jess didn't want to know his reasons. The business of private investigations occasionally skirted the law. Corlew would be no exception just because he was an ex-cop.

The department's budget was going to take a major hit. Something else to put Dan in the hot seat with the mayor and it was her fault.

For almost twenty years her job had been to help find the monsters among society. She had made the decision to put herself in harm's way by going into this line of work. It was just wrong for her family and friends to suffer because of her choices.

Don't dwell on what you can't change. Do what you have to do. Agonizing over what wasn't right in all of this wouldn't change a thing.

Jess reread the lines in her notes she'd reviewed twice already. The ability to concentrate eluded her. They were almost forty-eight hours into this investigation and she couldn't seem to catch up. Her mind wouldn't stay focused. She was relying heavily on her team for interviews and fieldwork. Generally, she preferred to be involved in as much of that work as possible herself. Not this time. As much as she wished she could blame it on hormones, it wasn't that at all.

What she felt was guilt. These people were dead because of her.

She set her notes aside and stood. Lisa Templeton had come here for a new beginning. A fresh start. Instead, she and the woman she loved became ensnared in Spears's evil scheme. Now both were dead. Burgess's family had come to Birmingham and identified her body. Templeton's, on the other hand, had chosen not to bother. Instead, they had ID'd the body from a photo faxed to the police department there. One last injustice to a woman who only wanted to live her life her way. When the body was released, it would be shipped like a box of fall bulbs to her childhood home to be planted.

Home. Jess closed her eyes. Wherever it was, it should be a place where you felt happy and safe. The homes these victims had chosen had cost them their lives.

Her eyes flew open and she stared at the faces on the case board. Fury blazed a path through her. And here she was feeling sorry for herself.

"The house where you and your sister grew up is here."

Harper's voice jerked her to attention. She adjusted her glasses and moved to the case board to view the map. He circled the Irondale address where she had lived until she was ten with her parents. The sergeant was wrong about growing up there. That part of her life had ended abruptly at age ten. She and Lily had been snatched away from their home and dropped off in Druid Hills to live with Wanda.

Even with loving parents and a cozy little home, they hadn't been safe from the ugliness that fate had thrown in their path.

"Your sister's home in Bessemer is right there." He made another circle. "This is Lori's old apartment and the one you rent from Mr. Louis." Harper circled those two, and then glanced at Jess. "The chief's house is here." One last spot on the map was ringed in red. "Did I miss anything, ma'am?"

"I wish I knew, Sergeant." How far back did she go? Did she consider the homes of kids she'd known in school? She'd had her share of sleepovers. It was impossible to guess how deep Spears would dig to find relevant details about her past. "With what little we have to go on, it seems reasonable to say he's targeted places where significant life events took place." She glanced over at Hayes. "Do we have someone at the Irondale house yet?"

Hayes was still on the phone but he gave her a thumbs up.

She breathed a little easier, but she feared their efforts would never be enough. "We're casting stones in the dark, Sergeant. Hoping to hit the objective."

Lori moved into their huddle. "I spoke to Chief Burnett's secretary."

"Is he on his way?" Jess cringed at how needy she sounded. Dan should know about this. Either his phone was dead or he was in a meeting. As much as she hated to admit it, now she knew how he felt when he couldn't reach her. She didn't like it.

"She said he and Chief Black are at Oak Hill."

"The cemetery?" Had there been another murder? She looked to Harper. "Is something going on over there?"

"Nothing I've heard about."

"Sheila said she'd give him the message." Lori held up her cell. "Do you want me to call him directly?"

"I guess not." If he was in the middle of a briefing or some meeting with city planners, there was no truly pressing reason to disturb him. Not at this point anyway. Jess rubbed at the lines on her brow. "Let's release the photo of the blonde to the public. See if anyone recognizes her. Call Gina Coleman. Maybe she can expedite things at her station." The city's television sweetheart could get the ball rolling. Coleman had been helpful to the department and to Jess in the past.

"That could be a problem," Hayes said as he approached, "if it turns out the women are nothing more than friends of one of the residents. People love filing lawsuits."

"No one in the building recognized her," Lori countered. "Or had guests who left at that hour."

"Maybe," he nodded toward the photo taken from the video footage, "if they're working girls it's possible no one wants to remember seeing them."

"Thomas most likely brought them home with him, but since no one we've contacted knows where he was earlier that evening, we can't confirm it." Jess wanted to scream. They'd had no luck tracing the number of the phone that sent the text with the video. They needed more. Something. *Anything*.

"Maybe Cook will find someone who knows where Logan was and who he was with," Harper suggested. "He's still pounding the pavement."

"Am I sending out the photo or not?" Lori looked to Jess for a yay or nay.

"Send it to Coleman first. Tell her to move fast, and then send it to the others." Jess wasn't waiting. These two killers—if these women were their killers—were working way too quickly. "Lieutenant," she turned to Hayes, "you and I are taking a walk down memory lane."

Hayes glanced at the map. "Irondale?"

"That's right." Jess walked to her desk and grabbed her bag. "Sergeant, you and Detective Wells go through the lists of friends and coworkers for all three victims. See if they have any in common. Run through those closest to the victims first and see if anyone recognizes the blonde. Somebody somewhere has to know her."

"On it, Chief," Harper assured her.

Jess hadn't been back to the Irondale house since she left Birmingham at eighteen. She hoped whoever resided there now was still breathing.

TWENTIETH STREET SOUTH.
IRONDALE, 4:05 P.M.

Lieutenant Hayes parked at the curb in front of the house that Jess had once called home. She hadn't expected it to be abandoned. The local detective Hayes had spoken to while they were en route said no one lived in the house. From the looks of things no one had lived here for a very long time.

One less surveillance detail.

166

Seeing the house this way startled Jess a little. It looked nothing like the home she recalled. Most of the windows were boarded up. Pale blue paint peeled from the wood siding. The yard was a jungle, overgrown with weeds more than waist deep. The house next door was gone entirely, leaving a chimney standing among the wilderness of tangled bushes. On the opposite side of the street an old store was boarded up. Memories of her and Lil skipping across that street for ice cream filtered through her mind. Pigtails flopping as they giggled and acted silly the way young girls will.

Summers were spent in the backyard climbing trees and running through the sprinkler her mother used to water the lawn. Alabama summers could be hell on lawns and gardens. Some days her mother would prepare a picnic basket and the three of them would spread out on a blanket beneath the big maple tree Jess loved climbing. Their father was always on the road. But his homecomings were vivid recollections of hugs and presents and special dinners.

Wanda's tales of how Jess's mom had been afraid of her husband, of how she feared for their lives, shattered the pleasant memories.

"Do you want to go inside, Chief?"

Jess shifted back to the present. There really was no need to even get out of the car.

"Yes," she decided. They were here. They might as well have a look.

Hayes went through the usual routine. He got out, surveyed the street, and came around to her side of the car. When he opened the door, she climbed out and spotted her personal BPD detail parked nearby.

Dan still hadn't called her. What could be so important at the cemetery that he wasn't taking calls?

Just wait until he nagged her again about ignoring his calls.

The sidewalk was cracked and grass had taken up residence wherever there was a gap in the old concrete. The heat and humidity were oppressive. She pulled at her blouse. August couldn't be over soon enough.

"Let's try the front door," she suggested. She had no desire to wade through the overgrown yard to have a look around back.

Two steps led up to the porch. Sagging boards creaked with their weight. A tree had sprouted in an area that was completely rotted through. Bird nests sat on every available ledge overhead and the tops of the doors and windows. Hooks that once supported a swing at one end of the porch remained, but the swing was long gone. The remembered sound of laughter rang in Jess's ears as images of her and Lil swaying back and forth on that old swing played inside her.

"Is this breaking and entering?" Hayes tested the door.

It was nailed shut but it didn't look as if it would take much effort to change that. "We have exigent circumstances, Lieutenant. Since this house fits the profile of our crime scenes, we have to operate under the assumption there may be a victim inside."

He scrutinized the door. "Works for me."

Jess glanced around the street. Not that there was anyone who might wonder what they were doing. When had this little section of the neighborhood died?

A lot could change in three decades. She'd always pictured this place as staying exactly the same. Even now, she half expected her mother to come out the door shouting for her and Lil to come in for dinner.

The door burst inward. Jess jumped. She stretched the kinks from her neck, squared her shoulders and followed Hayes inside. The house was as dark as a dungeon.

"I have a flashlight in the car."

"I'll just wait here in the shade, Lieutenant." One of the perks of being the boss was that someone else had to do the running. It was certainly cooler in here, musty and dank, but cooler.

She checked her cell again. Still nothing from Dan.

By the time she'd scrounged up her penlight, Hayes had returned with his flashlight. "Lead on, Lieutenant." This was one time she was more than happy to have someone else go first.

The front room was littered with trash. Discarded food containers and various items of clothing. No decomp smells, thank goodness. Whoever had left the mess it had been a while ago. The ash and remnants of firewood scattered across the hearth suggested the mess had been made last winter. Homeless folks often spent cold nights in abandoned houses. The floors were dirty and dusty but there were no tracks in the dust. Backed up the conclusion no one had been in the house for several months at least.

Moving toward the dining room, Hayes suddenly stopped. The beam of the flashlight he carried paused on the wall above the doorway that separated the living area from the dining room.

It took several seconds for the words scrawled on the wall to penetrate the state of shock and disbelief that instinctively swaddled her brain.

Welcome home, Jess.

6:01 P.M.

Jess sat on the top step as members of the crime scene unit went in and out around her. The sound of hammers and drills played like a twisted score to the comings and goings of the characters in this bad movie in which she was the leading lady. Lori and Harper had arrived. Harper and Hayes had decided to remove some of the boards over the windows to allow some light air inside. Local cops had shown up with the necessary tools. BPD's crime scene unit showed up eventually with lots more lights. Every crack and crevice of the house would be explored.

Lori had started with the closest neighbor to get some recent background on the property. When had the last residents lived here? Had they seen any strangers in the area? Any noise coming from the abandoned house or store?

The intruder who'd left the message had come in through the back door. The tracks in the dust on the hardwood in that part of the house were recent.

This was the only real home Jess had known as a child. Somehow, the intrusion felt more injurious than the break-in last month at her house in Stafford. This marred those early years—innocent years—and damaged the few precious memories she had of her parents. It made her sick to her stomach.

Equally unsettling was the realization that, until today, she'd had no idea she was born in her aunt's house, with said aunt participating in the delivery. The few pictures she had from her childhood were all taken here. Yet Wanda had photos that were taken at her old house—the one where the first two murder victims had been found.

A big black Mercedes braked to a stop amid the chaos in the street. Jess's heart lightened as Dan emerged from his SUV. She blinked at the sudden rush of tears and cursed herself. *Damned hormones.* As he walked toward her, she stood, fighting the urge to rush into his arms.

"Hey." He reached out and squeezed her hand and her entire being reacted.

"What happened at the cemetery?" She cleared her throat and dusted off her backside. She probably had dirt and grime all over the skirt of her new suit. Lil would scold her if she found out. "You were MIA for a while."

"Vandalism." He glanced toward the activity beyond the door.

"Vandalism?" The chief of police was called out for vandalism?

"It's a historic cemetery, Jess." He took her by the elbow and ushered her across the porch.

Vandalism kept him from calling? "Spears visited Wanda."

Her announcement gave him pause. "When did this happen?"

"Two weeks ago. Didn't you get your messages?"

"My secretary called but I…" He heaved a big breath. "I should've called her back."

"Or me," Jess admonished.

He held up his hands surrender style. "I won't let it happen again."

"How did you know to come here?" If he hadn't called his secretary back, how was he here now? This made no sense. Mainly she just wanted something else besides Spears, this place and the murders to be riled up about.

"Hayes called me."

She raised an eyebrow at him. "You took his call but not mine?"

"I was just about to call you back when he called."

What did it matter? "I'm glad you're here." She had no right to interrogate him just because he hadn't responded to her messages. God knew, she did it to him all the time. They weren't anywhere close to even on that score no matter how she tried to spin it.

"You want to go back inside?"

She nodded. "You should have a look."

They entered her childhood home together. Having Dan at her side made being here less disconcerting. Her detectives had been successful in uncovering several windows. The light filtering through their damaged and grimy panes didn't make the rundown conditions inside look any better. A crime scene tech was still setting up the lights that would make the search for evidence considerably easier.

The message left for Jess had been spray-painted in black across the once yellow wall. Rather than linger on the words, she moved through the house. The kitchen was in worse shape than the living and dining rooms. The backdoor hung onto its hinges by a prayer. The intruder had done a number on it.

Down the hall were the two bedrooms and the single bathroom. The room she and Lil shared was the first one. If she'd expected to find anything there besides more dust, cobwebs and disrepair, she was disappointed. The walls had once been pink. Now they were an unhappy green. A round rug with circles of bold colors had covered most of the hardwood when they were kids. She and Lil had had twin beds and two dressers because neither had wanted to share drawers or mirrors.

Why hadn't Lil told her the place had fallen into ruins? Surely she'd driven by at some point in the last twenty or so years. Not that it mattered, but it just seemed strange to see their childhood home like this and not to have known.

Dan came up behind her. "Let me take you home, Jess. There's nothing else you can do here."

He was right. She and three of her team were here, wasting time. Their resources were needed elsewhere.

Distraction was his goal.

She'd let Spears get to her with his antics and diversions.

Not anymore.

CHAPTER FOURTEEN

Naked and still damp from their shower, Lori collapsed onto the bed. She felt more relaxed than she had in weeks despite three totally freaky murders. It had taken years but she'd had to learn to turn off work when she was home. Protecting her mental health after the abduction by Eric Spears's apprentice had become particularly important to her sanity.

Chet swaggered toward the bed naked as the day he was born, and she grinned. He had helped her through some difficult times.

Mostly he had stolen her heart.

"That was fantastic." Chet dropped next to her.

She snuggled closer to him. "Yes it was."

The silence was comfortable. She could lie here all night listening to nothing more than the sound of him breathing and the feel of his heart beating as her body melded with his.

"The chief is really off her game this week," he said.

As much as she would prefer not to agree with him, it was true. "She has reason to be."

"That she does."

Lori raised up, settled her chin on his chest. "I wish we could do more. Why the hell can't the FBI find this piece of shit? He can't be that good."

Chet sent her a look. "I think you know better than that. Spears is not your run of the mill serial killer. He's some kind of genius. Not to mention he's rich. The guy probably has money hidden all over the world. It's hard to find someone who has those kind of resources at his fingertips."

She couldn't argue that either. "It just frustrates me. Jess has already suffered so much. It's not fair that he keeps torturing her this way. Every time somebody dies, you can just see the toll it takes on her. She feels like it's her fault."

"I know." Chet stroked her hair. "Have you noticed that since Hayes joined the team it feels like she's pushing us away?"

Lori knew where he was headed with that. "I don't think Clint is going to take your place or mine when it comes to our bond with Jess."

"I guess it's an ego thing," Chet admitted. "Feels like she's picking him instead of one of us whenever she makes a move."

Lori caressed his sculpted abs. He had one hell of a six-pack. "I think maybe she's trying to protect us. If she keeps us at a distance, maybe we won't be targets or something."

Chet hissed a curse. "I need to be protecting her. Hayes doesn't know her like I do. I should talk to her."

"Give her some time. She's trying to find her footing in all this insanity. Don't push." Lori raked the pad of her thumb over his flat, taut nipple. He shivered. She loved it. "I'll talk to her when the time's right."

"Before you start something I'll have to finish," he pulled her on top of him, breasts to chest, and wrapped his arms around her waist, "there's something else we need to talk about."

She was the one shivering now. "I might have trouble concentrating in this position." She ground her hips into his. They both shuddered.

"It's about Chester."

Lori stilled. Their weekend to have Chet's little boy was coming up. They'd had to miss tonight's visit. "Is Sherry trying to keep him home again?"

Chet's ex-wife had been behaving a little flaky lately. She was always coming up with excuses why Chester couldn't have his visits with his father. Lori got it. The woman was worried her three-year-old would like Lori too much. All she could say was that the bitch should have thought about that when she kicked a good man like Chet to the curb.

"I think she's calmed down now. She didn't go schitzo when I told her we were on a tough case and wouldn't be able to pick him up today. She even sounded disappointed he wouldn't get to spend time with us."

Lori wasn't going to sugarcoat her feelings about the woman. "I'm glad but I don't know if I'll ever trust her again."

He kissed her nose. "I understand. She tried to mess with your head and that was wrong."

"What were you going to say about Chester before I butted in?" She hoped the little boy wasn't sick.

"After what we found out today, maybe not having Chester around until this is over is a good idea." Pain clouded his handsome face. "What if that bastard got to him?"

Lori saw the torment in his eyes and couldn't bear it. "I hadn't thought about that. You're right. Spears or one of his pals could show up anywhere. None of us are safe from him. If he's behind these latest murders, there's no telling what he might do next."

"I should talk to Sherry."

"Good idea. We don't want Chester anywhere near this nightmare." If they couldn't stop this freak of nature, how would their lives ever be normal again?

"Did you hear what happened at Oak Hill today?"

Lori braced her forearms on his chest and searched his face for clues. "I didn't. Something happen with Burnett?"

"Detective Roark told me Burnett received a text from Spears. Said there was a preview of things to come at the Linn Mausoleum. Burnett rushed over and found a headstone with his name on it."

"Are you serious?" The image made Lori shudder.

Chet nodded. "I don't think Chief Harris knew. After what she found out today, he probably didn't want to tell her until they were alone."

"Damn." Lori shook her head. "Spears is getting bolder."

"For sure."

A rush of fear chilled her to the bone. "I want you to promise me you'll be careful. I don't want to lose you to this."

Chet hugged his arms tighter around her. "Why would you think you'd lose me? I'm not letting that bastard get to any of us. You can take that to the bank."

Lori prayed that was a promise he could keep.

He caressed her back, trailed his fingers long ribs. "I got a call today."

She shivered as he cupped her breast. "From?"

"My doc."

Her heart beat a little faster. "What did she say?"

"I have an appointment with the surgeon next week. He'll do the necessary tests and we'll go from there. We should know soon if the reversal is possible."

"Sounds to me like a celebration is in order." She went up on her knees, straddling his waist. "You up for it, Sergeant?"

"Always, Detective."

With him guiding, she eased down onto his erection. Her eyes closed and she moaned. She had never wanted anyone the way she did this man. No one was taking him away from her.

Not his ex-wife and definitely not Eric Spears.

CHAPTER FIFTEEN

Jess sat crossed legged on the floor in the library or office or whatever Dan called this room. She stared at the make shift case board she'd cobbled together. A strip of tape, the kind used for wrapping Christmas gifts, held each photo and note to the edge of a bookshelf. Made her feel right at home.

Almost. She still missed her place. Her stuff was there. Here she had Dan, a more than decent trade off considering she loved waking up next to him. The thought made her feel warm and safe, despite the images hanging in front of her.

Get your mind on the case.

The first victims were murdered in the house where she was born. But why hadn't she received a video as she had with Logan Thomas. Serial killers rarely deviated from their pattern unless an unanticipated occurrence or reaction forced change. Then again, were these two women really serial killers in the true sense of the word? Or were they merely thrill killers on a rampage, disorganized and manic in their murder methods but highly organized on entrance and exit protocols?

Had Templeton and Burgess been their first kills? Their fingerprints weren't on file in the usual databases. The blonde looked very young, nineteen or twenty. Was SPU witnessing the birth of pure evil? The evolution of cold-blooded killers?

Jess wrapped her arms around her waist. To protect the people she cared about, including herself, if given the chance she would kill Eric Spears. Right now, without hesitation. It wouldn't matter if he were unarmed or debilitated. Hatred hardened her heart. She would kill him.

Did that make her a monster, too?

Jess turned away from the images of innocence slaughtered and drew in a shaky breath. Two decades of experience analyzing killers had taught her that all humans possessed the potential for evil. Some never crossed that, at times, blurred line. Others not only crossed it but plunged into an abyss of darkness where right and wrong no longer existed. They thrived on desire, greed, fear and rage.

Crossing the line was always accompanied by motive, some precipitating event or emotion that served as an impetus to the act of evil.

But what about these murders?

If Spears had initiated these heinous acts, had he paid the killers or were these kills some sort of initiation into his twisted club? *The Eric Spears fan club.* Anger burst so fast inside her that her ribs ached.

With her whole being she hoped to live to see him die a slow, excruciating death of utter agony.

She hugged herself more tightly. There were lots of reasons she intended to see that Spears lost this game. To that end, she needed this time alone to sort through and analyze the events of the day. Dan had grudgingly taken her by the office so she could get the copies she needed for creating this homework board. Cook had caught her there and briefed her on what he'd discovered which was basically nothing. None of the friends or coworkers of the two female victims knew the male victim and vice versa and not one recognized the blonde suspect.

She'd had high hopes for that discovery.

"I see you found a way to do your homework."

Jess glanced over her shoulder. "I told you I can't think without my case board."

He sat down on the floor beside her and put his arm around her. "You should work at home more often. I like the outfit."

As tired as she was, as worried as she was, she had to laugh. After a nice, long hot bath she'd shoved her damp hair into a claw clip and grabbed the most comfortable thing she could find to sleep in. "This Crimson Tide t-shirt of yours has seen better days."

He leaned over, kissed her cheek. Goosebumps rushed over her skin. "I've had it forever."

"I know." She looked into those blue eyes that still had the power to make her heart beat faster. "I remember it." She knew exactly how it looked stretched across those broad shoulders and that gorgeous chest that was temptingly bare right now. How nice it would be to lose herself in Dan's arms and forget all of this but that wasn't possible.

Jess closed her eyes and willed back the emotions crowding in on her.

"He's trying to get to you, you know." Dan trailed the tip of his finger along her jaw. "Digging up the past, trying to make you feel guilty for what he's doing."

"I know." She opened her eyes and smiled at him. "He seems to know more about my past than I do." The idea made her heartsick. "We made love in that bedroom of your old apartment."

A faint smile touched Dan's lips. "Over and over. I wanted you more than I wanted to wake up the next morning."

"I was so angry with myself for wanting you that much." She angled her head, studied the face of the man who had never permitted her to fall in love with anyone else. Not even the man she'd married. She'd cared about Wesley Duvall, but she'd never been able to love him the way she loved Dan. "Once I was back in Virginia I couldn't look in the mirror for days."

"You were too hard-headed to admit you still felt something for me."

Ten years ago Dan Burnett had been a handsome mover and shaker in this city. He still was. It seemed impossible that he had experienced the same uncertainties she had. "I was afraid you were rebounding after your divorce. I couldn't take the risk."

"We wasted a lot of time."

They had. They really, really had. "Too much," she agreed.

He tilted her chin up and looked into her eyes. "We have the rest of our lives ahead of us. No one is taking that away. No fear, okay?"

She nodded and reached up and caressed his jaw. "You are the one thing in all this that I am absolutely certain of. I hope you know that."

He looked away for a moment before meeting her gaze once more. "Your trust means a great deal to me."

She smiled. "We will get through this. Spears thinks he's smart. Finding out where I was born wasn't so hard. He just asked my aunt. But," she felt a trickle of that old uncertainty, "how did he know about that night we spent together?"

"Maybe he didn't. Maybe he was showing us he knew where I lived, too."

"I don't know." She chewed her lip. "Seems like he chose those two places because they were significant to my life. I just don't know how he could know that one thing."

Dan dropped his head. She frowned. What was this all about?

"We need to talk." He lifted his gaze to hers once more.

She didn't like what she saw in his eyes. He couldn't know. Hayes wouldn't dare. "Bout what?"

"Today when you couldn't reach me—"

"You were at Birmingham's historic cemetery, I know." She twirled a finger in the air in a whoop-de-do gesture. "Was the mayor there, too?" The city's hierarchy loved making a production out of every little thing.

He shook his head and looked away again.

Uh-oh. "What is it you don't want to tell me?" Like she could chastise anyone for keeping secrets. She had become a consummate secret keeper.

A huge lump rose in her throat. She was going to have a baby. *His baby.* She couldn't keep putting off that conversation. "You're right," she admitted, "we do need to talk." She had put this off long enough.

"Spears sent me a text," he said.

Cold invaded the comfortable warmth being near Dan had provided. Why couldn't it have been something simple like a rendezvous with Annette, his most recent ex-wife? Then again why was she surprised? Spears had visited her aunt. God only knew what he would do next. She'd already checked twice tonight with Lily to see that her surveillance detail was in place and that she remembered not to take anything for granted. 'Be aware' had to be her mantra.

"What did he say?" Jess braced for the rest.

Dan tucked a loose strand of hair behind her ear. "He said he'd left something for me at the cemetery."

Tension coiled tighter inside her. When would this stop? She pushed the feelings away, had to be strong. Why was she having such trouble doing that lately? *Dammit.* "So you went to Oak Hill."

Worry darkened his eyes the way clouds blackened the sky right before a storm. "He had a headstone made with my name on it."

Any chance of holding back her emotions evaporated. She shot to her feet and started to pace. *Don't fall apart. Don't fall apart.* "Was there a date of death?" He wasn't telling her everything. She could see it on his face. Dan had never been any good at hiding what was on his mind.

"In a manner of speaking." He stood, set his hands on his hips. "Very soon. That was the date. *Very soon.*"

She stamped out of the room. Boy, did she need some coffee or Pepsi or something. Maybe one of those one pound Hershey bars.

Dan trailed behind her. As she rummaged through the fridge for her favorite cola, he waited patiently for her to calm down enough to be rational. That was another thing he did. Always.

She grabbed a bottle, twisted off the cap and had a long swallow of Pepsi as she elbowed the fridge closed. Then, she glared at him. Wished he didn't look so good. Wished even harder she didn't notice. If she hadn't been so flipping mad she would have told him how sexy he looked in those sweatpants even at a time like this. But she was too ticked off right now. And too damned scared.

She lowered the bottle and wiped her mouth with her forearm. "Did you call Gant?"

She certainly had. One of the first things she'd done after she left Wanda's house was to call Gant.

She followed the proper protocol since he was in charge of the Spears investigation. He hadn't said a damned word about this headstone business. Knowing Dan, he'd insisted that Gant let him tell her.

Somewhere beneath all the frustration, she understood she was the pot calling the kettle black. But that was irrelevant at the moment, at least in her mind.

"I did. He sent Agent Manning over for a look. Crime scene unit lugged the damned headstone to the lab. One of the clerks at Birmingham Monuments said the man who placed the order claimed he was my cousin. He said it was a joke."

Jess reminded herself this could be just another one of Spears's distractions, like the message at her childhood home. He wanted them off balance.

Except three people were dead. People Spears had never met before and who weren't his type at all. One woman was still missing. "What did Gant say about the headstone? He certainly didn't have anything new to tell me."

Dozens of young, beautiful women had been murdered by Eric Spears, aka the Player. The Bureau had been on the trail of the Player for years. Jess had figured out who he was… had almost nailed him. But she screwed up and he'd walked away, free to continue his sprees of torture and murder. But now he was a wanted man. Despite the Bureau seizing his company, SpearNet, and every other known asset, Spears evidently had endless resources they didn't know about, probably in countries that wouldn't cooperate even if they did know.

But the most terrifying part about all of this had nothing to do with his assets, it was the reality that he no longer had anything to lose.

His life as Eric Spears was basically over. If he intended to remain a free man, eventually he would need to use those many assets to fade into obscurity. This big production he'd set in motion was his end game. The final public curtain call for the serial killer known as the Player.

And Jess was the award for best performance.

How many people was she going to let die before she gave him what he wanted?

Fear, dread, rage, all of it swirled like a hurricane inside her. Only she couldn't give him what he wanted. Another innocent life was depending on her. Yet, if they didn't stop him while he was still playing this game with her, he might never be stopped. The concept of how many people he could potentially kill in his lifetime was inconceivable.

"Gant added the headstone to his growing list of moves Spears has made without leaving a traceable path." Dan shook his head, physically and mentally exhausted just as she was. They were both barely hanging on by a thread. "What else could he say?"

Jess set her Pepsi on the counter and went to him. Arms locked around his waist, mostly to keep herself steady or maybe just so she couldn't turn tail and run, she pressed her cheek to his chest. "There's something else we should talk about."

"This sounds serious."

"It is." She'd managed to find a hundred ways to put this off but now she looked forward to the weight that would be lifted. Lieutenant Hayes was right. Carrying this load alone was too much. She and Dan needed to do this together.

A vibrating sound echoed around them. Dan glanced toward the island. Jess didn't have to look to know it was his cell phone.

"Go ahead." She dropped her arms to her sides and stepped back. "It could be Gant." Dan hesitated. "Take the call," she insisted. Her secret would keep a few more minutes.

Jess put her face in her hands and rubbed her eyes. She was so tired. Maybe Spears's real goal was too wear her down. She was exhausted, that was true enough, but she wasn't allowing him to win. She might have suffered a few stumbles lately but she would regain her footing. The deep sound of Dan's voice soothed her frayed nerves. She smiled. Being here with him was right.

No matter what Corlew or Katherine or anyone else said, this was where she belonged, with Dan.

"On our way."

Those three words chased away the warm fuzzy feelings. She didn't have the wherewithal to even ask what had happened now.

"That was Gina."

"At this hour?" Jealousy reared its ugly head. *So sue me.* She was only human.

"One of the calls to the station's hotline panned out." He took Jess by the elbow and steered her toward the hall. "There's a man on his way to Gina's station right now who swears he knows who the blonde is and where she lives."

"Finally." Jess's tension eased a fraction. "Some good news."

It was about time they caught a break.

CHANNEL 6, THURSDAY,
AUGUST 26, 1:20 A.M.

Jeremy Kendall was twenty-five years old. He was good looking in that emo guy sort of way with his black skinny jeans and extra tight black shirt. Dark eyes and even darker hair cut in that swing style that hung low across an attractive yet pale face. The kid needed a little sun. He had two eyebrow rings and a tongue stud that affected his speech ever so slightly. He was also the manager of an ultra cool dance club, he claimed, called Raw for those who liked living on the edge.

"Jeremy, you understand that time is of the essence here," Jess explained, "if you're not certain about this we don't want to waste city resources trying to find this young lady."

He smiled at Jess. "You are so nice but—fair warning—she is not a lady." He tapped the blonde's image. "This one's a straight up hard core bitch who would not only scratch out your eyes she'd eat them, too."

The image of the blonde eating a heart flashed in front of her eyes before Jess could stop it. "Well, all right then. But you're positive this is the woman you know as Selma Vance."

"Umm-hmm. That's her." He sat back, pale arms crossed over his chest. "I had to throw her out of my place Saturday night."

"Really?" Jess readied her pencil.

"She and her sister started a fight with one of my preferred members."

"She has a sister?"

"Yeah, that's probably her there. Olive." He tapped the brunette in the photo, the one with her back turned to the camera. "She doesn't say much, but I've heard rumors she's even more twisted than her sister."

"Do these sisters live together?"

He nodded. "After I saw the eleven o'clock news I reached out to a few friends to get the four-one-one on their habitat. They live over on Victoria Road in Mountain Brook. Really rich parents who live in France most of the time. The sisters have the run of the place and of their plastic."

"Do Selma and Olive have jobs? Go to school?" With mommy and daddy's plastic at their disposal maybe not.

He leaned forward and braced his elbows on the table. "Think the Kardashians, only way creepier."

Well, that explained everything. "What was this fight on Saturday night about?"

He shrugged. "They were blitzed. Celebrating some major happening the next night."

Jess supposed murdering two women and ripping out their hearts would qualify as a major happening. "Are Selma or Olive bisexual?"

Another shrug. "Isn't everyone?" He gifted her with a knowing smile. "Society is evolving. Boundaries are changing."

That was the truth. "Do the sisters have any friends they hang out with on a regular basis? Maybe someone was with them Saturday night?"

"The only time they have friends is when they're buying. No one wants to hang with those foul bitches unless they're laying out the cash."

"Thank you, Mr. Kendall." Jess gathered her pad and pencil. "I may want to speak with you again. Would that be all right?"

"That's cool. You can find me at Raw from dusk to dawn."

No wonder he was so pale. He probably slept all day.

Jess walked him to the door. He hesitated before leaving the room. "You should watch yourself with these two. They would do anything," he looked her straight in the eyes, "*anything* for excitement. They're mental, for real. Hitchcock psychos."

"Thank you." Jess gave him a smile. "I'll remember that."

Gina, decked out as if she were about to go on the air, thanked the young man for doing his civic duty as she showed him out of the studio. Jess groaned. She'd pulled on a pair of sweats with this old tee. She stared at her flip-flops. She couldn't even remember the last time she'd had a pedicure. Another groan escaped her as she slung her bag on her shoulder. She needed some me time.

She clopped out to the corridor to find Dan, who looked amazing in those same sweats and a plain white tee, chatting with gorgeous Gina.

God, she hated beautiful people. Not really, she was just feeling sorry for herself. Again. Gina was smart and actually pretty nice. One day Jess would get over being jealous of the women who'd had relationships, however superficial, with Dan.

Lori and Harper appeared just then. Jess had never been so glad to see anyone.

"Hayes and Cook are on the way," Harper confirmed.

"We have an ID on the two women on the video." Jess smiled, thankful for a small triumph. "And an address."

"Do we need a search warrant?" Lori was already reaching for her cell.

"Let's do a drive by and check it out first."

"You riding with us, ma'am?"

Jess shook her head at Harper. "Dan's coming. I'll ride with him."

She didn't want him out of her sight. Not after that delivery from Spears.

Now who wanted to hover?

Before heading out, Jess thanked Gina again for coming through. As jealous as she was of the woman at times, she was a sort-of friend, too. Like Sylvia. Jess had always been too busy to have many friends.

All of a sudden she had several... sort of. Maybe that was why she had so much trouble deciding if they were really friends or not.

"Keep me posted," Gina called after them.

Jess gave her a wave. "The exclusive is yours." It always paid to have someone in the media on your side.

"Love the tee, by the way." Gina pointed at Jess, then gave a thumbs up. "Roll Tide!"

Super.

CHAPTER SIXTEEN

The sisters hadn't come home all night. Lori, Cook and Harper were attempting to track down friends or family who might know their whereabouts or what they had been up to since Sunday.

With the rest of the team pounding the pavement and banging on doors until midnight, Jess and Dan had kept an eye on the Vance residence for the night. They'd slept in shifts. She could not remember when her body had been this sore. Sleeping in a vehicle, even one as nice as Dan's Mercedes, was no stay at the Ritz.

Around three this morning she'd considered having that talk with Dan. But it seemed as if each time the moment appeared to be right one of their phones would ring. Flustered, she'd finally given up.

When Cook arrived to take over surveillance, Jess was immensely grateful for a chance to run home, grab a quick shower and change of clothes before coming to the office. At least they had movement in the investigation. Using her DMV photo, the blonde

196

had been positively ID'd as Selma Vance. Since she was on video leaving a crime scene with a large bag during the victim's estimated time of death, a BOLO had been issued for her as a person of interest in the investigation. With no way to identify the sister as the other person in the video, the 'be on the look-out' didn't include her.

Hayes was on the horn with Boston PD again attempting to prod information out of the detectives who had worked the case involving Ellis's neighbor. It was a closed case, a very old and very cold one. No one wanted someone new to poke around and find something they had missed.

Then again, maybe Boston PD hadn't missed a thing. Ellis might be a dead end, but Jess had a feel-ing about the guy.

First thing this morning when she arrived at the office she had called Paris and spoken with the Vance sisters' father. The trouble his daughters might be in seemed to rattle him. When she'd asked for permis-sion to search his home, he'd hemmed and hawed and insisted he must speak to his wife first. Unless his wife was also his attorney, Jess suspected he was calling his attorney right this minute.

Whether he agreed or not, they were going in. The odds of getting a judge to sign the warrant were very good, in Jess's opinion. For now, the house was under surveillance in case one or both sisters showed up.

Jess walked the length of the official case board, studied the faces there. They now had both Selma and her sister Olive posted under the persons of interest column. Selma, twenty-two, had attended college right here in Birmingham, so had Olive who was two years older. Neither had bothered to stick with a major long enough to achieve anything close to a degree. Both daughters were party girls. Living the Sex in the City life right here in Birmingham. By all accounts, clothes and parties were their primary interests.

Every parent's dream.

Jess pressed a hand to her waist. Parenting was hard work. She'd heard Lil say it often enough. Sometimes even children of good people, who had done everything right, turned out to be criminals or ended up dead way too young.

How did you know if you were doing it right? Her instincts worked pretty well when tracking down a murderer. But that didn't mean she'd be any good at guiding a child through life. Dan would be better at that than she would.

Another truckload of worry dumped on her, prompting a weary sigh. Whether they solved this case or not she had to find time to talk to him about this. Last night she had tried, she really had, but ultimately the point of a stakeout was to stay vigilant. Allowing that kind of distraction would have amounted to dereliction of duty.

They needed privacy and time.

Time, apparently, was her enemy. When she'd dressed this morning in her favorite red suit, she'd noticed the waistband of the skirt was a little tighter. Was that supposed to happen this early? God, she hoped not. If that was the route her body intended to take, she was doomed.

Her cell rang and she was glad for the reprieve. Lori's image flashed on her screen. Jess's pulse automatically shifted into a higher gear. "Did you locate the sisters?"

"Not yet, but the detective in Paris called."

Now there was a surprise. The French National Police rarely responded so quickly. "Anything useful?" Jess reached for a pencil, ready to jot down a few notes.

"Ten years ago three students from one of the premiere art schools went missing about a month apart. Each body was found a few days after the victim's disappearance. All three had been brutally murdered, chests cracked open and hearts removed."

Jess dropped the pencil back onto her desk. "Did Ellis teach at this school?"

"He did, but he was never connected to the crimes in any way. The cases remain unsolved."

"See if the detective will fax or email us the case reports," Jess wanted to kick something, "or anything that shows Ellis was a person of interest on that case. We need something tangible to put in front of a judge in the event we want to go into the gallery and his home."

"There's more."

Jess stilled. "I'm listening."

"Two years before the murders in Paris a couple of students disappeared from a small town in the Ukraine. And it doesn't end there. Two years prior to that, three students went missing in Hungary and before that one in Romania. There may even be more, those are just the ones he discovered long after Ellis had left Paris. But none of the missing students could be connected to Ellis and they all remain unsolved. The detective has been able to loosely connect travel by Ellis to the general area in those three cities, but nothing concrete."

"Call the judge." This was enough, Jess felt confident. "Get me a warrant for the gallery and his residence, in case we need it. Lieutenant Hayes and I are heading to his home now." The gallery wasn't open yet. Maybe they'd catch him at his house.

Jess ended the call and grabbed her bag.

Hayes was already waiting at the door. "You have an address?"

"Clairmont Avenue. It's in Forest Park," she told him.

Hayes opened the door as she reached him. "I know the area well."

Jess resisted the temptation to ask if he'd had clients in the wealthy neighborhood back when he was working his way through college.

Not nice, Jess. Maybe the detective had friends there. She knew from his personnel file that he didn't live in that posh neighborhood.

CLAIRMONT AVENUE, 9:15 A.M.

Hayes rang the bell again. There was a Jaguar, presumably Ellis's, in the driveway near the detached garage. If he was home, Jess wished he would come to the door already. It was hot as blazes out here and it wasn't even ten o'clock.

The impressive Tudor style home was quite beautiful and large. The house sat amid lush landscape facing Triangle Park. It didn't take a lot of imagination to know it would be equally grand inside.

"Did you hear something?" Since the noise sounded like footsteps, she hoped it was Ellis coming to the door.

"I did," Hayes confirmed. "Someone's coming."

The door opened and Ellis looked from Jess to Hayes and back before offering a smile. "Good morning, Chief Harris." He glanced at Hayes again.

"Mr. Ellis." She gave a nod. "This is Lieutenant Hayes and we'd like to speak with you a moment if you have the time." Since she didn't have a warrant yet, playing nice was the only way to go.

"Of course. Come in." He drew the door open wide in welcome. "I was just about to have one last cup of coffee before going to the gallery. Would you care to join me?"

Considering he was one of three suspects in her ongoing murder case, the answer to that would be a resounding no. "Thank you but I've had way too much caffeine already this morning."

Ellis shifted his attention to Hayes. "Lieutenant?"

"No, thanks."

"Join me in the parlor." He led the way through the ostentatious entry hall with its own little gallery of artwork to a room on the right.

The interior was elegantly decorated. "You have a lovely home." Jess produced a big smile. "You live here all by yourself?"

He gestured for her to have a seat then he and Hayes followed suit. He sat in a throne like chair, one leg crossed over the other. "I do."

"It must get lonely?" She'd bet her beloved Coach bag in which she carried the necessities of daily life, that he had at least one maid and a lawn service.

"I travel so frequently I rarely have time to be lonely."

"Your work at the gallery and the school keeps you busy as well," Hayes commented. "I've spoken with a number of your students. They all idolize you."

Jess gave the man high marks for joining the conversation rather than merely observing. He'd apparently hit a nerve since Ellis's jaw tightened noticeably. Clearly, he wasn't happy to learn that questions were being asked about him.

"I'm flattered. My greatest hope is that I can instill passion. Art without passion is dead."

"Have any of your students mentioned Lisa Templeton's or Alisha Burgess's untimely deaths?" Jess found it odd that he hadn't asked how the investigation was going the moment they arrived.

"We haven't spoken of it." He glanced at his untouched coffee waiting on the table next to his chair. "I've been watching for updates on the investigation in the news. Do you have any leads?"

"We do." Jess watched his face and eyes carefully as she spoke. "We believe we've identified the murderers."

His eyebrows reared up in surprise. The reaction wasn't reflected in his eyes. "There's more than one?"

"Two. Females. They were caught on the security camera at the apartment where they brutally murdered their last victim. They're wanted for questioning."

"That is good news."

"Mr. Ellis." She leaned forward just a bit and clasped her hands in her lap. "From what I've seen so far, you're a man of passion. What kind of passion do you suppose drives a person who would murder another human being and then take their hearts right out of their chests?"

He took a moment to sip his coffee. The delicate bone china cup and saucer looked right at home in his long fingered hands. This was a man who enjoyed the finer things in life. He wasn't pretending to be hoity-toity, he was. All the way down to his expensive hand-tooled leather shoes. But those hands of his weren't soft and smooth… they were rough. Maybe from working with tools—like the ones used to crack open the chests of his victims.

"I'm sure you would know better than I," he said at last. "Clearly, it would take a person driven by strong emotions."

Jess nodded in agreement. "Did you hear about the three murders, exactly like these, when you lived in Paris? I think the victims attended the school where you taught art."

There was a hint of a shrug and the inevitable averting of his gaze. "Paris is a very large city, Chief Harris. I do recall hearing something about the murders but I didn't know the students personally."

"The odd thing is," Jess went on, "there were several murders exactly like these, always a couple of years apart and in different cities. You didn't hear about those?"

"Not that I recall, no." He set his cup aside, rested his hands on the ornately carved wooden chair arms and stared directly at Jess, game face on. "Where did these murders occur?"

"I don't remember the names of the cities." Jess made a big production of blowing off the whole subject. She reached into her bag and retrieved the photos of the Vance sisters. She showed them to Ellis. His face remained impassive but there was something in his eyes… approval or pride. "Were either of these women ever students of yours?"

"No." He shook his head.

"You're certain?" Jess pushed.

"The bond that develops between teacher and student in art is far different from, let's say, English or Math," he explained in a tone just shy of arrogant. "I would remember any student I've had the pleasure of teaching." The glee or pride she'd noted in his eyes when he viewed the photos of the sisters was still there.

"They travel a lot to Europe." Jess studied the photos. "We've spoken to the detective in Paris who was in charge of the cases there. He's thinking of reopening them. He wants to see if he can connect the murders that occurred there with the ones happening here. He plans to start with the Vance sisters."

Jess felt confident the detective would as soon as she passed along their identities.

"I'm happy to help any way I can, Chief." Ellis stood. "Unfortunately, now I have to get to the gallery. I'm sure you understand."

Jess rose from her chair. "Certainly. I didn't mean to keep you so long."

As he walked them to the door, Ellis assured Jess he would be available if she had any other questions.

Outside, she hesitated at the car. "I want Ellis followed," she told the lieutenant. "He lied about not knowing the Vance sisters." He not only knew them, Jess was certain he shared that bond he'd spoken of so fondly with them. Her instincts were humming. He was part of this… somehow.

Hayes glanced toward the Jag backing away from the garage. "That might be difficult unless you want me to follow him."

"Send our surveillance detail. He's headed to the gallery. We'll catch up with them there. I have a stop to make first."

"Chief Burnett won't be happy about that."

Ellis's Jaguar was already rolling down the driveway and here they were debating an order on the street. "Do it. Now, Lieutenant."

"Yes, ma'am."

Jess settled into the passenger seat of Hayes's Audi. Her frustration mounted as she watched Ellis's Jag fading out of sight. Finally the BPD cruiser rolled out after him. "Jesus." She took a couple of deep breaths.

Hayes settled into the driver's seat. "Where to now?"

"The morgue." Maybe Lori would have that warrant for the gallery and Ellis's home soon.

No doubt word had traveled to the Vance sisters by now. They were wanted women.

Ellis's cage had been rattled. Time to find out what else the victims had to say.

JEFFERSON COUNTY CORONER'S OFFICE, 10:50 A.M.

"It took some time," Sylvia Baron announced, "but I found the culprit your killer used to disable the victims."

"Not one of the usual date rape drugs?" Jess glanced at the lieutenant who seemed perfectly fine standing next to Mr. Thomas's body on a cold steel slab.

"Nope." Sylvia pointed to a spot on the victim's upper thigh, near the groin. "This is the injection site. I found one on the shoulders of the other two victims."

"They disabled him with the stun gun and then injected him with…?" Jess prompted.

"Curare. A skeletal muscle relaxant. One of those organic compounds you have to be looking for to find." Sylvia waved her hand and made a face. "It wouldn't show up in a routine tox screen. I looked for the most common paralyzing agents until I found the one used. Just the right amount of Curare paralyzes. A little too much and the respiratory system shuts down."

Jess couldn't wait until the county saw the bill for that one. Police business was like most others these days, trying to find ways to cut costs. "So we were right about Templeton and Burgess not being able to fight back."

"*You* were right," Sylvia corrected. "You pointed out the fact that neither victim fought their restraints. Good catch, Harris. I gave you full credit on the orders for testing. Now I won't have to listen to my boss complain about my decisions."

Jess flashed her a fake smile. "That was thoughtful of you." What a friend! "You have the cause of death on Thomas yet?" She'd said earlier that the triple stun gun hit hadn't been the culprit.

"Drug induced asphyxiation. They gave him too much of the Curare."

Hayes checked his cell. "I'll take this in the corridor," he said to Jess as he backed out the door.

Her thoughts were on the Curare. The ways the Vance sisters may have gotten their hands on the drug ticked off in Jess's mind. Making it was risky business, but it could be done.

"So you're staying at Dan's now?"

Jess frowned at the ME. "What? Yes. Just until we get this Spears thing under control." She wasn't about to feed the rumor mill.

Sylvia peeled off her gloves and headed for the sink. "Gina and I have a bet on how long it'll be before the two of you are married. I think I might win."

"Is that a fact?" Jess checked her cell, wished she would get a call, too. Where the heck was Hayes?

"Are you going to be one of those over forty women who start having babies right away?" Sylvia tossed a paper towel into the trash. "You don't want to let all those eggs shrivel up and die and, of course, we wouldn't want vaginal atrophy to set in. Women like us are behind the curve, Harris."

Now she was just fishing. If Jess weren't standing here already pregnant, she would have been offended. Maybe she was anyway. Dammit. But she gave Sylvia grace. After all, her husband had left her for a younger woman who immediately gave him a child. What they needed was a subject change.

"Officer Cook seems to be quite smitten with you."

The abrupt change of subject startled the ME, but she quickly regained her mental footing. "I'm aware."

"He's young and naïve."

Sylvia smiled. "He is young. I don't know how naïve he is." She inclined her head. "Get to your point, Harris. Do you have an issue with older women dating younger men?"

"Absolutely not." Jess held up her hands. "It's just that he's on my team and I don't want any work issues cropping up."

"You have my word there will be no issues."

"Good. Cook is a nice guy. Don't break his heart."

Sylvia smiled. "It's not his heart I'm interested in."

Hayes poked his head in. "We have to roll, Chief."

Dread pooled in her belly. "We have another murder?"

Hayes shook his head. "The lab found traces of linseed oil, vermilion and cinnabar in the bleached blond hair from the Homewood house." At Jess's look of confusion he added, "Elements commonly found in the oil paint artists use."

That was the best news Jess had heard all morning. Maybe it was coincidence that Selma Vance had paint in her hair. Maybe Ellis had never laid eyes on her or her sister before today. But now Jess had an excuse to push him a little harder.

109 BROADWAY, 12:30 P.M.

The tail she'd put on Ellis had lost him. Of course, rather than coming to the gallery as he'd said, he disappeared. Ellis was not here or at his home. He was not answering his phone. He was gone. Dammit.

Now what she needed was evidence. She couldn't put a BOLO out on him without some way to connect him to the crimes or some aspect of this investigation that suggested he was in danger.

She had zip on the guy, except for two uniforms and a detective wasting time out here on the sidewalk waiting for a search warrant to be inked. Jess was ready to explode.

Dammit all to hell!

Hayes's phone rang. Jess held her breath while he took the call.

"Thank you," he said to the caller, then he put his phone away. "Warrant's signed. We can go in."

The door was open in under a minute.

"There's a second floor," Jess said as they entered the gallery. "We don't want to miss anything."

The two uniforms rushed ahead to get to the stairs. "Lieutenant, I'll look around down here. See if there's a hidden storeroom or a basement around here."

Hayes gave her a two-fingered salute and headed toward the rear of the gallery.

Jess checked behind the paintings hanging on the wall. She lifted them away just enough to ensure there were no hiding places. Then she moved on to the sitting areas. A few minutes were required to check for any thing hidden under the sofa and chair cushions. She did discover a small office, but the desk and a lone file cabinet were locked.

Looked like they were going to need a locksmith.

"Chief!"

She followed the sound of Hayes's voice. "Yes, Lieutenant?"

"Found a storeroom."

Jess followed him to the back of the gallery where Ellis had been speaking to the visitors from Montgomery. A massive painting of Birmingham, three or four feet wide and six or seven feet in height, hung at one end of the room. Hayes pulled the painting away from the wall. To her surprise, it was hinged like a door.

Jess moved closer to the room he revealed. The light inside was already turned on. The space was set up like a small gallery. The walls, ceiling and floor were black. On those black walls were a dozen or so paintings. Savage death scenes from someone's gruesome imagination were captured on the canvas. At least she hoped it was only their imaginations.

Her breath caught when she spotted one of Logan Thomas. The image was just as she had found his body in the bedroom of Dan's old apartment. In the painting, the view of downtown Birmingham was framed in the bedroom window. She moved back through the paintings she'd just viewed, looking for landmarks, until she found one that showed what appeared to be the Eiffel Tower in the distance outside a window.

"We need photos of these paintings sent to the detective in Paris." Some of these could very well depict victims from the murders he had told Lori about.

"Chief."

Hayes was at the far end of the room staring at a painting she hadn't reached yet. He glanced at her, and something in his expression told her he'd discovered something significant. Before she realized she'd taken a step, she was moving toward him.

The painting was of her… asleep in Dan's bed. The tufted headboard, the paisley comforter, the crystal lamp on her side of the bed…

Dan was there, too. Blood was everywhere, all over the covers. She forced her mind to wrap around the rest of what she saw. Dan's chest had been pried open and inside there was nothing but a dark empty void where his heart should be.

An image of the headstone Dan had told her about jumbled into the mix of horrible scenes in this room.

She leaned closer to get a better look at the bottom right hand corner of the painting. Her heart thumped harder as she read the artist's signature. *Selma.* Jess straightened, took a deep steadying breath. "Lieutenant, let Detective Wells know we have sufficient evidence for the search warrant of the Vance home. She and Sergeant Harper are to conduct that search immediately."

Her chest felt so tight it was almost impossible to take a breath. *Keep it together.* "Also, have a BOLO issued for Ellis. Let Agent Manning at the local Bureau office know we have a potential international suspect they're going to want to talk to. Immediate action is necessary since Ellis is a flight risk." She stared at the painting. "I think maybe he has considerable experience slipping away from trouble."

Hayes was already talking to someone. Lori probably. Jess needed to call Dan and Gant. Her entire being felt numb now. They needed a crime scene unit at Dan's house. Someone had been watching them there.

A new kind of fear planted firmly, deeply inside her.

CHAPTER SEVENTEEN

Crime scene unit folks were exploring every room in Dan's house. Jess sorely wished she had picked up a bit before she left this morning, but she'd had little sleep and her mind hadn't been on housekeeping.

Then again it rarely was.

Now everyone would know what a slacker she was around the house. Funny, her office and notes might look chaotic to others but were actually highly organized. Maybe she could convince all those sifting through her things right now that this was in reality a carefully choreographed order.

She imagined most of those prowling through Dan's house wondered why she was living here. At this point, the rest of the department and the mayor could think what they would.

Spears had made it clear what his intentions for Dan were. Her heart ached, the fear crushing it against her ribs. She could not let that happen. Her stomach clenched, reminding her that there was even more at stake now. She could not allow Spears to catch her off guard.

Besides department personnel, Dan had called in a friend who worked in security systems. Benton Thompson helped out the BPD in situations like this. Between Thompson and their own tech wizard, Ricky Vernon from the lab, they usually found their way around any issue involving electronics and the World Wide Web. Add to the horde, Jerry Griggs the supervisor from the security company who monitored Dan's house, and it was a regular circus around here.

"Got something here!"

Hugging her bag like a lifeline, Jess followed the voice to the guest room. Dan came in right behind her. Thompson was on a ladder digging something from the ceiling above the bed near the light fixture. Tiny flakes of drywall and finishing compound dust fell onto the covers. Ricky Vernon held an evidence bag ready as Thompson dropped a white object hardly larger than a nickel into it.

Jess's brow puckered, adding more wrinkles to the ever increasing number already there. "Is that a camera?"

Beside her Dan said nothing, his expression dark with fury.

Thompson climbed down from the ladder. "An eyecam. Smallest one I've seen in this kind of setting. Typically they're black. Someone had this one designed specially to incorporate into white ceilings. Wireless, built in transmitter. I can only guess at the range and other capabilities until I've had a chance to test it." He looked to Dan. "But I can tell you it's uber high tech. Whoever planted this could potentially be watching you from most anywhere, across the street or across town."

Jess felt sick. She had slept in this room.

"We have another one in here!"

The voice came from Dan's bedroom—the one they shared. The bottom dropped out of her stomach though she shouldn't be surprised. The painting had captured the bedroom in far too much detail to hope the invasion into their privacy hadn't extended there.

A chorus of shouts followed. The eyecams were in every room. How long had Spears been watching? How many times had they discussed work and him, dammit, in this house?

As if that weren't bad enough, this and the painting suggested the murders this week were all connected to Ellis and Ellis was connected to Spears.

That reality settled heavily onto her shoulders.

"How did he get into my house without triggering the alarm?" Dan demanded, his frustration now aimed at the men from the security company.

"I think we have that answer for you, Chief." Griggs led them through the house and out the kitchen door.

Jess's legs felt too heavy and uncoordinated. The whole scene was far too surreal. They would be checking her apartment next.

Beyond the porte-cochere, Griggs gestured to the end of the house. All Jess saw was the vent that allowed airflow in and out of the attic. She was certain there was a more technical term but it escaped her just now. Another guy, from the security company Jess deduced, was examining the vent.

"The vent's been removed recently," the guy on the ladder shouted down to Griggs. "Some of the screws are missing. Whoever did it was in a hurry to get out of here when he finished."

"We should have one of our forensic techs have a look before you go any further," Dan said. He shook his head, disgusted.

Within half an hour, the attic had been designated a crime scene.

Someone had entered via the vent in the gable end of the house. A video surveillance system, including a signal booster, had been put into place that monitored every room in the house including bathrooms. A wave of revulsion washed over Jess.

She wandered back to each room and had another look. As careful as those removing the cameras had been, they still left a bit of a mess. Who had cleaned up that mess when the cameras were installed?

Did Dan have a maid?

If she remembered the white dust they might be able to narrow down when the cameras were installed.

She located Dan and pulled him away from the huddle of those discussing how to properly secure his home after such a breach. "Do you have a maid?"

He nodded. "She comes in once a week."

"You should call her and ask if she noticed anything unusual like that white dust? That could give us a time frame for when the cameras were installed." Knowing Spears, he arranged for the work to coincide with the cleaning lady's scheduled workday.

"There may not have been any detectible residue left behind," Thompson said, joining their conversation. "Didn't mean to eavesdrop but a system this high tech was most likely installed by someone who knew what he was doing. The tool he used to make the necessary opening in the drywall probably had a vacuum attachment. I doubt you would've noticed whatever trace amounts of debris he left behind."

So much for that theory.

The sound of her cell phone ringing tugged Jess away from the conversation. Lori's image appeared on the screen. Jess moved into the only room that was clear, the hall bath and closed the door. "Did you locate the sisters?"

They needed to find those two women before anyone else was lured into their trap. The surveillance details at her sister's home, Dan's parents' home and Mr. Louis's home were on heightened alert. The same alert had gone to the detail at Wanda's house. Jess couldn't forget her no matter how often she had wanted to in the past.

She caught a glimpse of her reflection and cringed. Too bad it wasn't Halloween, she'd fit right in. Then again, maybe it was. Spears had certainly turned her life into a nightmare.

"No one has seen either of the Vance sisters since Saturday night. Apparently once they started their killing rampage, they closed everyone out."

Their faces had been plastered all over the news. If they were still in Birmingham, hopefully someone would spot one or both soon.

"We're in the Vance home now," Lori went on. "There's an art studio behind the house. Apparently the daughters inherited their interest in art from the mother. And guess where she took classes?"

"Paris?" Jess wilted onto the closed toilet lid and let her bag slide to the floor. Of course, the mother's age was right. "Ellis was her teacher or a fellow student."

"I think maybe he was a whole lot more than that."

Jess perked up. "Ellis and the mother had an affair?"

"I think so. I'm still combing through things but I found several photos of Mr. and Mrs. Vance with Ellis. The way Ellis looks at Mrs. Vance, it's more than friendship. None of the photos I've found so far are recent. I'm guessing they were taken twenty or more years ago."

"We need to talk to the mother."

"There's more."

Jess slipped a shoe off and rubbed at her aching foot. "You heard from the detective in Paris again?"

"Actually, I just got a call from the wife of that Boston reporter I told you about."

Jess reached into her bag for her pad and pencil. "Did she recall something about that murder Ellis witnessed?"

"She did. Her husband, Steve Cooley, died of cancer just two years ago. His death was slow and painful. One of his last requests was to speak with the brother who survived the sister's murder."

"Did the brother agree to speak with him?" Anticipation burned through Jess.

"He did but Cooley never repeated the conversation. He didn't even bring it up again until the night he died."

"This is the reporter who insisted there was a cover up? Why the hell would he let it go?" *Dumb question, Jess.* Knowing you were living your final days would assuredly change ones perspective. She kicked the idea that Spears had insinuated that Dan's days were numbered out of her head. She refused to let that idea take root.

"The same," Lori confirmed. "He didn't share a word until the night he died when he told his wife he'd been right all along."

Jess's hopes fell. "But what does that mean?"

The door opened and the officer coming in jumped when he saw Jess. "Excuse me, ma'am."

Jess gave him a perfunctory smile. "There's another one that way," she told him in case he needed to use the facilities.

Face red, he nodded then closed the door.

"Cooley never believed the father killed his daughter," Lori continued. "He was convinced the brother did it and the father covered for him."

"What was the father's motive?" It was true that parents often covered for their children but this was taking it to the extreme. The father's first instinct would have been to protect his remaining child and his wife from the threat—even if the surviving child was the threat. The father killing himself took him completely out of the equation. Not the natural reaction of a parent hoping to protect his child.

"She didn't say much about the father," Lori went on, "Cooley's theory revolved around the brother and Ellis."

Now Jess was really confused. "How was he tying Ellis into the shooting?"

"He believed Ellis and the brother were caught in the act of doing something bad to or with the sister since her body was nude. The official report found no indication of sexual activity, but forensic science back then wasn't what it is today. Anyway, then the father came in and things got crazy."

That was a nice theory but too circumstantial for building a case. Jess needed more than that. "Does the brother have a record?"

"No record. Not much of a life either, for that matter. He never married and keeps to himself. Had Polio when he was a kid, wore the braces. No friends. He lives alone with his elderly mother."

"We should try and talk to the brother." Jess couldn't guarantee how much good it would do, but it couldn't hurt At this point, everything about Ellis's past was relevant.

"I'll see if I can set something up with the brother."

"Thanks, Lori."

Jess ended the call and tugged her shoe back on. Spears had his followers coming out of the woodwork. If she'd had any doubts whatsoever that he had roused the Man in the Moon, those doubts were all but gone now.

How could they hope to catch up to Spears let alone get a step ahead of him?

A quick check of the hall showed the search was ongoing in the rest of the house. They didn't need her for that. Jess decided to stay put and to call her sister. This might be her only chance to actually talk to Lil for the next few days.

When Lil answered Jess smiled at the sound of her voice. "Hey."

"I'm doing exactly what you told me to do," Lil informed her, "the last time you called. And the time before that."

"I'm not calling about your surveillance detail." Her sister was right. They'd hardly spoken lately unless it was related to Spears. "I just wanted to say…" What did she want to say? "I'd like to get together for lunch, maybe this weekend if you have the time."

Silence.

Now she was just punishing Jess.

"Sorry," Lil grumbled. "I had to pick myself up off the floor."

"Ha ha. Do you want to have lunch or not?" Hopefully, by then she would have had *the* conversation with Dan and she could tell Lil.

"Yes, I'd love to have lunch. Whatever day works for you. How's your day going, by the way?"

Lil did not want to hear the answer to that. "Great. We have three persons of interest in the case. Any time now we should be able to wrap this one up." Jess could dream.

"Wanda called."

Jess leaned toward the mirror and grimaced at her reflection. "That's nice."

"Sorry I forgot," Lil griped, "you want to pretend she doesn't exist even though you ate fried chicken with her."

Jess had known she would live to regret that temporary lapse in sanity. "I know. I know. She's changed. She's our only living relative. We should forgive and forget." There were things Lil didn't understand. Jess hadn't told her sister about Wanda's accusations. She needed to determine if there was any truth to the allegation that their mother was afraid of their father before she went mending any fences or telling her sister.

"She's not getting any younger, Jess. You'd feel really bad if she died with this unresolved between you."

"You think?" Good grief. Just because she hadn't been married half her life and didn't have kids or go to church every Sunday didn't mean Jess had no compassion for others.

"I'm sorry. I just want us to be a family. All of us."

"Can we talk about this later?" For the love of God. Spears had been watching her pee! Not to mention having sex with Dan. *Oh God.* She closed her eyes and tried to block the frustration and humiliation. At least she hadn't taken a pregnancy test here.

"I know you have to go find bad guys," Lil relented. "I love you. We'll figure out the Wanda situation eventually."

Jess appreciated the reprieve. "Love you." Her chest ached at the idea that she had put her sister and everyone else she cared about in danger.

"Love you more!"

Lil ended the call before Jess could one-up her.

Why in the world had she stayed away so long? Jess had missed so much. Oh yeah, she'd been too busy with her career.

She sighed. Why was it that every decision she'd made in her entire existence had to be revisited and overanalyzed at this stage in her life? So far the forties were anything but fun and fulfilling.

A rap on the door jerked her back to the here and now. "Jess, you in there?"

Dan. She opened the door and presented a smile. "I had to check on Lil."

"I have a meeting back at the office." He looked so tired. She just wanted to hug him. "You done with things here?"

She nodded. "Your security people will get this place secure again?"

"Thompson gave me his personal guarantee that he would oversee the work himself. As soon as they're finished here, they're going to tackle your apartment."

"Good." She dragged her bag onto her shoulder. "Do you have time to drop me off at the gallery on Broadway so I can catch up with Lieutenant Hayes? He's finishing up there."

"I can do that."

Her phone made that loopy little sound that warned she had a text. She could check it in the car. Right now, she wanted out of here.

Once she was settled in his SUV, she dug out her phone. Dan maneuvered between the official vehicles parked every which way in his driveway and yard.

The text was not from a number in her contacts list. Tension rippled through Jess. Not again. *Please.* She opened the text and found a video.

The video showed a man, fifty or older. He was visibly inebriated. His speech was slurred. He wore a business suit. What was that in the background? A bed? Was he in a bedroom? Jess stared at the small screen and tried to see any other details.

"We could go back to the pool." The man in the suit grinned, or tried to. "Take a swim."

Was he in a hotel room? Jess got a glimpse of the phone on the bedside table. Definitely a hotel room.

"You're both so pretty," he slurred.

"What the hell?" Dan hit his brakes and turned to Jess.

"I never did a threesome before," the man in the video mumbled.

Fear rammed into Jess. She turned to Dan. The sisters were with this man and Jess knew exactly where they were—or, at least, where they had been.

"The Howard Johnson Inn where I stayed when I first got here."

Why hadn't she thought of that place? Jesus Christ she should have known.

"Heading there now."

Tires squealed as Dan whipped out onto the street.

Jess started to enter the number for dispatch but a call from Harper interrupted.

"Chief, we're en route to the Howard—"

"So are we." Her voice sounded empty. But agony was brimming inside her. "We'll meet you there."

Jess felt sick.

The murders were growing more blatant. Each one added another layer of guilt to the mountain already sitting on her shoulders.

Spears intended to win this battle… even if it was his last.

CHAPTER EIGHTEEN

Are you having fun yet, Jess?

That was the message on the wall above the bed. It appeared to be written in the victim's blood. Even after more than half an hour, Jess couldn't stop glancing back to look at it again. The words had been videoed, photographed, and swabbed for evidence.

The room was a bloody mess.

Since each victim's heart had ceased to beat before the mangling of the torso, there was no reason for blood to be all over the room. What were they doing? Using the victim's blood like lotion or body paint. Jess shuddered. Hadn't she seen a movie or read a book about a blood countess in Hungary or somewhere in Europe? Legend or historical fact she couldn't recall. Were these two killers performing the same sort of rituals?

Had Ellis studied more than the Old Masters while in Europe? Maybe he'd decided to relive some of the folklore he'd learned.

Were the Vance sisters his pupils in the art of death?

Another shudder rocked Jess. Too many questions and not enough answers. She pushed aside her raw emotions and focused on the details of the scene. Just about a month ago, this room had been vandalized along with all her things. It certainly hadn't taken the motel long to get it refurbished. Too bad for Mr. Theodore McCrary of Nashville, fifty-nine and widowed with one grown son.

He had come to Birmingham for a business meeting yesterday. According to an associate whose business card was found at the scene, after a long meeting McCrary and several others had gone to dinner and then to a bar. When they'd parted around ten-thirty, McCrary had called a taxi to return to his motel. He was supposed to fly back to Nashville today. His son had gone to the airport to pick him up at one o'clock but his father hadn't been on the flight. When repeated calls to the vic's cell had gone unanswered, the son had called the motel.

Imagine the manager's surprise when, after much prompting by the son, he'd found this unholy mess.

Mr. McCrary had come back to his room last night, but the sisters had probably been waiting and intercepted him at the pool. He'd said something in the video about going back to the pool. To reach this room, passing the pool in the inner courtyard was necessary. To a man McCrary's age, away from home and feeling lonely, having two beautiful young women flirting must have been very flattering. A few more drinks, a little Curare, and the poor man was done.

"Same array of tools as before," Harper reported.

"Brands are sold at Lowes and Home Depot," Hayes added.

Cook and Lori were interviewing guests in the surrounding rooms.

"Do we have information on the son for a next of kin notification?" The motel manager had not called the son back to relay the news.

"Nashville Metro is contacting Mr. McCrary's son." Harper checked his cell. "Dr. Baron says she's on her way."

"I hope she's not driving and texting." Jess was a little annoyed with the ME. She'd watched Cook's face light up every time he heard Baron's name. Jess didn't know when she'd decided saving the youngest member of her team from heartbreak was her job. She had enough on her plate already.

Maybe it was the idea that Sylvia had ignored Jess's wishes on the matter. When had professional courtesy gone out of style?

Or maybe it was her, Jess mused. She couldn't seem to focus. Her emotions had hopped on a roller coaster and refused to get off.

She was not herself. How much of her fluctuating emotions were hormones? She had no idea. The better question was when would it pass?

She moved to the door of the small bathroom and surveyed the smears of blood. There were few footprints this time. The room's new carpet had seen to that. The place was going to need another refurbishing. When Jess had arrived the manager had taken one look at her and shaken his head. You'd think she would be used to that kind of reaction by now.

"Sergeant?" Jess turned back to the room at large. Harper moved toward her. "I'd like you, Detective Wells and Officer Cook to focus on finding the Vance sisters and Ellis. Ensure we have surveillance on their homes and the gallery twenty-four/seven. Lieutenant Hayes and I will wrap things up here."

"Yes, ma'am."

"Lieutenant, where's Chief Burnett?" He'd been here a few minutes ago. Jess didn't usually have this much trouble keeping up with the folks at her crime scenes.

"He's just outside taking a call. Do you need him?"

She shook her head. "I'll talk to him in a minute." Mostly she just needed to confirm he was close by and safe.

She wished she had the luxury of just falling into Dan's arms and closing out all this ugliness. How would she ever make a decent life for this child? Her entire existence revolved around murder.

"See if there's anyone else we need to interview here, Lieutenant. I'll see what our ME has to say and then we'll be on our way. I have a few things I need to do at the office." Then she was going home and she and Dan were going to talk. No matter what happened. The rest of the world was just going to have to take a time out.

Hayes hesitated. "You won't—"

"I'll be right here, Lieutenant. I'm not going anywhere."

When she'd shooed him away, Jess stared at the poor man on the bed. *I am so sorry.* Chances were he had never even heard of Jess Harris. Now he was dead because of her. For the first time in her career, she wanted to cry right here in the middle of a crime scene.

"What has your crazed serial killer done to get your attention this time?"

Startled from her troubling thoughts, Jess turned to the ME as she breezed into the room. "You're late."

Sylvia arched an eyebrow. "I didn't know you were keeping tabs on my response times."

Jess looked her up and down. Even under the disposable paper lab coat the formfitting dress was eye catching. The soft muted color of orange, not the garish one, even looked good with her red hair.

"Nice dress," Jess said begrudgingly.

Sylvia shrugged. "If you haven't heard, orange is the new black."

If tangerine counted Jess was in vogue and she hadn't even tried. At the moment, she didn't care. "Thanks for the fashion tip."

Jess wasn't cutting the ME any slack this afternoon. She was too tired, too disgusted and way out of patience.

Sylvia waved a gloved hand toward the bed. "Let's have a look at the vic."

"I think the sisters are growing weary of this game." Jess surveyed McCrary once more. "His clothes are still on." His shirt had been ripped open. Buttons were scattered everywhere. Yet, his trousers remained fastened, including the belt. Shoes and socks on his feet. The sisters hadn't given this guy the full treatment the other victims had received. Maybe they'd taken short cuts because he was too old for their taste.

"No foreplay, eh?" Sylvia set her bag aside. She peeled back the shirt in the area of his left shoulder and leaned down to have a closer look.

Jess frowned. What was up with all these sexual metaphors? Was the woman just horny or what?

"How about making yourself useful, Harris, and checking the other shoulder?"

Jess put aside her irritation and hurried around to the far side of the bed and uncovered the victim's right shoulder. "Are we looking for an injection site?" She pushed her glasses up the bridge of her nose with the back of her hand.

"We are."

Jess searched the pale, gray skin of his shoulder and upper arm. "Found it."

Sylvia came around to her side of the bed and had a look. "That's it." She straightened. "I'll confirm but I think we'll find an overdose of the Curare was cause of death." She moved back to the other side of the bed and rummaged around in her bag.

"He appeared inebriated in the video I received." Jess looked down at the man whose chest had been cracked open just as brutally as the others. Wrong place, wrong time. Loneliness had made him vulnerable. "They prodded him with drink and lured him to bed with the promise of sex."

"Been there, done that a few times," Sylvia muttered as she prepared to take the body's temperature.

"The lurer or the luree?" The ME had walked right into that one. Jess wanted to discuss Cook with her anyway. Now was as good a time as any. Or maybe Jess was just in the mood to pick a fight.

Sylvia shot her a look. "Since both parties usually regret it the next morning, is that even relevant?"

"Depends," Jess tossed right back, "whether or not both parties understood what they were getting into in the first place."

Sylvia checked her thermometer. "Are we talking about someone in particular?"

"Aren't these conversations always about someone in particular?" Jess argued. She wasn't Cook's mother or his sister, but she did not intend to have a member of her team emotionally compromised just to fulfill Sylvia Baron's sexual fantasies.

"I see." Sylvia assessed her in that condescending manner only those born to privilege could pull off. "You *do* have issues with older women choosing younger men."

"I absolutely do not. Unless," Jess glanced down at the murder victim lying between them, "it costs one of those involved more than he intended to pay."

"Who says anyone is going to pay anything?" The ME was more than a little put out now.

"We both know someone will." Jess lowered her voice since the crime scene unit was still going over the room. Why didn't Sylvia just back off? This was a conflict of interest, for Pete's sake. She should just pick some other younger guy.

Sylvia scoffed. "Besides, I never make the first move, Chief Harris."

Now she'd just made Jess mad. "Like you don't dress for attention. Every male in the vicinity watches you enter a room. That's a first move if I've ever seen one." She gestured to the woman on the opposite side of the bed. "Take that dress, for instance. Or those shoes. Not to mention the hair. You're dressed for a dinner party or a night out on the town, not a homicide scene."

"And you don't," Sylvia threw right back at her, "in your hot red suit and sassy Mary Janes with their four inch heels? I don't see any of the other division chiefs dressing that way."

Well. She had Jess there. Dammit. It was her one vanity. She liked clothes and shoes and her bag. But she wasn't trying to get attention… she was just…. It was not the same thing.

Sylvia lifted her chin, pretending to recheck the thermometer. "Be advised, Harris, if you think this is how I dress to go out, you are sadly mistaken."

Jess resisted the urge to grab that damned thermometer and shove it where the sun didn't shine. "The point is someone's going to get hurt."

"Not in this situation," Sylvia argued. "This is a mutual decision by intelligent, consenting adults."

"Ha!" Jess leaned toward Sylvia, shook her finger at her. "He is not an adult when it comes to that. Men never are until they're at least thirty-five!"

A throat was cleared. She and Sylvia glared at the sound. Lieutenant Hayes, the perpetrator, jerked his head toward the two forensic techs. Both appeared to be busy with their work but apparently had been paying more attention to the exchange over the dead body in the room than the collecting of evidence.

"Judging by the body temp and the state of rigor," Sylvia announced as if they hadn't just waged war over a corpse, "I would estimate time of death between ten last night and one this morning. Since the air conditioning in the room is less than adequate for the heat we've experienced today, that time may be off a little."

Jess squared her shoulders. "Thank you, Dr. Baron. I look forward to your preliminary exam results as soon as possible."

Sylvia faked a smile. "Of course, Chief Harris. I'll get the report to you later tonight or first thing in the morning, depending on my schedule."

Jess turned her back and headed out of the room. She didn't have to wonder if Hayes followed. He was already too well trained to allow her out of his sight.

Outside the door, Jess paused long enough to rip off her shoe covers and gloves. Dan closed his phone and headed toward her. He looked furious. Briefly she wondered what had happened now, but mostly she thanked God he hadn't witnessed the fiasco that would no doubt be all over the department's grapevine before dark.

"I have a meeting with Black. Are you heading back to the office now?"

"Lieutenant Hayes and I will be along after we finish up here." She exhaled a big breath and tried to calm herself.

Dan gave her a nod. His eyes told her he wanted to do more but couldn't. They were on the job and Jess had already allowed her professional composure to slip with Sylvia. Why was it after a confrontation like that occurred, within mere minutes all the fire and conviction she'd experienced suddenly evaporated.

Now she just felt like a fool.

"Don't let her out of your sight, Lieutenant," Dan said to Hayes.

Under normal circumstances Jess would have scolded him for the comment, but he was right. She scanned the many windows and doors around the courtyard. There were far too many opportunities for someone to get too close.

As she watched Dan walk away, wishing he would take the same precautions, she made him a silent promise.

Tonight she was going to tell him about the baby.

CHAPTER NINETEEN

This day couldn't be over fast enough to suit Dan. The security company had fortified his house. At some point, he would need someone to come in and make the drywall repairs. No hurry on that one. Right now, the last thing he wanted was any more strangers in his home. Thankfully, Jess's apartment had been clear. No bugs, no cameras.

His mother had called twice. Dealing with a surveillance detail unsettled her. She couldn't see why Dan wouldn't come home and stay with them. After all he was the chief of police and they were his parents. They needed him.

He could just imagine how that suggestion would go over with Jess. Not that his mother had mentioned Jess. His mother pretended Jess was not living in his house. Eventually she would come to terms with the idea that Jess, if he could persuade her to agree, was going to be his wife.

Or she wouldn't. The decision would be his mother's loss.

As for protecting his parents, the worst move he could make would be to put the danger closer to them. Jess was right about that part. Spears had targeted her and anyone in or near his path to that objective was in danger.

Dan's jaw tightened. He had sent the bastard a message via the same number he'd used to text Dan about the cemetery delivery. If Spears had received the promise, he didn't bother replying.

I'm sending you to hell. Soon.

He hoped Spears comprehended that, unlike him, Dan was not playing.

The intercom buzzed. "Chief, Supervisory Special Agent Gant is on line one."

"Thanks, Sheila." It was about time. Dan took the call. "I hope you have something at least resembling good news for me."

"I'm afraid not, Dan."

Dan closed his eyes and shook his head. "I'm listening."

"Our one lead on the Net has disappeared again. We were closing in on a location near you and now the link is gone. We're picking up nothing at all. No talk about Jess. No talk about Spears. Nothing."

"How close did you get before the link vanished?"

"Too close, Dan. Within a ninety mile radius. Whoever was using that link is practically your neighbor. Since we have two confirmed sightings of Spears in the past two weeks right there in Birmingham, I'm concerned that he's the one who used that link."

Dread hardened like a rock in his gut. Fear for Jess filled his chest, but so did anger. "Just keep trying to find him, Gant. I know you have other cases, but we need to know you're on this."

"We're not pushing this one aside, Dan. You have my word on that. We're doing all we can to find Rory Stinnett and Spears. We don't want him or his friends claiming any more victims. If it makes you feel any better, we're getting help from several other agencies, like Interpol. We have to get this guy before he disappears for good."

"I'll pass that along to the citizens of Birmingham. Four people have died in as many days. His friends are popping up all over the place down here and he's orchestrating the gathering." The mounting frustration and worry forced Dan out of his chair.

God Almighty. How the hell was he going to stop this?

"I feel you, Dan. This is a bad situation. To be honest with you, I've never seen anything like it. Spears has started something we may not be able to stop any time soon. All we can do is react. The ball is in his court and he's keeping it there. Judging by what's happened the past few days, he's hyper focused on Jess. We're hoping that will be his downfall."

As long as he didn't take Jess with him, that worked for Dan.

"I appreciate your people doing what they can." There was no point in giving Gant a hard time. The one thing Dan knew with complete certainty was that it would take all of them working in concert to stop this son of a bitch.

"If anything changes," Gant assured him, "you'll be the first to know. I have people focused on finding Spears twenty-four/seven."

Dan thanked him and dropped the phone into its cradle. He paced to the window and stared out at the commuters rushing to get home. Spears could be out there, watching them run in circles and laughing at them.

A rap on the door was followed by, "Dan, you have a few minutes?"

He flinched, then faced Harold Black and gave him the expected welcoming smile. "Come in. Have a seat."

"That was quite an ordeal at your house this afternoon." Harold settled into one of the chairs in front of Dan's desk. "Has your security system provider been able to get things straightened out?"

"That's what they tell me." Dan wasn't so sure he would feel truly secure any time soon. More importantly, he wouldn't feel Jess was as safe as she should be even with him. He'd insisted she move to his place to facilitate her safety and this was how things turned out. Her safety had only been further compromised. At least she wasn't fighting him so hard on being extra careful. She'd actually been cooperative with her surveillance detail. Whatever the reason, he was thankful.

"I'm confident you're mindful of what a thorough job our crime scene unit does. Our forensic techs and detectives are some of the best in the nation. When they're called in to assist with a search such as what took place at your home today, they leave no stone unturned." He put a hand to his chest. "I, for one, feel good knowing I can count on them not to leave anything behind."

"Where're you headed with this, Harold?" They were both far too busy to be having this kind of conversation. Dan was well aware of the topnotch work the crime scene unit did. He'd handed out plenty of awards in his four years as chief of police.

Harold placed a clear evidence bag on Dan's desk. "One of the techs found this in the grill on your patio."

Dan reached across his desk and picked up the bag. "What is it?"

"A wedding band."

"This," he frowned, inspecting it more closely, "was in my grill?" He'd grilled steaks earlier this week.

Harold nodded. "There's an inscription, Dan."

Dan stared at the ring. Obviously it was a man's. He turned it and started to read the inscription.

"To Ted with all my love," Harold recited.

"This is Ted Allen's wedding band?"

Harold nodded. "When he first went missing we asked for all sorts of ways to identify him. Birthmarks, scars, jewelry. His wife gave a description of the ring."

This was like the phone, except far worse. "So, you think because you found this in my grill—which stays outside on the patio, accessible to anyone who decides to walk into my yard—that I put it there in hopes of destroying evidence?"

"I didn't say that, Dan."

He tossed the bagged ring back across his desk. "Didn't you? I grilled steaks Tuesday evening. Jess and my parents can confirm that for you. I haven't been near that grill since. I don't see any signs the ring has been exposed to a heat source which tells me that someone placed it there after Tuesday evening."

"I know," Harold began, "and you know this is a set up. But my hands are tied, Dan." The department's ranking division chief shook his head. "I have no choice but to pursue any leads that come available to me. Ted Allen is one of our own. A veteran cop in this department. I cannot ignore anything at all that might help us learn what's come of him."

Outrage rendered Dan momentarily unequipped to hold his tongue. "I can tell you what's come of him, in case you haven't figured it out by now. He's dead, Harold. Either that or he's involved in an elaborate plan to fake his death and to pin it on me."

"Please." Harold held up his hands. "I don't want to hear a statement like that from you again. We're going to pretend you didn't say what you just said. This is no longer just between you and me. This," he nodded to that damned ring, "is part of the official investigation and if Allen is dead, that makes it a homicide investigation. Don't go losing your temper and saying things you don't mean and can't possibly know."

This was ridiculous. "You want to hold a press conference? I'll tell the citizens of Birmingham the same thing. I had nothing to do with his disappearance and you know it."

Harold visibly braced. "Chief Harris has access to your home."

Now he'd gone too far. "We're not going there. We've talked about this before. Jess is not involved in his disappearance either. You know that as well." He was done here. "Anything else you want to talk about?"

"You need to listen to me carefully, Dan."

He couldn't place what had changed in his old friend's demeanor but something definitely had. Whether it was the somber expression on his face or the troubled tone in his voice, this was no longer a casual or friendly conversation between lifelong buddies.

"The mayor has been after you to get rid of Harris from day one," Harold held up a hand to stop him when Dan would have argued, "he's keeping close tabs on what's happening. Every time somebody dies at Spears's hand, Pratt chalks that up as one more loss of life related to Harris being in this department. He's keeping score and he's going to use the final tally to be rid of you and Harris. Whether it's Spears setting you up or someone else, you need to pay attention to what I'm saying to you."

The reality of his words clicked for Dan then. "Pratt has called you to his office."

Betrayal always stung, but Dan wasn't surprised. Mayor Joseph Pratt didn't like it when his wishes were ignored and Dan had been ignoring him since Jess returned to Birmingham.

"I'm not the only one he called, Dan." Harold heaved a big breath. "Trust me when I say this is going to get ugly."

Dan nodded his understanding. "You have to protect your position. I wouldn't expect you to do otherwise."

"I'm too close to retirement not to. My wife and I are depending on that retirement." He heaved a big breath. "As much as it pains me to say it, I have an obligation to protect our future. Surely you must understand?"

"I do." What kind of person would he be if he didn't? "I want you to do your job, Harold. I have nothing to hide. Jess has nothing to hide."

"We wouldn't be having this conversation if I thought otherwise. You know me better than that." Worry furrowed Harold's face, deepening the lines that several decades in law enforcement had earned him. "I believe with all that makes me a cop that you're being framed—more importantly, I believe it with all my heart. We've been friends a very long time. I don't want to see this end the way I fear it's going to unless drastic measures are taken."

Dan gave his head a shake. "I told you I don't have anything to hide. What is it you're getting at?"

"Tomorrow morning around ten o'clock I'm going to ask you for permission to conduct an even more thorough search of your home."

Indignation lashed through Dan again but this time he kept it contained.

"If you refuse, a warrant will be issued."

"Why the hell would I refuse?" Now he was just plain pissed off and damned well offended.

"I'm not suggesting you would refuse," Harold urged. "I'm only explaining what's going to happen. This is out of my hands now, Dan. The search will take place." Harold rose from his chair.

"Why wait until tomorrow? Do it now." Dan shot to his feet. "I'll make the call myself." He reached for the phone, exasperation making it difficult to stay rational.

Harold reached across the desk and placed his hand over Dan's. "Listen to me," he added emphasis to each word. "Tomorrow morning. Ten o'clock. Do whatever you need to do tonight. Are we clear?"

His words penetrated the layers of denial that had protected Dan until now. "Crystal."

"Good."

Their gazes held for a moment longer before Harold took the incriminating evidence and walked out.

Dan surveyed the office he had worked so hard to achieve. As if he had nothing else to worry about, the thought of how disappointed his mother would be if this all went to hell made him laugh. *If*? What was he thinking?

He braced his hands on the window ledge, the laughter dying in his throat. It was already going to hell. Spears had set the course and every piece was falling into place.

Dan grabbed his cell and walked out of his office, maybe for the last time. He was taking Jess home.

That was one thing Spears would never be able to do.

CHAPTER TWENTY

Lori sat on the floor with reports spread all around her. Chet crossed the room, a cold beer in each hand. He passed one to her and sat down beside her. "Found anything new?"

She shook her head then took a long draw from the beer. "Not one thing." She turned to Chet. "You checked everywhere, right?"

It wasn't bad enough that they were both banging their heads against the wall on this homicide case, now there was the added worry that Spears might be watching every move they made right here in their own home. After what happened at Burnett's, they had a right to be worried. "Everywhere I know to check."

He had searched the whole house, top to bottom. No hidden cameras, no listening devices.

She sighed. "That's a relief." Yet there was little relief in her expression as she turned back to the reports. "I wish I could say the same about this case."

"Let's go over it again," Chet suggested.

"According to their known associates," Lori rubbed at her neck as if an ache had started there, "the Vance sisters have fallen off the grid. The feds say they haven't left the country. Their parents haven't heard from them. But then, they rarely do."

"They're laying low somewhere," Chet suggested. He reached up and massaged her shoulders and neck. "Waiting for further instructions, maybe."

Lori reached for his hand and held onto it. "I don't ever want us to be that way. I call my mom and sister every day. I want it to be like that with our kids even when they're grown and sick of hearing from us."

Chet smiled. Why couldn't he have found this woman first? "We'll never be like those people. I promise." He would gladly promise her the world. He loved her that much. He prayed the tests the new doctor would conduct before proceeding with the reversal of his vasectomy turned out the right way. He wanted to have babies with Lori.

Sisters and brothers for Chester.

They just had to get through this thing with Spears. In spite of everything the bastard was throwing at them, Lori didn't look scared. Worried, for sure, but not afraid. Chet was glad. After what she'd gone through with that Reed guy it was a miracle she could deal with being a part of this investigation. She was brave and strong. He admired her so much.

"Jess still isn't herself." Lori turned to face him. "She's too distracted. She's the strongest woman I know. But this is breaking her down."

As much as he hated to admit it, Chet had noticed the same thing. "She's definitely not herself."

"You were right." Lori took another swallow of her beer. "She is pushing us away."

"Did you talk to her?"

Lori shook her head. "I will. I didn't want to add to her stress today."

Chet hated the toll this insanity was taking on his boss and on Lori. He would like nothing more than to be the one to put a bullet right between Eric Spears's eyes. Though he'd understand if the chief insisted on that privilege.

"You think these two chicks are just thrill killers doing whatever Ellis tells them to do?" Lori picked up the photos from her pile of reports. "Or do you think they're working directly for Spears?"

He mulled over her question for a second or two. "I think Ellis is the one interacting with Spears. He and Spears seem" Chet shrugged "I don't know, cut from the same cloth. That whole arrogant attitude combined with enough money not to care what anyone else thinks."

"Ellis may be one of those guys who gets off just watching." Lori shuddered. "Speaking of watching, I'm going to try and reach William Upshaw tomorrow. He's bound to know something."

"Upshaw? That's the brother of the murdered girl up in Boston?" Lori and Hayes had been working that lead. Chet wasn't as familiar as maybe he should be with that cold case.

Lori nodded. "I think Ellis did more than witness the murder."

"Maybe the sister was his first kill?"

"That's possible."

On the coffee table Chet's cell phone buzzed. He and Lori exchanged a look. He hoped it wasn't another dead body.

Chet pushed to his feet and reached the phone just before it went to voice mail. His ex-wife's image flashed on the screen. *Sherry?* Why would she be calling at this hour? Worry twisted his gut. He hoped his son wasn't sick. "Hey, everything okay?"

"I want you to listen, Chet, but I don't want you to get excited."

His pulse slung into overdrive. "What's going on?" He could hear television sounds in the background.

"Everything is fine. Chester is fine."

Somehow that wasn't reassuring. "What's going on, Sherry?" Lori moved up next to him. He shrugged, uncertain what the hell was up.

"With all that's going on with your job and your new girlfriend, I've been really worried, Chet. And now this business of assigning a cop to watch the house, it's too much. I decided it was better if I took Chester away for a while."

The fear he'd been holding at bay surfaced. "What does that mean, Sherry? Where are you?"

"We're fine, Chet. Chester and I are staying with friends until this is over. You don't need to worry. We're safe."

Damn. "Sherry, where are you?" She didn't sound drunk. His ex-wife hardly even drank a glass of wine.

Had she lost her mind? Was someone forcing her to make this call? His heart started to pound.

"I'm not telling you where we are, Chet. Our son is safer that way. He's not safe with you right now. We'll be fine. When this is over, we'll come back home."

"I don't think—"

"I'll call you again soon. Bye, Chet."

The call ended. "What the hell?" He tried to call her back three times but it went to voice mail each time.

"What's going on?"

"Sherry took Chester somewhere." He closed his eyes and took a slow, deep breath.

"She's protecting him."

Chet opened his eyes and glared at Lori, wanted to be angry. But she was right. "I don't like it."

Lori put her arms around him and leaned her cheek against his shoulder. "As much as I hate to agree with anything she says or does, she is right. If Chester isn't around, he's unlikely to become a target." She raised her head to look him in the eyes. "We don't know what's going to happen next, Chet. He's safer this way. We talked about this. You were the one who brought it up first. She's only doing what you would do if the circumstances were reversed."

"We did." He exhaled a big breath. What would he do without this woman? He might be a grown man and a homicide detective but right now what he wanted to do more than anything was cry.

As if she knew exactly how he felt, she stood on her tiptoes and kissed him. "Come to bed. We've had a long day. A good night's sleep will make everything clearer."

"I just hope it puts us one day closer to stopping Spears."

CHAPTER TWENTY-ONE

Jess stared at the ceiling. She couldn't sleep. Dan slept soundly next to her though she didn't see how. He'd been distracted all evening, prowling around the house like he'd lost something besides their privacy. But then, who wouldn't be? Every time she'd started to bring up the news she had to share, he seemed to withdraw.

How could she blame him? She had turned his life upside down. She hadn't intended to come back here and wreak such havoc. Her sister and her brother-in-law weren't safe in their own home. Dan's parents weren't either. Wanda had been visited by the killer who wanted Jess for some twisted reason.

The people she cared about most, the friends she had made since coming here, all of them were in danger because of her.

That didn't even include the baby.

Her stomach did one of those rolls that warned she'd better head to the bathroom.

She pushed the covers down and eased out of bed, snagging her cell phone as she went. Cringing with every step, she padded into the bathroom. When the door was closed, ever so gently, she turned on the light.

She sat on the side of the whirlpool tub and waited to see if her stomach would settle. Everything was such a mess. Lately it felt like each day brought some new complication.

Like being pregnant.

Her attention settled on the full-length mirror on the back of the door. She stood, turned side ways and pulled her nightshirt tight over her belly. No noticeable change yet. But there were a million things to do starting with finding a doctor.

When the baby was born, where would they live? Here? Would Dan insist on a big wedding? How would she handle that? There was no question, she wanted to spend the rest of her life with him but she wasn't entirely comfortable with sharing their private lives with the world.

The image of that headstone cut through all the worrisome thoughts. The painting came next. She trembled. Spears had shown them just how close he could get with such ease.

How did she protect Dan or this baby?

She'd asked herself that question a thousand times and she still had no answer. Her hand flattened against her tummy. Whatever happened, this new life was depending on her.

A soft knock made her jump. "You okay in there?"

She opened the door and made an apologetic face. "I didn't mean to wake you. I couldn't sleep."

How could the man roll out of bed after the kind of day they'd had and look that good? His hair was mussed, he wore nothing but his boxers and he could still rock the cover of a fashion magazine. Every inch of him was well muscled and beautifully toned. So not fair. She sighed.

He took her by the hand and tugged her along. "Let's find some hot chocolate. That'll help you sleep."

"You have hot chocolate?" Her stomach let her know it was interested.

"It may be left over from Christmas."

She followed him into the kitchen and scooted up onto a stool at the island. "You have hot chocolate at Christmas?"

"I do," he said as he searched the cabinets. "Don't you remember?"

With her elbows on the counter and her chin in her hands she searched her memory. It took a little longer than it used to. Then she smiled. "I remember the first winter we were away from Birmingham. We had hot chocolate and marshmallows every night." How had she forgotten that? Boston had been cold as hell compared to here.

"Ah ha!" He turned back to her, container of instant hot chocolate in his hand. "It was so cold in Boston we stayed under blankets in that tiny apartment all winter." He laughed, the sound more cathartic than anything she'd experienced in weeks.

"I remember thinking I never wanted to see snow again."

"Very different from Alabama winters." Jess laughed. They had been so young and so madly in love.

"That's putting it mildly."

"Shoveling out the car was the worst." She had vivid recollections of that chore.

He groaned. "Don't remind me." He filled the teakettle and set it on the stove. There was a click, click, click and the flame lit beneath it. "I thought I had died and gone to hell."

While he rounded up cups, measured out the proper amount of mix into each one and then gathered spoons, Jess wished she had some of the photos that were stored in Virginia. She still had a few from those days in Boston.

He leaned on the counter to wait for the water to boil. "I also remember the snow that Christmas you came back here for a visit."

The mischievous twinkle in his eyes warned that he was recalling one part in particular. "I was on my way to Lil's house when I ran into you."

He grinned. "We hadn't seen each other in…"

"Ten years," she supplied. "A whole decade."

"I can't believe we let that much time pass."

"Then we let another decade pass before we saw each other again." It didn't seem possible so much time had slipped away. Dan had called and asked for her help on a case. She'd needed desperately to get out of Virginia. The Spears investigation had just gone to hell and it was her fault—at least the world had thought so.

"You think maybe destiny is trying to tell us something?"

"That we have truly odd timing?" she suggested with a laugh.

He reached toward her, let her hair filter through his fingers. "Like maybe we belong together and no matter how we've tried to pretend otherwise, we are destined to be a couple."

Or a family. This was the time. "We need to have that talk I've been trying to have with you all week."

The kettle whistled.

"Hold that thought."

Dammit, she couldn't keep holding this one! She slid off the stool and rounded the island as he poured the steaming water into the cups. While he set the kettle back on the stove, she stirred.

"Can we talk now? Give it time to cool?" Most people would think they were crazy for having hot chocolate in August. It was hot as blazes outside. The humidity was unbearable. But she needed the comfort only heated chocolate could give.

"All right. I'll go first."

"You want to go first?" Had he been keeping a secret too? Was she never going to get to tell hers?

"Come on. We have to do this right." He carried their cups and led the way.

Jess followed him into the living room. He sat down on the hearth. She sat beside him and accepted one of the cups.

"Shall we light the gas logs?"

He gave her a sideways glance before sipping his chocolate.

She savored a swallow of hers and waited for him to begin. It gave her another minute to rally her nerve. *Yeah, yeah. More excuses, Jess.*

"While the crime scene team was here today they found something besides all the cameras."

A new kind of worry needled its way beneath her skin. "No one said anything."

"Harold came to see me just before we left the office."

No wonder he'd seemed so distant tonight. "What did they find and what does Black have to do with it?" Harold Black did not like her. No matter how he pretended to, Jess understood that he did not. He'd made that clear from the beginning whether Dan wanted to see it or not.

"Remember last week they found Allen's cell phone in my garbage?"

She nodded. It didn't matter that the cup she held was warm, her hands felt suddenly cold.

"A search of Allen's office uncovered a report he'd supposedly written with the intention of filing a complaint against me for threatening him."

"What? You didn't threaten him." She winced. "Did you?"

"I did not threaten him."

This was sounding more and more as if someone was trying to frame the chief of police. But they were framing the wrong chief. Jess was the one Allen hated.

"So today they found something else? Here?" Jess couldn't believe it!

He nodded, set his chocolate aside. "They found Allen's wedding band in my grill."

"His wedding band? In the grill you used for the steaks the other night?"

Another nod. "The inscription confirmed it was Allen's."

That would have been her next question. "Black doesn't think you put it there, does he?"

Dan braced his forearms on his knees. "I don't know what he thinks. He insinuated he believed me when I said I didn't put it there."

"He probably thinks *I* put it there." If either of them had motive, it was Jess. But she had not put anything in the grill.

"Whatever he thinks," Dan went on, "because they found the ring, they want to do a more thorough search of the house and yard."

"What?" Jess almost spilled her hot chocolate. Dan took the cup from her and set it beside his. "They want to search your house? Oh my God!" She shot to her feet and started to pace. This was beyond insane.

"I have nothing to hide."

"You need a lawyer." This was wrong. "If Black isn't setting you up, then Spears is… *somehow*. Either way, you need a good attorney to protect you, Dan. You can't take this lightly."

He stood, caught up with her and pulled her into his arms. "I do not need an attorney. I have nothing to hide. Whoever planted that ring and the phone is barking up the wrong tree. No one is going to believe I killed anyone."

He had a point there but this was so unfair.

"This is my fault." She looked up at him, anguish tearing at her heart. "This has to be Spears. He's trying to destroy you because of me."

"He's going to fail, Jess."

She tried to pull away to prevent him seeing her tears. She hated crying.

He held her tighter. "This isn't your fault. You are not responsible for what he's doing. He's a psychopath."

"Sociopath," she corrected. "He has a lot of traits of a psychopath but, deep down, he's a sociopath."

"Whatever he is, he wants you to feel guilty."

As true as his words were, they didn't lessen the responsibility she felt. And dead was dead. Her ability to recognize where guilt belonged was not going to bring all those victims back to life. Even worse, it wasn't going to prevent Spears from killing again and again until someone stopped him.

Since no one could find him, that made him unstoppable.

"Well, he succeeded," she confessed. The guilt she felt wasn't going away.

"Your turn," Dan prompted, obviously ready to change the subject.

Uncertainty and plain old fear tightened her throat. She needed to tell him. She should have told him already. Now here she was with just the right moment and she was terrified. Up until now, she could be Deputy Chief Jess Harris and everyone saw her that way. Nothing had changed from the outside. Once she said the words out loud... once everyone knew, her life would be different. Everything would change.

That scared the hell out of her.

"Jess," he smiled down at her, "surely you know by now you can tell me anything."

She didn't know how he could smile at a time like this. He could lose his job. He could be falsely accused of murder. Still, he smiled for her.

"You said you want children." She hoped he couldn't feel her body trembling.

"I've done some thinking about that." He cupped her cheek with his right hand. "I understand if you don't. I will not allow anything to come between us again, Jess. You make me happy. We don't have to have children to be happy."

"Yes, we do."

A line formed across his forehead. "We do? You changed your mind? You want to have children? When did this happen?"

Jess moistened her lips and told her heart to stop its frantic pounding. "I don't know, maybe a month ago."

"Why didn't you tell me?" He held up his hands surrender style. "Not that I'm pushing the issue. Whenever you're ready. I'm just glad you want to... consider it. If, that's what you're saying. I know how a child—being pregnant—would affect your work. I really do understand you may not want that."

He was rambling. She took his hands in hers. "Dan, I'm trying to tell you that we're pregnant."

He stopped. Moving. Breathing. He stared at her as if he was struggling to grasp what she meant. "You're… are you positive?"

"Four pregnancy tests, Dan. They all showed the same results. Positive."

"We're pregnant?"

"Yes."

His expression remained guarded. "And you're not upset?"

She shook her head, and then shrugged. "I'm getting used to the idea."

"*Oh my God.* We're… having… a baby?"

"Yes." She nodded this time just in case he wasn't getting it. She pressed his hand to her belly. "We are pregnant. We are having a baby in about seven and a half months or so."

He took a breath, then started to speak but stopped. Confusion and surprise played across his handsome face. "Are you okay? I mean… are you *really* okay?"

"I'm okay."

"Have you seen a doctor?" All that emotion was suddenly shining in his eyes.

"I have to get that scheduled. Soon," she promised.

"And you want to do this?"

She nodded. "I do. Yes."

He swept her into his arms. "I don't know the right words to say." He kissed her hard on the lips. "I love you, Jess."

"I love you, Dan."

She melted against him then, too overwhelmed and too exhausted to talk anymore. He carried her to his bed. He kissed her temple. Whispered plans about the future as he undressed her and then himself. The happiness and excitement in his voice was all the confirmation she needed to know this was right.

No matter what else happened, they—the baby—was right.

His lips moved down her throat, leaving kiss after kiss against her skin. Tiny shivers spilled over her body and need throbbed between her thighs. He reached her hip and paused. His caressed her belly first with his hand, then with his lips. He whispered to their baby and her eyes filled with tears.

He settled between her legs and rubbed her intimately with his hardened length. "Thank you."

She couldn't speak. The tears wouldn't be restrained. She hugged her arms and legs around him and savored the sensation of being filled by him. He made love to her so tenderly her very soul cried out with the sweetness of it.

Later, when he had fallen asleep once more, she slipped from the bed and made her way through the darkness until she was in the study with her makeshift case board.

She paced the floor and argued with herself about what she should do. There had to be a way to stop what was happening to Dan. This was so wrong. There was only one person she could turn to for help. Corlew was probably in bed by now. But this couldn't wait.

She exhaled a weary sigh. "Last chance, Jess." Can you really trust him?

Did she have a choice?

She made the call. Corlew answered on the second ring.

"What's up?"

Mustering up a sociable tone, she said, "You sound better."

"I feel better. Fever's gone." He yawned. "What's going on with you? You can't sleep?"

She glanced at the door. Listened for any sound. "Remember when you told me there were things about BPD I didn't know. You made some shallow innuendoes about Chief Black."

"Hey. Shallow is one thing I'm not," he argued.

Depended upon who was doing the measuring, she supposed. "Do you have resources that could look into something inside BPD?"

"I knew you'd see the light," he said, triumph in his voice. "I told you I lost my job because of Dan and his cronies in the department."

"This is serious, Buddy." A beat of silence passed. She hadn't called him by his first name since they were in seventh grade.

"Okay, okay. I know Dannie boy is a pretty decent guy. Maybe it wasn't him. What's so serious?"

As much as she needed his help, she couldn't bring herself to trust him with all the details. "I want you to dig up what you can—without anyone in the BPD finding out preferably—on Captain Ted Allen."

"The cop who went missing?"

"Yes." She checked the hall. "Don't think I expect you to do this or the investigation into my parents' accident for free. I'll pay your going rate." When he started to object, she cut him off, "I insist. This is business."

"Okay, okay. Got it. And, yes, I have a contact inside the department. I'll see what I can get."

Jess moistened her lips and went for broke. "I want you to check into Chief Black as well." The thump, thump beneath her sternum made it hard to breathe. She was taking a major risk here.

Corlew laughed. "Hell, I'll do that one for free."

Jess wished she didn't have to do it this way but she couldn't ask Lori or Chet to put their jobs on the line. "You have to be careful. No one can know. I mean it."

"You have my word." All signs of humor vanished. "No one will know what I'm doing or who I'm doing it for. I just have one question."

Jess couldn't wait to hear it. There was no telling what he would come up with. "If I can answer it, I will."

"What's Black done to get on your bad side?"

For a long second she hesitated but there was no way to keep him entirely in the dark. "I think he's trying to hurt Dan."

More silence.

God, she hated this. Her attention shifted to the door again. Dan would be upset with her if he learned she was trusting any part of this to Corlew.

"That's all I needed to know. I'll get on this ASAP."

"Thanks. Call me as soon as you know anything."

"You got it. Get some sleep, kid."

Jess watched her screen go black. It was done. She prayed this wouldn't turn into another complication.

Things were already complicated enough.

CHAPTER TWENTY-TWO

11:59 P.M.

It was only moments until midnight.

The final canvas had been chosen. The perfect medium for the work. And the subject, of course. The subject was the pièce de résistance.

Richard wondered if Jess Harris had any idea just how spectacularly important she was in this passionate endeavor.

He watched the two beauties he had trained so well as they added the final touches to the masterpiece that would be his gift to one of the greatest killers the world would ever know.

Selma came to him. Wrapped her arms around him, her soft skin warm against his. "Will he like it?"

Richard smiled. "He will love and treasure it for the rest of his days."

He motioned for Olive to join them. Though she possessed little artistic talent, she was loyal and dedicated to his cause. She curled her arms around his. "We are ready for tomorrow?" he asked.

Both smiled and looked to him with such admiration. "It will be amazing," Selma enthused. "I can hardly wait to begin the next part of our journey."

Olive puckered her lips in a pout. "Don't keep us waiting long for you, Richard."

He was such a fortunate man. To watch two magnificent savants emerge from their shells and open to the passions that only he could show them. He had shown many the wonder and beauty of true art. He had taken those who yearned to feel the deepest of passions and immortalized them. But none had been as important as these two young women.

Together they were *his* final masterpiece.

Now everyone would know his utter brilliance and the depth of his immense passion. His own beauty would no longer be hidden in the shadow of others.

And the woman, the mother of these two lovely creatures, would forever remember the heart she had shattered and tossed away.

He looked from Olive to Selma. "No one has ever loved you the way I do."

"No one," they echoed in unison.

"You must promise me that you will not fail," he urged. "This is the moment I've always waited for. The moment *he* is waiting for. You must not disappoint us. You are the instruments of our destiny."

"You have my word," Selma promised. "We will not fail."

"We will not," Olive vowed.

He kissed each one on the cheek. "I will be right behind you, my darlings."

CHAPTER TWENTY-THREE

"Jess!"

Her eyes opened but she didn't want to wake up. "What time is it?" she murmured.

What was that smell?

"We have to get out of the house!"

She sat up or he was hauling her up, she couldn't say for sure which. "What's that smell?"

"Smoke. We have to get out!"

Smoke?

Jess came wide awake. Adrenaline rocketed through her veins. Smoke was thick in the air. She coughed. Her eyes burned.

What happened? Where was Dan? She reached out... tried to get her bearings. She couldn't see. Why didn't he turn on the lights?

The roar of flames whispered through the darkness. *Fire.* Oh God! They had to get out of here. She stalled. *The baby.* She shouldn't be breathing all this

270

smoke. She tugged the neck of her nightshirt up over her nose and mouth. "Dan!"

Hands clutched at her. She jumped.

"Right here. I've got you."

His arms went around her. He picked her up and held her tight against his chest. She blinked repeatedly, trying to see. Suddenly they were at the window. He helped her climb out and get her feet on the ground.

"Go," he ordered. "Get away from the house."

She ran bare foot across the dew-dampened grass, Dan right behind her. At the far side of the backyard she stopped, she doubled-over coughing. Tears streamed down her cheeks.

"You okay?" Dan asked between his own bouts of coughing.

She nodded. What the hell had happened? The sun wasn't up yet and the stars and the moon were doing little to light the sky. It was eerily dark around the house. All the exterior security lights were out.

The house was on fire. She saw flames through the kitchen window. The reality shook her all over again. "Oh my God."

Where were the sirens? Why had no alarm sounded?

Dan dragged in a big breath. "I need to call for help."

The house—and everything in it—was going up in flames. Jess groaned. "My bag is in there." She whirled toward Dan. "My Glock. My phone."

"Oh hell." He ran his hand through his hair. "Mine too."

There was nothing they could do… they couldn't go back inside.

Dan's home, all his things, including the pictures of them he'd kept from all those years ago, were being destroyed as they watched.

A memory clicked into place. Ten years ago, the farmhouse outside Ruckersville… the cages and those young women.

Spears.

The epiphany hit with such impact that she swayed. He'd been digging in her past again. The night before she'd come home for Christmas ten years ago, she'd solved a case involving five missing women. They had been held in cages, just like the three he'd held captive in Tennessee only days ago.

Ten years ago that old farmhouse had burned down with Jess and one other survivor barely escaping.

He was taunting her with all that he knew about her, breaking her down bit by bit and giving her a preview of things to come.

She turned to the man at her side.

Spears intended to destroy Dan just to get to her.

7:50 A.M.

The fire was out.

Jess stood in the middle of the backyard staring at the smoldering rubble that had been Dan's home. Lori had brought Jess a change of clothes and a ponytail holder for her hair.

Her bag was gone, along with the world she carried inside it.

She sucked in a breath, swallowed against her dry, sore throat. But they were okay. The paramedics had checked both her and Dan and they were fine. She'd asked the paramedic about the baby. He'd suggested she see her obstetrician as soon as possible but didn't believe she had any reason to worry since they'd escaped the house basically unharmed.

Chief Black and Dan were having words. Judging by the body language it wasn't a casual conversation. The crime scene unit was here. Cops were everywhere. Dan's parents had showed up but he'd ushered them away.

"What do you suppose that's all about?" Lori asked, following Jess's gaze.

"Doesn't look friendly," Harper suggested.

Jess turned to the two detectives who were far more than just members of her team. "They found Captain Allen's wedding ring when they were looking for spy stuff in Dan's house yesterday."

Lori expression showed the shock she felt. "You're not saying they believe Chief Burnett had anything to do with his disappearance?"

Jess just wanted to cry. "I honestly don't know."

"Unbelievable." Harper shook his head.

"Tell me about it." Part of her wanted to share the other news with her friends, but just now she needed everyone focused on the case. "Anything from the brother in Boston?" she asked Lori.

"I have a call into him. I'm hoping he'll agree to a Skype interview."

Jess didn't hold out much hope but it was worth a try.

"No hits on Selma or Olive Vance's passports," Harper reported. "If they've left the country they used an alias. We've checked with the bus station, AMTRAK and rental car agencies. No hits there either. Same goes for Ellis. They either had some other form of transportation or they're laying low right here in Birmingham."

"All right." Jess crossed her arms over her chest. She was still shaking. "Nudge the Vance sisters' parents again." She thought about that for a second. "Better yet, have Agent Manning do it. The feds will be taking this case anyway if the international connection we suspect pans out. Maybe the parents will react to the threat of a federal investigation."

"I'll make that call right now." Harper stepped away, his phone already in hand.

"Lori, you and Cook follow up with the ME. See if there's anything new with the latest victim. Check with all the surveillance details and with Gina Coleman at Channel 6. Maybe someone has seen or heard something new that we don't know about yet."

"You staying here?" Lori glanced around at the chaos.

"Just until Hayes picks me up. I need a new badge and a weapon and…" She groaned. "My bag and all my notes. My phone. It's all gone."

Lori gave her a hug. "All those things can be replaced." She glanced at Dan. "You and the chief are irreplaceable."

"You're right. I should be happy to be alive." She wasn't sure she would ever be happy again until Spears was dead.

"I know this isn't the time," Lori ventured, visibly hesitant.

Jess frowned. "What?" If either she or Harper was thinking of moving out of SPU, they could forget it. *Wouldn't they be better off away from you?*

"I'd like to go with you today. Hayes can work with Harper and Cook."

Expecting anything but that, the request puzzled Jess for a second, and then she understood. "I guess you saw through my big plan." No use denying it.

Lori nodded. "You've been keeping us at arm's length." She reached out, squeezed Jess's hand. "We're in this together. We want to help keep you safe."

That confounding tidal wave of emotions swelled up again. When had she become such a blubbering bundle of emotions? "I just don't want—"

"We know. But this is what we want. We want to help end this."

Jess managed a shaky, watery smile. "Okay. You're with me today."

"I'll pass along your instructions to the others."

Jess watched Lori cut through the crowd around Dan's house. She was wrong to try and protect her team. They were more than capable of protecting themselves.

Hopefully today they would get a break in the case. Ellis's part in this was still unclear to Jess. He would have a motive for being involved beyond simply following orders from Spears. The Vance sisters were young. They might very well have less of a personal motive and more of a grandiose reason for being puppets for Ellis and, by extension, Spears. Whatever their reasons, Jess intended to find them.

Her attention shifted back to Dan. Black stamped off, visibly angry or upset. Dan headed her way. She hoped the news wasn't as bad as it had looked.

"You okay?" The smile that tilted his lips under the circumstances made her heart stumble.

"I'm okay." She searched his face and saw the strain there. "The question is, are you okay?"

"Guess so." He glanced back at this house. "It looks like we'll be finding a new place to stay for a while."

"We'll stay at my place."

He shrugged. "Thompson gave the place the all clear. We can do that."

Suited Jess. "You're okay with my place?"

"As long as we're together it doesn't matter where we stay." His gaze slipped down to her belly before returning to meet hers. "I need you to be extra careful, Jess."

"I will," she promised. "Everything I do is about more than me now."

He reached for her hand and squeezed it. "It's about us. All *three* of us."

She wished she could leave it there. But she had to know. "What's Black saying this morning?"

Dan swiped what was likely soot from her cheek. "Besides insinuating that I burned down my own house to destroy evidence?"

"Please tell me he's not really going there?"

Dan shook his head. "I don't know, Jess. I think this might not be going away so easily."

The hope she'd held out wilted. Whether Dan chose to blame her or not, she had devastated his life. He was being framed and his home had been destroyed. The painting of them in bed together and the headstone crept into her thoughts.

Her being here had already cost him so much. Whatever happened she intended to see that she wasn't the reason he lost his life.

BIRMINGHAM POLICE DEPARTMENT.
11:59 A.M.

Jess stared at her new smart phone. It looked and felt almost like her old one, but all the photos and contact information were missing. She should have signed up for that backup plan she'd been offered. Oh well. Lori was forwarding contact numbers to her.

"I hate this." Jess set the phone aside and studied her new Glock. "I hate this even more." She'd had the other one, her second weapon in her entire career, for twelve years. This one looked basically the same. The weight was the same or very close, but it felt different. God, she despised change. She couldn't imagine how Dan felt.

"The call with Upshaw is in five minutes," Lori announced.

At least something was going right this morning. "I'm ready."

Dan was back in his office. He'd stopped by to check on her after his trip to the AT&T store. He had a flashy new phone too and a new weapon. That was one of the perks of living in the same city where you grew up—you had contacts. Dan had put in a call to a friend and weapons were delivered to them at the office. The forms were filled out, the background checks done and they were good to go.

Except it was all different.

She glanced at the temporary bag on the floor next to her desk. The clerk at the phone store had felt bad for Jess and provided her with a nifty tote bag that sported the AT&T logo. Until she had time to shop, it would have to do.

She grabbed a bag of M&Ms from her drawer and decided a snack was in order. Lori had insisted on taking her to a drive through for breakfast after leaving Dan's. She hadn't been hungry but Lori had been right to insist. Jess needed to eat.

The whole morning had passed in a whirlwind of smoke and purchases. It was lunch already and she felt as if she'd moved backwards rather than forward. Hayes had gone for burgers. Jess rolled her eyes. This kid was going to be addicted to chocolate and red meat before he or she was even born.

She was going to be a horrible mother.

Another chirp from her new phone and Jess jumped. Every time her phone made the sound indicating she had received a new contact it startled her. Mainly, because her thoughts were all over the place. She didn't want to think what would've happened if Dan hadn't woke up this morning.

Though she doubted killing her in a simple house fire was what Spears intended, she felt certain he was attempting to create havoc and more distraction. He had certainly accomplished that objective.

When the fire marshal's report was in they would know the point of origin and the cause of the fire.

Was Spears the reason Captain Allen had disappeared? There was always the chance someone in the department wanted to get back at her or at Dan, but still the idea that it was Spears wouldn't stop nagging at her. Maybe she was getting paranoid but she didn't think so.

Harper and Cook were in the field, knocking on doors and making calls, following up with friends of the victims as well as those of the suspects. The Vance sisters and Ellis had to be somewhere.

Jess's attention settled on Lori. She would be disappointed that Jess had kept the pregnancy a secret from her. But she couldn't tell Lori before she told her sister. There was an etiquette to these things.

As if she'd felt Jess's eyes on her, Lori turned to her. "We're almost ready."

"I was just thinking," Jess admitted. "We've hardly had a minute to catch up this week."

Lori looked at her for a moment without speaking. "Sherry took Chester to a friend's until this is over. She refuses to tell Chet where they're at. How's that for catching up?"

Jess winced. "How's Chet handling it?"

Shoving her hair behind her ears, Lori gave an uncertain shrug. "We were both upset at first, but then we kind of decided she'd probably made the right decision even if she went about it the wrong way."

Made sense. "I think you're onto something there." Jess closed her eyes and gave her head a little shake. "We can't predict where this is going."

"Are you holding up okay?" Lori asked gently.

Jess shrugged. "As well as can be expected." *Under the circumstances.*

"All right, here we go," Lori announced. "Our guy is calling early."

Jess washed down a gob of M&Ms with a chug of water before joining Lori at her computer. William Upshaw was calling from his cell phone but Lori had forwarded hers to the computer for the larger screen. Skype was one of those new ways for teleconferencing Jess had ignored.

"Mr. Upshaw, this is Detective Lori Wells and Chief Jess Harris."

Jess produced a smile for the man. He was mid fifties with gray hair, brown eyes. He had no wife and no kids. The really strange part was that he still lived with his mother in the house where the murder had taken place. He worked at a grocery store stocking shelves in the same job he'd had since he was seventeen.

His face told the story. This man had died the same day his sister did.

"Mr. Upshaw, I appreciate you taking the time to speak with us. We need your help very badly." Jess hoped his silence was not an indication of how this was going to go.

He cleared his throat. "You've read the statement I gave to the police when my sister died?"

"Yes, sir," she confirmed.

"I haven't changed my story in all that time. Why would I change it now?"

Good question. She could try a psychology trick or two for prompting his cooperation but she had a feeling that wasn't going to work with this man. "I don't expect you to tell me anything different about your actions, sir. It's Richard Ellis I wanted to talk to you about."

He flinched and averted his gaze. "What about him? I haven't spoken to him since that day. I don't even know if he's dead or alive."

"He's very much alive, Mr. Upshaw. We believe he's responsible for the gruesome murders of four people just this week."

He shook his head. "I can't help you with that. I don't read the papers or watch much television. Current events don't interest me."

For a guy who professed such indifference to the media and the news the smart phone he was using at this very moment was just as high tech as the one Jess owned. He could text, Google or virtually anything else he wanted to do right from the palm of his hand. He had never used Skype before but he knew what it was. He'd added it to his phone for this interview.

He wasn't fooling Jess. He knew exactly what was going on in the world around him, he'd just opted not to be a part of it any more than necessary.

"Ellis and two of his friends murdered four people but that wasn't enough to satisfy their appetites," Jess informed him. "Once the victims were dead, they butchered their bodies and ripped out their hearts. Anything you might recall about him could be useful to our investigation, Mr. Upshaw. We don't want him to keep getting away with murder and I'm certain you don't either."

There was a flicker of something like remorse then he blinked it away. "You read my statement. I haven't remembered anything else."

"Ellis did this same thing in Europe for years," Jess went on as if he hadn't spoken. "They didn't find enough evidence to charge him so he got away with all those murders, too. He'll keep getting away with it and using people to do his dirty work. People who might not have otherwise harmed another person. People like you, Mr. Upshaw."

He jerked. "I don't know what you mean by that statement. We were neighbors. That's all. Neighborhood kids hang out together, you know."

Jess had taken a risk going with her gut instinct. She decided to push a little harder. "Richard Ellis did something to cause your father to react the way he did. You were there, Mr. Upshaw. You know what he did."

"I didn't…" His voice trailed off.

"If you help us, I might be able to stop the man who devastated your family."

Emotion brightened his eyes and Jess knew she had him.

"I knew he was still out there… doing those despicable things. I was going to write a letter." He shrugged. "That way by the time the police started asking questions it wouldn't matter."

"Are you going somewhere, Mr. Upshaw?" He hadn't left Boston in all this time so she doubted that was the case now. Maybe he was sick.

He shook his head. "My mother's dying. Her doctor said maybe another couple of months. I promised her I would never tell what happened. She doesn't want my sister's name sullied."

"I'm sorry about your mother, Mr. Upshaw, but you must know every minute we waste is one that could cost someone else their life."

"I can't do that to her." He shook his head. "I've already taken everything else she had. I won't take that, too."

Jess tried a different strategy. "If you tell me the truth, I won't put that information in my reports. You can take it to the Boston PD yourself, when you're ready. There's no reason for me to do that as long as I can get Ellis on the murders here. To make that happen, I need your help."

The hesitation that followed had Jess's hopes sinking.

"I was fifteen. I had nothing but cars and girls on my mind."

Jess nodded. "That's probably true of all fifteen year old boys."

"Rick didn't like my sister. She yelled at us all the time. She didn't want us near her friends. And I think something happened between her and Rick and he really hated her after that."

"You have no idea what happened between them?"

"I think it was about that picture he painted of her. He had a crush on her and wanted to impress her. He worked really hard for days and days painting her portrait. When he gave it to her, she laughed. She told him he was pathetic and that he didn't have enough talent to paint a door much less a portrait."

"Did Ellis change after that incident?"

Upshaw nodded. "He did. Started trying to turn me against her. There was a lot going on with my family, too. They were laying off at my dad's factory. I overheard my parents talking about how they didn't know what they'd do. They'd used up their savings on my medical bills. I had Polio and it was tough for all of us."

He didn't speak again for a bit. Jess struggled to be patient.

"My sister got mad at me for something dumb I'd done and she told me that mom and dad hated me. She said it was my fault they were so worried about bills. She said she wished I'd never been born."

"Siblings say that sort of thing sometimes." She and Lil had said horrible things to each other from time to time.

"I know," he agreed hollowly. "Rick used it to convince me that my sister was evil. He hatched this plan about how he could prove it to me. He said that if he got her into bed and then I joined them I'd see how evil she really was. I mean, what kind of sister would have sex with her brother, right? My family's devout Catholics. Just talking about it was enough to send us to hell."

He shook his head. "Rick bought some weed and we all got high. It wasn't like the weed I'd smoked before. This was powerful. We all ended up in bed together kissing and touching." He scrubbed a hand over his face. "My father came in and he went ballistic. Rick laughed and told him he should join us. My father suddenly had his shotgun." He shook his head. "I don't know how he got the gun. I was really messed up by the weed. My sister was screaming and telling us to get out of her room."

More silence elapsed.

"The next thing I knew my father aimed the shotgun. Rick pushed my sister at him just as he fired. The sound was like a bomb exploding in the room. There was blood everywhere and my sister was lying on the floor. My father and I tried to help her but there was nothing we could do. She was dead. There was a big hole in the middle of her chest... like where her heart should be."

"Where was Ellis while you were trying to help your sister?"

"I didn't figure that out until later. He was reloading the shotgun. My father was so devastated that when Rick put the shotgun back in his hands and started talking to him, he just went into a coma. Rick told him to pull the trigger and he did. It was like something from the movies and all I could do was watch."

The horror the man had likely suffered over and over since that day was unimaginable. "Thank you, Mr. Upshaw. You have no idea how much you've helped us. You have my word, we'll do all we can to stop him."

When the connection ended, Jess stared at the faces of the victims on the case board. They were all just like William Upshaw's sister. Innocent... led to slaughter by a devil, a hole left where their hearts had been.

Jess shuddered.

Hayes walked in with a bag of burgers and a disposable tray of soft drinks. "Lunch is served, ladies."

Jess held up a hand to Hayes. "Put it over there." Her appetite was MIA at the moment. "We need to figure out if Ellis had anything to do with Lisa Templeton and Alisha Burgess getting into that house in Homewood. I'll bet," the rest of the scenario unfolded for Jess, "Rod Slater kicked Templeton out of her apartment because Ellis paid him to do it."

Ellis wasn't an artist. Not a single one of the paintings in his gallery or in his home carried his name. Jess got the picture now. He wasn't a painter at all. He was a director and these murders were his stage plays—his works of art.

"Are you thinking Ellis intended for Templeton and Burgess to be the ones to die there?" Hayes suggested.

Jess nodded. "Burgess, Thomas, and McCrary may have been murdered simply because they were in the wrong place at the wrong time, but I think Templeton was an intended victim. Just as Upshaw's sister was." Jess considered the idea that most of the victims left in Ellis's wake were art students. Did they all have one thing in common? Perhaps the ability to paint better than Ellis could ever hope to? "The Upshaw girl was guilty of making him feel inferior when she degraded his work. Templeton did the same thing when her talent outshined his."

"In the end," Lori surmised, "the victims in Europe may have been guilty of nothing more than being better painters."

"Envy can turn a person into something vicious," Hayes offered, their lunch getting cold on his desk.

"That's exactly right," Jess agreed.

All they had to do now was find Ellis and his little murdering helpers. She wondered if Selma and Olive were as innocent as William Upshaw had been. Or were they just as evil as their teacher?

Her new cell made that puny sound that announced she had a text message. Jess frowned.

She needed to change that. Corlew's name flashed on the screen. She opened the text.

We need to meet. Something you need to know.

Worry had her heart rate picking up. *Where*, she responded.

He sent the address of a restaurant in Five Points.

Jess grabbed her temporary bag and a burger. To Hayes, she said, "Lieutenant, catch up with Harper. I'd like the two of you to talk to the Homewood landlord and to Slater. Detective Wells, come with me. I have a meeting."

"I could tag along," Hayes proposed. "Make the calls en route."

Lori grabbed one of the burgers and a drink. "I got this, Lieutenant."

Hayes didn't like it but he backed off.

Jess would smooth that tension over the first chance she got.

Like maybe sometime in the next century.

JIM 'N NICKS. FIVE POINTS. 2:19 P.M.

The burger she'd scarfed down on the way over was not sitting well. Jess stared at the door, wondering what the hell was keeping Corlew. He'd asked her to meet him here and then he was late.

That was the trouble with Corlew. He operated under one set of rules—his own. Though most of his work was good, that was only the case if *good* didn't get in the way. If he had to choose between what he wanted and in doing the right thing, what he wanted would win every time.

Lori sat at the bar, keeping watch. Jess appreciated that she understood the meeting with Corlew was private—at least for now.

Her cell rattled on the table. She'd turned off the ringer so she and Corlew wouldn't be interrupted. Harpers's name appeared on her screen. Maybe she'd get lucky and Ellis had turned himself in, along with his two protégés.

"Tell me something good, Sergeant." Jess kept an eye on the restaurant's entrance.

"Hayes and I connected and we have a couple of real bulletins for you, Chief," he announced. "Are you sitting down?"

Jess perked up. "I am."

"First, Slater admitted that he booted Templeton out of her place because Ellis paid him to do it. Ellis also set up the lease with the owner of the house in Homewood. He provided Templeton with the money she needed for the move by buying her painting."

"Ellis has been a very busy man." Jess could not wait to take him down. Like Spears, he had gotten away with his evil deeds for far too long. Whether he was the murderer or the orchestrator of murder, he was guilty of taking lives.

"Busier than you know," Harper went on. "The Vance sisters' mother just called. Apparently, her conscience started to weigh on her. She and her husband will be back in Birmingham tomorrow. They're leaving Paris tonight."

"She's feeling bad for leaving her spoiled daughters at home alone?" Too bad she hadn't thought of that maybe twenty years ago.

"I do believe so," Harper confirmed. "She admitted to having an affair with Ellis while she and her husband lived in Paris the first time. Ellis wanted her to leave her husband but she refused. The affair ended badly when she told him that he didn't make enough money to support her."

"Oh. That's cold. Another blow to his tender ego." Jess could see where this was going.

"She also confessed that Selma is Ellis's biological child. She's afraid he might be levying a little payback."

"I guess she chose the wrong psychopath to have an affair with." Jess couldn't see this ending pretty for anyone involved.

The call ended and Jess placed her cell back on the table. Now all the players were lined up. The sisters were likely so thankful for all the attention the charming older man lavished upon them that they would do anything he asked. Though twisted, the sisters were victims of his egocentrism, just as Templeton was. The others were just collateral damage to satisfy Spears's wishes.

What would make a killer like Ellis or Cagle do Spears's bidding? Cagle mentioned something about doing what he did for his daughter. Maybe Spears had threatened the man's family. But what about Ellis? What could Spears possibly have on him? He had no family.

Except Selma Vance. Yet, Ellis was using her to exact his own kind of payback.

Maybe Ellis was enjoying being a part of Spears's big finale.

"Sorry to keep you waiting, kid."

Jess about jumped out of her skin. She hoped Corlew didn't notice. She'd been so lost in thought she hadn't seen him come in and she was facing the door, for heaven's sake. "I ordered you a Pepsi." She sipped her own. "And that burger you ordered last time we were here."

He made a face at the drink. Probably would have preferred beer. "Thanks." His eyebrows drew together. "What's this I hear about Dan's house burning down?"

She nodded. "We figure it was Spears. We're hoping the fire marshal can shed some light on what happened."

"Damn." Corlew shook his head. "He probably has good insurance."

"I hope so." She hadn't even thought of that. As responsible as Dan was she couldn't imagine he didn't have good insurance. But money couldn't buy everything he'd lost. "You have news?"

The waitress arrived and plunked a plate on the table. Big burger and a mountain of fries. "Anything else?" she asked.

"We're good." Jess smiled, hoped the vivacious woman would run along. Since she was cute and big breasted Corlew would have her sitting down with him if she lingered.

To Jess's surprise he was too busy manhandling that enormous burger to ogle the waitress. The smell of it made Jess's stomach churn. What was on that burger?

He chewed a couple times and then swallowed. Before he said a word he surveyed the place, nodded at Lori. When his attention finally settled on Jess once more, he said, "You were right to be worried about Black. He's investigating Dan. The jackass officially labeled him a person of interest in Allen's disappearance."

"What the hell is he thinking?" Jess couldn't believe Black would go that far.

Corlew tore off another bite of burger. When he'd washed it down with Pepsi, he leaned forward and spoke more quietly. "My contact says the mayor is pushing Black to get this done. Fast. He wants Dan out."

Insane, just insane. "Are you certain you can trust this contact?"

He leaned closer still. "One hundred percent." He searched her face for a moment, his own dead serious. "Danny boy is in real trouble, Jess. Real trouble."

The smell of onions and grilled beef hit her in the face and her stomach contracted hard.

Oh Lord.

"I'll be back." She grabbed her AT&T bag, scooted out of the booth and headed for the bathroom.

Lori slid off her stool and caught up with her. "You okay?"

Jess paused at the ladies' room door and took slow, steady breaths to try and calm her belly. "I think I ate that burger too fast."

"Let me have a look inside," Lori suggested, "and then I'll get out of your way."

Jess nodded. She didn't trust herself to open her mouth again. Lori entered the ladies' bathroom and had a look around. As soon as she was back in the corridor, Jess hurried inside.

Lori walked back to the bar. She took her seat but kept her attention on the entrance to the short corridor that led to the bathrooms. Jess had looked damned pale. The fire had obviously shaken her more than she realized. It was a miracle she could get through the day with all that was going on. The stress was taking a serious toll.

Corlew strolled over to the bar and ordered a beer. He took a slug and sighed. "Better." He jerked his head in the direction Jess had disappeared. "She okay?"

"I think so. It's been a rough couple of days."

He made a sound of agreement. "I've got a feeling it's not going to get better any time soon."

Lori suspected he was more right than he knew. Buddy Corlew was a private detective now but he'd once been a BPD cop. He'd gone to school with Jess, and Lori sensed he still had a thing for her. He was a good-looking guy, but nothing like Dan Burnett. Corlew was the jeans wearing, ponytailed type. For all his cocky attitude and tough guy exterior he was damned good at his job. He'd earned himself the nickname the Tracker. But if he had his sights set on Jess, he was wasting his time.

"Buddy Corlew!"

Corlew turned toward the door. Lori leaned past him to see who had shouted his name. It sounded like... *Chief Black?*

As Lori watched, Chief Black, followed by two of his detectives and four BPD uniformed officers, crossed the room.

"Buddy Corlew," Black repeated as he stopped a few feet away, "you are under arrest for bribery and obstruction of justice."

Corlew laughed. "That's a good one, Black, but this isn't April Fool's day and I'm in no mood to play with a joker like you."

Roark, Black's ranking detective, stepped forward and recited the Miranda Rights.

Corlew glanced at Lori. "Get Channing Cole on the horn. Tell him I need to call in that marker he owes me. *Now.*"

Lori nodded and reached for her cell.

What the hell was happening here?

Jess had barely made it to the toilet before the burger retraced its path. She grabbed another wad of toilet paper and wiped her mouth. The wheeze and whine of the hydraulic closer on the bathroom door warned that someone had entered. It was a three-stall facility so that was no surprise. Still, she reached into her bag for her weapon as she got to her feet and readied to face whoever had paused at the open door of her stall.

"Don't be afraid, Deputy Chief Jess Harris."

Jess didn't need eyes in the back of her head to know who had decided to pay her a visit. The fingers of her right hand closed around the butt of her new Glock as she straightened. She turned, her weapon leveled on the first person to come into view.

Selma Vance. The barrel of the blonde's handgun was already aimed at Jess's face.

Well hell.

Behind Selma, her sister Olive leaned against the bathroom door, her weapon trained on Jess as well.

Maybe this was why she'd always resisted the idea of children. Jess was barely pregnant and already this kid had her in trouble.

No problem. As long as she was still breathing, Lori would be making an appearance any second now.

"Why would I be afraid, Selma?" Jess smiled as if all were right in the world. "My job is to serve and protect. How can I help you and Olive?"

The sisters exchanged a glance.

That couldn't be good.

A hard rap on the door followed by, "Chief, you okay in there?"

"Careful," Selma whispered.

"Just that barbecue I had for lunch, Lori. I'll be out in a minute." Jess prayed Lori got the message.

"You need some Tums, ma'am," came her detective's response.

"Give me *two* minutes for Christ's sake." She rolled her eyes before meeting Selma's again. "I never get a minute to myself. Now, where were we?" Jess worked hard at appearing calm, but her heart was about to beat its way out of her chest. Her stomach was churning like there might be an encore coming. She sure wished those sleek black barrels weren't so damned close.

"We were chosen as messengers," Selma explained. "Our task is almost complete."

"You have a message for me?" Jess tightened her hold on her Glock. Told her heart to slow just enough so she could hear herself think over the blood pounding in her ears. "Why don't we put these guns down and talk about it."

Ignoring the suggestion, Selma passed her weapon to her sister. Olive promptly leveled it back on Jess while her sister pulled a necklace from beneath her blouse. A small glass vial hung from the silver chain. Looked like blood inside it.

Was it tainted with Curare? Jess steeled herself. Considered whether or not to take the shot. But then the sister would fire one or both of the weapons she held.

Not a good outcome for anyone involved.

"I kept it close to my heart so it would stay warm," Selma explained.

Jess's throat tightened. *Shit.* "Is that for me?"

Selma nodded. "It's *his* blood." She opened the vial, poured a little on her fingertip and reached out to dab it on Jess's forehead.

Jess held her breath. She could yank Selma into the stall as a shield and just start shooting at Olive.

"And the blood shall be to you for a token." Selma drew circles on Jess's forehead, using the blood like paint.

"When they see the blood," the sisters chanted together, "they will pass over you and you shall not suffer death as his enemies are destroyed one by one."

Selma lowered her hand and stared into Jess's eyes. "For you are *his*, now and forever."

Jess braced for the finale. "Why don't we lower our weapons and talk about this? Your parents are on their way home, Selma."

Olive passed Selma's weapon back to her.

"Your mother's very worried about you," Jess said a little louder. "All you have to do is put your weapons down and we can clear both of you of wrongdoing. You're not responsible for what Ellis forced you to do."

The sisters smiled and started speaking in unison again. "Our quest is complete. Good-bye, Deputy Chief Jess Harris."

Before Jess could fathom their intent the sisters turned to each other, embraced and kissed, each jamming the barrel of her weapon beneath the other's chin.

Jess shouted for them to drop their weapons. The bathroom door burst inward. The handguns discharged simultaneously. Jess jerked with the sound. Blood and brain matter splattered the walls and the Vance sisters' bodies dropped to the floor.

Reminding herself to breathe, Jess turned to Lori. The front of her blouse and her face were speckled with blood. She looked as rattled as Jess felt.

Lori abruptly bolted toward her. "Oh my God. Are you hurt?"

Jess shook her head, the emotions she'd been holding back bursting forth now. "I'm... not. No."

Lori suddenly hugged her. "I let you down. You could've been killed. I'm sorry. I'm sorry."

Jess's gaze landed on her reflection in the mirror over the sink.

The circles on her forehead were entwined... the infinity symbol.

For you are his, now and forever.

CHAPTER TWENTY-FOUR

1 0 : 3 0 P . M .

Eric stood back and admired his gift. "It's magnificent, Richard." He turned to his old friend. "You have outdone yourself this time."

"My pleasure, Eric." Richard smiled. "It's not everyday a man such as myself has the privilege of working with a true master."

Eric made a sound of satisfaction. His entire body responded to the painting. The likeness was so real... stunningly so. Jess had been captured standing on a sidewalk, the sun making her skin glow, the wind toying with her long blond hair. The dress hugged her slender body. He hardened just looking at her.

"Your daughter's work is exquisite, Richard."

"She sacrificed a great deal to find just the right mixture of passion and excitement. She and her sister bathed in the inspiration I helped them discover." Richard smiled. "As you well know, the true beauty of life is only found through death. It was an incredible journey for all of us."

"I'm certain it was."

Eric lifted the beautiful painting and carried it to the place of honor he had reserved. The small Band-Aid in the bend of his elbow reminded him he'd forgotten to remove it after giving the vial of blood to Richard. He ripped it off now and stuffed it into his pocket. A shiver of desire went through him at the idea that Jess had been marked with his blood.

The entire event had been timed perfectly. His friend in Birmingham's police department had not let him down. Eric's attention went back to the exquisite painting. "The frame is perfect, Richard."

As was the one now surrounding Chief of Police Dan Burnett.

"It had to be." Richard picked up the tumblers of scotch from the bar and joined Eric at the fireplace. "Such a superb piece of art deserves nothing less."

Eric accepted his glass. "Where to now?"

"Some place in the Caribbean, I think. I'm looking forward to sandy beaches and warm water. I'm confident I'll find students eager to learn."

Eric smiled. "I'm certain you will."

"And you," Richard inquired, "how long will you be staying in the Magic City?"

Magic City. Perhaps it was quite magical. "Just until my work here is finished."

Richard tapped his glass to Eric's. "To your success in all things."

"Hear, hear."

They downed their scotch and Eric showed Richard to the door. Once his old friend was gone, he locked up and returned to admire his painting.

He poured himself another splash of scotch and lifted his glass. "To you, Jess." His heart beat a little faster as he admired her image. "You'll be mine soon."

CHAPTER TWENTY-FIVE

Jess poured the second bag of popcorn into the big plastic bowl.

"I've got the Pepsis," Dan said as he kneed the fridge door closed.

"You don't have to drink Pepsi just because I am," Jess reminded him.

He kissed her cheek and grinned. "I want to. I plan on sharing the entire experience."

Jess laughed. "Do you plan to wear the empathy belly, too?"

"Maybe not quite that much sharing." He reached for her tummy. "But I'll be happy to rub yours. And your back and shoulders. Legs. Wherever you need attention."

"I plan to hold you to that, mister." She'd heard her sister complain about all sorts of pregnancy aches and pains. "You know we have to tell Lil tomorrow." She absolutely could not put that conversation off any longer. "She's invited us to lunch."

"We'll tell my folks, too." He plopped down on the sofa and grabbed the remote. "They've invited us to dinner tomorrow night."

Jess bit back a groan as she trudged barefoot over to join him on the sofa. "Can't we do that later? Like next year?"

"Be nice. My mother will be over the moon."

Jess poked her hand in the bowl of warm popcorn. "That's what I'm afraid of."

"She'll want to know when the wedding will be."

Jess scoffed. "She does not get to plan anything about our future. Are we on the same page with that, Burnett?"

"We're on the same page." He grabbed a handful of popcorn. "This is about us and our son."

"Daughter," she countered. *No boys.* She would be totally lost and Katherine would use that as an excuse to plow her way into Jess's business. She could hear her now: *I raised Dan and look how well he turned out.*

"The insurance adjustor is coming on Monday," Dan said. "According to the fire marshal, the house is a total loss."

Jess turned to him. "You heard from the fire marshal?"

He nodded. "Arson. There'll be an investigation but we all know who's responsible."

Jess wished her throat didn't feel so tight. "What about Black? Is he backing off?" Corlew was out on bail. She felt terrible about his arrest. Her efforts to help Dan had further complicated things, it seemed.

She had told Dan what Corlew learned. Dan didn't trust him and was nowhere near ready to throw Black under the bus. Jess was past ready.

"He can't back off. He's in charge of the investigation. He has to prove I didn't burn my own house down to destroy evidence."

"I cannot believe he would even suggest such a thing!" She wanted to shake Dan.

"He has to do this by the book, Jess. Just because we're friends doesn't mean he can cut me any slack."

"Right." Jess shoved more popcorn into her mouth to prevent saying something she would regret.

"Manning called while you were in the shower."

"You're just telling me this now?" She'd taken a shower at least two hours ago. If he started protecting her from phone calls, she was really going to give him what for. "Any news on Rory Stinnett?" Jess held her breath, prayed they had found her safe and sound.

Dan shook his head. "Nothing on Stinnett. Manning called about Richard Ellis. He tried to leave the country this morning. They caught him."

"That's good news! Why didn't you tell me this before?"

"He was in holding less than an hour when he attacked another prisoner and was killed."

Anything he might have been able to tell them about Spears was lost. Dammit. "They should've put him in a cell by himself."

"True."

Jess shuddered each time the double suicide of the Vance sisters replayed in her head. Dan had done the next of kin notification. Jess was grateful. Lori was still blaming herself for being distracted when she was supposed to be watching Jess. Whatever anyone else thought, Jess wasn't buying the idea that Black's arrival had been coincidence.

Was there *anyone* besides Dan and her team and maybe Corlew that she could trust?

How could Spears reach into the department like that? Or maybe Dan was right and she was being paranoid.

Another shudder quaked through Jess at the thought of the vial of blood Selma had marked her with. It was supposedly Spears's blood. Whoever it belonged to, it was at the lab now.

Selma's cell phone held several other videos. One of Templeton and Burgess at a club before their murder. Ellis had been captured seated at one of the tables in the background. Jess assumed that was the reason she hadn't received a video prior to those murders as she had with the others.

There were two videos of Jess and dozens of photos. The sisters had been following her well before the first victims were found. That was probably the part that bugged Jess the most.

How many other freaks out there were doing the same thing?

"The game's about to start." Dan adjusted the volume on the television he'd insisted on buying for her apartment. It was a guy TV. Big, with all the bells and whistles. Jess didn't really mind. It made him happy. She wouldn't complain about it as long as he didn't complain about her homework case board.

Dan's arm went around her and he pulled her close. "Thank you for agreeing to watch the first game of the season with me."

"Just don't expect me to watch them all."

He laughed. "We'll be too busy building our new house and picking out nursery colors."

And obstetricians and maternity clothes.

The popcorn suddenly turned into a massive lump in her stomach.

The alarm sang out, warning that someone was coming up the outside stairs that led to her door.

Dan shot to his feet and went to the monitor. He winced. "It's your landlord." He glanced at Jess. "He's carrying a package."

Jess set the popcorn on the coffee table and hopped up. She straightened her t-shirt and made her way to the door. She ran her tongue over her teeth. Damned husks.

The bell rang and she opened the door. "George! Come in."

Dan was right. He was carrying a package. A large white one wrapped with a pink bow.

"I don't want to disturb you," he said with a glance toward Dan, "I know it's almost game time."

"You're not disturbing us. Have a seat. You're welcome to watch the game with us." It was the least she could do for a lonely old man.

"Thank you." He settled on the sofa next to Dan the big white box in his lap.

"Would you like a Pepsi, George?"

"No, thank you. I have to watch my sugar intake."

"Water?"

He nodded. "Please."

Jess grabbed a bottle of water from the fridge and joined the two men on the sofa. "What's in the box?"

"Oh." George set the water on the table and offered the box to Jess. "This is for you. Your friend dropped it off."

Fear clamped like a vise around her chest. She instinctively drew away from the package. "My friend?"

"What did this friend look like?" Dan was on his feet reaching for the package. "When was it delivered?"

George frowned, holding onto the box like a kid who didn't want anyone else to play with his toy. "She was tall with red hair." He looked from Dan to Jess and back. "She was here just a few minutes ago. I was watering my flowers. She said she didn't want to interrupt your afternoon."

"She?" Jess told herself to breathe.

George nodded then adjusted his glasses. "The coroner lady who drives the nice car. A Lexus, I believe. I've seen her here before." He seemed to lean closer to Jess as he peered up at Dan again. "She was very nice."

Jess slumped with relief. "Sylvia Baron."

"That's the one." George smiled. "I think she was in a bit of a hurry."

Dan ran a hand over his face. Jess was relatively certain he'd been as terrified as she was. Good grief they were both going to have heart attacks!

"You want to open it?" George offered the box to her again. "There's a card."

"Yes, thank you." Jess accepted the box. She removed the small envelope tucked beneath the bow. Harris was scrawled across the front. Definitely Sylvia. Jess pulled the card from the envelope. One word was written there.

Truce?

Jess batted back silly tears. She was so emotional lately. So this was Sylvia's way of apologizing? Jess owed her an apology as well. Hers and Cook's love lives were really none of Jess's business as long as it didn't interfere with work.

Suddenly aware that both men were watching her and waiting, Jess removed the bow then tore off the paper. The box opened easily, no taped sides, thank goodness. Inside was a black leather Coach Bleeker bag just like the one she'd lost to the fire.

Unable to help herself, she gasped. "Oh my gosh!" Jess had bought that bag for her fortieth birthday otherwise she would never have spent so much money. "What was she thinking buying me a gift like this?"

"That you're friends," Dan offered.

Jess smiled up at him. "Guess so." She gave George a hug. "Thanks for delivering my gift."

He looked anywhere but at her, his cheeks flaming with embarrassment. "I heard about the fire on the news." He glanced up at Dan. "I'm really sorry about your house." He turned back to Jess then. "But I'm glad you're back home."

Jess blinked back more foolish tears. She grabbed the bowl of popcorn and thrust it at her landlord. "You boys enjoy the popcorn. I'm going to organize my new bag."

She didn't give Dan time to complain though he did manage to send a frown and a frustrated gaze her way.

By the time Alabama made a touchdown, he'd forget all about dear old George perched on the sofa next to him.

Jess reached for her phone to send a pic to Lori. There was a text message from a number not in her contact list. Her heart dropped into her stomach as she opened the message.

The picture of a young woman, long dark hair, tall and slender filled the screen. *Not Rory Stinnett.* Someone new, but exactly the Player's type.

Spears had taken another victim. Jess opened her mouth to call to Dan but another text notification appeared. She tapped the screen.

We're waiting for you.

Don't miss the next thrilling installment of the Faces of Evil. VILE is coming! Read on for an excerpt!

VILE

For the vile person will speak villainy,
and his heart will work iniquity…
~Isaiah 32:6

CHAPTER ONE

Ellen Gentry was mad as hell. She had worked at this floral shop for five years and not once had she called in sick. If her name was on the schedule, she was here—unless, of course, she was in the hospital or the morgue.

Apparently, she was the only employee around here with proper work ethics. She'd had to run around like a chicken with its head chopped off to fill this morning's orders all by herself. Nearly every single one had been for an anniversary—not that she was complaining about that part. Anniversary arrangements were good for business and almost always included generous tips. Husbands, even the not so nice ones, typically went all out for that annual celebration. A big old bouquet of flowers could get a guy out of hot water faster than just about anything.

Ellen placed the final arrangement in the walk-in cooler and breathed a sigh of relief. "Done."

It wasn't brain surgery, but her work gave her a sense of accomplishment. Speaking of surgery, she wouldn't mind snagging a doctor. There were plenty of them in Birmingham. She smoothed a hand over her hair and straightened her apron. These black slacks and the white blouse were her favorites. They fit exactly right. She'd added a nice little red scarf for an accent. Looking her best wasn't just something she did for work. It never hurt to showcase her assets especially since all those husbands would be coming in to pick up their orders. Married guys were always telling their single friends about the hot chicks they ran into. She looked pretty good even if she was about to turn thirty. There was still time to snare a husband.

"Before all the good ones are gone," she grumbled. *Or maybe they already are.*

Time for a break—if she could find her drink. A quick survey of the counter and she spotted her Coke Zero right where she'd left it behind the cash register.

As she guzzled what she fondly called her coffee in a can, a frown scrunched its way across her brow. Why was that child still standing on the sidewalk outside the shop? The traffic was lighter now that the morning commute was over and done with, but there were still plenty of cars whizzing along Sixth Avenue.

Ellen tossed the empty can into the trash and wandered to the door. The little blond haired girl had been standing in that same spot for at least half an hour. Where in the world were her parents?

Irritation lit in her belly. Some people were so stupid they didn't deserve to be parents. Ellen pushed through the door and the bell jingled overhead. The hot, humid air enveloped her instantly. It was going to be another scorcher. Just a few steps outside the door and she was already sweating.

The little girl didn't turn around. She stared out at the street as if she were lost. Was someone supposed to pick her up? Had a parent dropped her off and then driven away?

"Hey there." Ellen crouched down, putting herself at eye level with the little girl who couldn't possibly be older than four. "What's your name, sweetie?"

The child turned to Ellen and then drew back in fear. Her little face was red from crying.

"Don't be afraid," Ellen said gently. "Where's your momma?"

The child just looked at her without saying a word. A piece of plain white paper had been folded and fastened to her pink dress with a big safety pin. Ellen reached for the note. Surprisingly, the child held still as she removed it.

This was totally spooky. Ellen's heart beat faster as she unfolded the page. The words there were formed with cut out letters pasted together. "What in God's name?" She read the lone statement again.

Take me to Deputy Chief Jess Harris.

Look for the other books in the Faces of Evil Series:

ABOUT THE AUTHOR

DEBRA WEBB, born in Alabama, wrote her first story at age nine and her first romance at thirteen. It wasn't until she spent three years working for the military behind the Iron Curtain—and a five-year stint with NASA—that she realized her true calling. A collision course between suspense and romance was set. Since then she has penned more than 100 novels including her internationally bestselling Colby Agency series. Her debut romantic thriller series, the Faces of Evil, propelled Debra to the top of the bestselling charts for an unparalleled twenty-four weeks and garnered critical acclaim from reviewers and readers alike. Don't miss a single installment of this fascinating and chilling twelve-book series!

Visit Debra at www.thefacesofevil.com or at www. debrawebb.com. You can write to Debra at PO Box 12485, Huntsville, AL, 35815.

Printed in Great Britain
by Amazon

85708366R00187